'Dunstan is no friend of Warehaven.'

She explained what he already knew.

'Why would you deliver me to him?'

Her tone rose with each word.

He heard her inhale sharply before asking, 'Who are you?'

He tightened his hold round her, lifted her feet from the ground and resumed their walk towards the beach. He was certain from the tightness of her voice that she'd already guessed the answer.

Dipping his head, so he could whisper into her ear, he responded, 'Who am I?' He brushed his lips along the delicate curve of her ear. 'Why, fair maiden of Warehaven, I am Richard of Dunstan.'

She trembled against him. 'Why are you doing this?'

'Glenforde must pay for his crimes.' Richard hardened his voice. 'And you, as his intended bride, will ensure he does.'

Praise for
Denise Lynn:

'Lynn captivates readers
with a rich, intense romance.'
—*RT Book Reviews* on
PREGNANT BY THE WARRIOR

'Lynn weaves an intricate tapestry full of
royal intrigue, slavery and revenge.'
—*RT Book Reviews* on
BEDDED BY THE WARRIOR

'Lynn carries on her tradition of
producing love stories full of suspense,
romantic characters, humour and
a can't-wait-to-read-it happy ending.'
—*RT Book Reviews* on
FALCON'S HEART

THE WARRIOR'S WINTER BRIDE

Denise Lynn

First published in Great Britain 2014
by Mills & Boon, an imprint of Harlequin (UK) Limited,
Large Print edition 2015
Harlequin (UK) Limited, Eton House, 18-24 Paradise Road,
Richmond, Surrey TW9 1SR

© 2014 Denise L. Koch

ISBN: 978-0-263-25536-2

Harlequin (UK) Limited's policy is to use papers that are natural,
renewable and recyclable products and made from wood grown in
sustainable forests. The logging and manufacturing processes conform
to the legal environmental regulations of the country of origin.

Printed and bound in Great Britain
by CPI Antony Rowe, Chippenham, Wiltshire

Award-winning author **Denise Lynn** lives in the USA with her husband, son and numerous four-legged 'kids'. Between the pages of romance novels she has travelled to lands and times filled with brave knights, courageous ladies and never-ending love. Now she can share with others her dream of telling tales of adventure and romance. You can write to her at PO Box 17, Monclova, OH 43542, USA, or visit her website: www.denise-lynn.com

Previous novels by the same author:

FALCON'S DESIRE
FALCON'S HONOUR
FALCON'S LOVE
FALCON'S HEART
WEDDING AT WAREHAVEN
   (part of *Hallowe'en Husbands*)

DEDICATION

For Mom, with love.

Chapter One

Warehaven Keep—autumn 1145

Men were no better than toads, hopping mindlessly one way and then the next without warning. Before, she'd only wondered about it, but now she knew for certain it was true.

The cool night air did little to soothe her raging anger. Isabella of Warehaven shouldered her way through the throng of people crowded in her father's bailey. She needed some time alone before returning to the celebration about to take place inside the keep.

Her betrothal and upcoming marriage to Wade of Glenforde had been painstakingly planned for months. Each detail had been overseen with the utmost of care. Every line of the agreement had been scrutinised with an eye to the future—her future.

And in a few moments' time she would toss all of her father's planning into the fire. Her parents would be so upset with her and she hated the idea of disappointing them, but she just couldn't, she wouldn't marry Glenforde. He could wed the whore she'd seen him kissing while he pulled the giggling strumpet into a private alcove.

Thankfully, her mother and father had given her, and her younger sister, Beatrice, the rare blessing of choice. And while she'd dragged her feet until her father, out of impatience, took it upon himself to find her a husband, Isabella was certain he would not force her to go through with this betrothal or marriage. Especially when she shed light on Glenforde's unseemly behaviour.

Isabella picked up her pace as the recent memory renewed her rage. It was one thing for him to have a whore, but it was another entirely for him to so openly flaunt the relationship inside her father's keep. And to do so on the evening of their betrothal was beyond acceptable.

Adding this indiscretion to the way he'd pushed her to the ground in anger earlier this afternoon when discussing her sister was more than Isabella was willing to accept.

If he acted in such reprehensible ways now, what would he do once they were wed?

She had no intention of discovering the answer to that question. She was certain that once she explained all to her parents, they would understand her misgivings about this arrangement and she'd never have to worry about the answer. They would more than likely be upset that they'd been so duped into believing he was a suitable choice by her aunt. Her father's half-sister, the Empress Matilda, had insisted Wade of Glenforde was not just suitable, but the perfect choice all round: he was young, wealthy, available and, more importantly, supported her claim to the crown over King Stephen's. To sweeten the pot, the empress had promised to supply Wade with a keep, demesne lands and a title worthy of Isabella. How could her parents turn down such an offer?

Fisting her hands, she lengthened her stride in an effort to get clear of the guests milling their way to the keep. Isabella nearly choked on the urge to scream.

The sound of a splash and the ice-cold wetness seeping into her embroidered slippers made the scream impossible to resist. 'My God, what more ills will this cursed day from hell bring me?'

She slapped one hand over her mouth, lifted the long skirt of her gown with the other and then ran at an unladylike pace towards the stables at the other end of the bailey. No one would hear her curses there.

Quickly gaining the privacy offered by the stables, she ducked to the far side of the building. With her chest heaving from the effort and speed of her escape, she lowered her hand from her mouth. This far away from the keep no one would hear, or see, what was about to be one of her finest bouts of temper since she'd gained adulthood.

Isabella closed her eyes and took a deep breath before parting her lips. Only to have a large work-worn hand slapped firmly over her mouth.

She opened her eyes wide in shock as she swallowed the scream she'd been so eager to let fly.

'My, my, what have we here?' the man standing behind her asked softly over her shoulder.

He ignored her struggles to free herself to ask, 'Why, I wonder, would Warehaven's whelp travel this far from safety in the dark?'

He leaned closer, his chest hard against her back, his breath hot across her ear. 'Unescorted and unprotected.'

The deepening timbre of his voice acted like a bucket of ice-cold water sluicing down her body, making her tremble as she suddenly realised the danger in which she'd placed herself.

She'd been a fool to have flown the keep so rashly. Alone, without protection, she had foolishly risked her life. Her family had repeatedly warned her about her rashness. They'd gone to great lengths to frighten her with terror-filled tales of what happened to headstrong maidens who cavorted about in such a thoughtless manner.

Was she now about to be killed—or worse—for paying no heed to their dire warnings?

His deadly soft chuckle served to increase her tremors. 'Do you smell that?' He inhaled deeply. 'It's the scent of fear.' Pulling her closer against him, he stroked the flat edge of a blade against her cheek adding, 'Are you afraid, Isabella of Warehaven?'

Of course she was afraid. It was a time of anarchy and unrest, when no one could truly be safe. With the great number of people who'd been invited to Warehaven for this betrothal ceremony, countless criminals—men who had no sense of honour or decency—would surely follow.

Cut-throats and pickpockets alike would flock to Warehaven simply to take advantage of the opportunity to line their pouches with gold, jewels and any other item that might garner them a goodly sum.

Her breath caught in her throat. Would not the lord's daughter gain such a man much wealth?

The ground beneath her feet seemed to sway. She desperately tried to gasp for breath, but his hand over her mouth and nose prevented her from drawing in the air she needed. And his arm, now wrapped so tightly around her waist, made even normal breathing nearly impossible.

Isabella kicked back, frantic to free herself from his hold, and more frantic not to swoon. She had to escape. There was no telling what this unchivalrous knave intended.

Richard of Dunstan did his best to ignore the misplaced bit of guilt pricking at him as he held tight to Glenforde's betrothed. He tamped it down, squashing it as one would a bothersome gnat. Useless things like morals and guilt were best left to those who still cared about the niceties of life.

Guilt had provided him with nothing more than a way to avoid doing what needed to be done. And morals had only held him back from exacting vengeance for what had been done to his family.

The only thing Richard cared about any more was satisfying his need for revenge—Wade of Glenforde had seen to that by his murderous actions on Dunstan.

With that solitary end focused sharply in his mind, Richard and one of his men had slipped into Warehaven's bailey with the throng of arriving guests, intent on discovering a way to kidnap Glenforde's bride-to-be after their betrothal ceremony.

He and his man Matthew had quickly stepped away from the throng to take a position alongside the wall and survey the lay of the bailey. That was where Richard had overheard two of the guards, on the wooden walkway above them, talking to each other about the bride-to-be. It appeared that the lady in question was currently alone in the bailey and the two men were debating if they should be overly concerned for her safety or not.

To Richard's relief the older-sounding guard had set the other man's worries at ease by asking what could possibly happen with so many of Warehaven's armed guards on duty. Who, he had asked, would be daft enough, with so much manpower in evidence, to harm Lady Isabella?

Who indeed?

However, he'd never seen either of Warehaven's daughters, so he'd paid close attention to the guards' discussion, hoping they'd supply the information he needed. It was imperative he seize the right daughter. Thankfully, it didn't take long for them to provide enough detail for him to realise the richly dressed young woman rushing towards the stables was the woman he sought.

This had been an opportunity he couldn't afford to ignore. And once the guards broke apart to go their separate ways, he'd put his hastily revised plan into action. With his prey so near at hand that very moment, it had made no sense to wait until after the ceremony. Certainly not when it had seemed to be divine intervention. It was as if God himself had blessed his quest for vengeance by placing this woman neatly in Richard's hands.

Eventually, Glenforde would get the death he so deserved, but first he would suffer. He would be outraged that his bride-to-be had been taken. If he cared for the woman at all, he would suffer torment as he thought of the horrors his beloved might face.

And if Glenforde didn't hold any feelings for her, he would still be in agony at the lost riches Warehaven's daughter would have brought with her into their marriage.

Lord Warehaven possessed land and gold aplenty. He was aligned through blood with the royals on both sides of this never-ending war. There was little doubt that his daughter would bring not just wealth, but also political advantage to a marriage—the combination would be too much for Glenforde to willingly set aside.

Yes, Glenforde's pride and greed would draw him to Dunstan. He would come intent on rescuing the woman and retaining a secure hold on his future. But success would be far from his reach. He would arrive on Dunstan to find his beloved already wed and instead would be greeted only by the sharp blade of Richard's sword.

By luring Glenforde back to the scene of his

heinous crime, the spirits of his innocent victims would have the opportunity to lead the blackguard's worthless soul to the gaping mouth of hell.

The woman in his arms struggled yet again, drawing Richard's attention back to his captive. Her apparent youth almost made him regret the future she was about to begin, but a fleeting memory wove through his mind. The vision of a perfect blonde curl resting against a lifeless, blood-streaked cheek chased away any regret.

Warehaven's daughter would accept what fate decreed for her—or she would perish. That choice would be up to her.

He hadn't come this far, or taken such a risk, to turn back now. For months he had set aside duty and responsibility, existing solely for vengeance.

Now that the key to his revenge was securely in his arms, he wasn't about to let go. At this moment she likely thought him nothing more than a knave seeking to take advantage of her. Little did she know exactly what type of advantage he would take.

Against her ear, he warned softly, 'We are leaving the keep and if you scream, if you so much as think to draw attention to us, I will slit your throat.' He paused, allowing his threat to settle into her mind, then asked, 'Do you understand me?'

Richard waited until she nodded before moving

them slowly back towards the shadows behind the stable where his man waited.

A hand touched his back, bringing him to an instant halt. Light from a torch fell across them. Richard tensed, prepared to defend himself and somehow still retain his unsuspecting captive.

'Lord Richard, all is ready.'

He relaxed his defences at the sound of Matthew's voice. However, the woman in his arms stiffened. Richard tightened his hand over her mouth and placed the edge of his dagger against her throat. 'Your betrothed thought nothing of killing an innocent, defenceless six-year-old girl. Rest assured, I can easily even the score if you so much as sneeze.'

He loosened his grasp over her face slightly, relieved that she kept her lips together. 'You will live as long as you remain silent.' He waited a moment to let his threat take hold, then ordered, 'Nod if you understand me.'

She nodded. But something in the stiffness of her spine warned him that she wasn't going to be as compliant as he'd hoped. He would deal with that later—for now he only required her silence.

Matthew held up a hooded cloak. 'For the lady.'

As Warehaven's daughter, she would be too easily identified. The long, dark woollen garment would conceal her form and features. Richard uncovered her mouth, grasped her shoulder and pulled her further into the shadows, away from the glare of Matthew's torch, before releasing her. 'Stand still.'

He draped the cloak around her shoulders, secured it in front and pulled up the hood. After tucking her hair inside the fabric, he checked to make sure there was nothing visible to mark her as Warehaven's daughter.

Richard held his blade up, pointed towards her face and explained, 'You are feeling unwell and as your concerned brothers, we are escorting you home. If you give warning of any kind, you will forfeit your life before the guards can take mine.'

To his relief, she nodded her understanding without being told to do so again. With one arm across her shoulders, he motioned Matthew to her other side. Richard pressed down on her shoulder. 'Slump over as if you are ill.'

He could only hope she feared him enough to follow his orders. But when they took their first step, she tripped over the excess fabric of the cloak.

With a soft curse, he slid the dagger back into his boot and then swung her up into his arms.

She gasped, jerking away from him.

He held her tight against his chest. 'I won't warn you again. Rest your head against me and be silent.' With a nod towards Matthew, he ordered, 'Lead on.'

* * *

Isabella wasn't sure who deserved her curses more. While she knew that Wade of Glenforde was far from a gallant knight, she didn't think he'd stoop low enough to harm innocent children. But for whatever reason this man thought he had. So, Glenforde also deserved a portion of her curses.

And she was most certainly deserving of them—it was her own rashness that had got her into this situation. Or did the unkempt lout holding her deserve the curses more?

His man had called him *Lord Richard*. So, he was not a lowly cur as she'd first feared. He didn't lack status, nor did he lack the ingenuity to be armed.

Most of the revellers—invited or not—had left their weapons in the tents they'd erected outside the walls of the keep. Since it was easier to control an overlarge crowd when they were unarmed, those who hadn't stowed their weapons were relieved of the items upon entering Warehaven.

From the dagger in this man's possession, at least one guard had lacked thoroughness with his given task. A serious lapse in duty of which her father should be made aware.

The man holding her tightened his grasp as they neared the gate. She understood the silent warning and hoped they wouldn't be stopped. Not for a single heartbeat did she think the man wouldn't carry through with his threat to kill her.

Isabella took a deep breath to keep her fear at bay. She knew this warrior—this knave—would interpret any tremors on her part as a weakness he could use to his advantage. She could only pray that he released her before she could no longer suppress the need to quake with dread.

To her relief no one paid them the least bit of attention. Yet, as they passed beyond the gates and towards the open field now littered with tents and larger pavilions, the man didn't release his hold.

She thought he would hold her captive in one of those tents until Glenforde, or her father, came to claim her. But he kept walking and seemed to gather her even closer—impossibly close. His heart beat strong beneath her cheek. She felt the steady rise and fall of his chest with each breath he took.

His fingers pressing into the side of her breast drew an unrestrained gasp from her lips. Even through the layers of her clothing and the cloak, the heat of his touch seemed to scorch her skin before it skittered along her nerves, escalating her need to escape.

She twisted away and shoved at his shoulder, trying to lunge from his hold. 'Where are you taking me? Put me down.'

Richard stopped at the head of the trail leading down to the beach. If she screamed now, they would be close enough to board his ship before anyone from the keep could come to her rescue.

And that was the whole point of this unorthodox kidnapping—he wanted Warehaven to know who had taken his daughter, but he did not want to get caught. More importantly, he needed Glenforde to know who had possession of his betrothed. Otherwise, if they didn't know where to find the lady, this entire task could prove a waste in more ways than one.

He relaxed his hold on her legs and let her slide down the length of his body until she stood on her feet. But he had no intention of releasing her. 'Where am I taking you? You are going to be my guest for a time.'

She frowned, rightfully confused by his statement. 'Your guest?'

Anxious to be away, he ignored her to motion Matthew ahead with the torch. Then Richard turned the woman around so her back was against his chest and, with his arms wrapped about her waist, bodily forced her down the path.

Only then did he answer, 'Yes. You are going to Dunstan.'

He wasn't surprised at her cry of dismay or at the

way she dug her heels into the ground in a feeble attempt to halt their progress. He'd expected some type of struggle from her, especially after he'd divulged the first part of his intentions.

'Dunstan is no friend of Warehaven.' She explained what he already knew. 'Why would you deliver me to him?' Her tone rose with each word. He heard her inhale sharply before asking, 'Who are you?'

He tightened his hold round her, lifted her feet from the ground and resumed their trek towards the beach. He was certain from the tightness of her voice that she'd already guessed the answer. Dipping his head, so he could whisper into her ear, he responded, 'Who am I?' He brushed his lips along the delicate curve of her ear. 'Why, fair maiden of Warehaven, I am Richard of Dunstan.'

She trembled against him. 'Why are you doing this?'

'Glenforde must pay for his crimes.' Richard hardened his voice. 'And you, as his intended bride, will ensure he does.'

She jerked her head back, most likely to slam it against his nose. He was quicker and easily dodged her attempt to injure him. 'Come now, you can do better than that.'

However, her heels drumming sharply into his

shins and kneecaps was a distraction he feared would send them both crashing to the ground. Unwilling to take a chance of either of them being injured, he lowered her to the path, with the intention of taking her hand to lead her to the beach.

Her scream, loud and piercing, changed his mind. By her glare of mutinous rage and fear, he quickly realised there would be no leading her anywhere. Instead, Richard hauled her over his shoulder and ran down the narrow path. He shouted at Matthew just ahead, 'Move faster, before Warehaven's men catch up to us.'

He was fairly certain they were far enough away from the keep that while her screams would be heard, just as he had planned, her plea for rescue would go unanswered long enough for him to reach his ship. But it was a risk he didn't want to take.

'Lord Richard, here. This way.' Bruce's voice tore through the darkness ahead. A younger man from Dunstan stepped out from the cover of the overgrown vegetation. After lighting his torch from Matthew's, he held it aloft, illuminating a winding, narrow path down the face of the jagged cliffs.

'It's steeper than the path we climbed up.' He glanced at the burden slung over Richard's shoulder, adding, 'But quicker, if—'

Richard waved off his man's unspoken concern

of him falling with his wildly fighting bundle and ordered, 'Go.'

Just before they reached the beach, Richard paused at a sound behind them. Apparently the woman's desperate screams *had* been heard. However, Warehaven's men were closer than he'd expected.

He swallowed a curse, then barked an order at the men in front of him. 'Move. Faster.'

'There they are!'

At the shout from Warehaven's guards, Matthew and Bruce dropped their torches and scrambled over the final sets of boulders. Richard none too gently lowered the still struggling woman over the last boulder.

Just as her bottom hit the wet sand, he flung himself over the rock to land beside her.

But when he reached down to haul her back over his shoulder she quickly rolled away, shouting, 'No! Help!'

Determined to get away safely, without losing his captive, he tried to grab her again.

Slapping at his reaching arms, she shrieked, 'Warehaven, to me!'

Richard could now hear the jangle of mail and weapons from the men racing to their lady's aid.

Out of time and out of patience, he stomped on the length of cloak he'd wrapped around her, effectively holding her still long enough for him to reach down to grab her.

Still screaming, the lady had enough sense to curl her fingers tightly and ram her fist upward towards his nose. Richard turned his head to avoid the contact and the force of her punch caught him in the eye.

He cursed, chagrined that he'd let this slip of a woman plant him such a stinging blow. Without pausing to wipe the watery blur from his sight, he pulled her up and once again slung her across his shoulder.

His captive somewhat secured, Richard shouted to his men in the small rowing boat that would take them out to his ship anchored further offshore, 'Shove off!'

Bruce and Matthew nearly dived into the boat as it bobbed in the water. Bruce manned an oar, while Matthew notched an arrow in his bow and let it sail.

Richard splashed through the knee-deep water, dodged the sweeping oars and unceremoniously flung the woman into the boat before scrambling in behind her, ordering, 'Put some muscle in it, men.'

When she tried to sit up, he pushed her back down. 'Stay put, lest you want one of Warehaven's arrows to accidently end your life.'

He grabbed his own waiting bow, then turned towards the beach. Another curse escaped him at the sight of her father amongst the men shooting at them. Warehaven's death might delay—or prevent—Glenforde from coming to Dunstan.

An arrow whooshed past his ear. Richard ducked. His own life and the lives of his men were at stake, he would do what had to be done. He notched an arrow and let it sail towards the beach along with another volley of arrows from his men.

'No! Oh, dear Lord, no!' the lady cried from where she knelt on the bottom of the tiny boat as one of the arrows found its way to her sire's chest, dropping the man on to the wet sand.

She screamed again and wrapped a hand around Richard's leg. Before he could free himself, an arrow from one of Warehaven's archers pierced his shoulder. Richard jerked back in pain, only to trip over the woman still clinging to his leg.

Chapter Two

'Hold him down!'

Isabella stared at Dunstan's rough-looking soldier as if through a heavy, thick fog. They had killed her father. The tightness building in her throat and stomach intensified. She could barely imagine the pain and agony her mother must now be suffering. What would she do?

'Help me!'

Help him?

He wanted her help with his commander? Isabella shook her head, brokenly whispering, 'No.'

She couldn't—she wouldn't help any of them. They'd stolen her from Warehaven, killed her father before her eyes and had forcibly dragged her from the rowing boat into this ship as if she'd been nothing more than a sack of grain.

And then, when she'd tried to climb back over the high side of the vessel, intent on reaching the beach to help her father, this man—this filthy, ragged-haired, scar-faced knave—had bodily carried her into Dunstan's small cabin beneath the aft castle.

'Damn you, woman, help me.'

'No. Get one of your men to help.' Dunstan's well-being would be better trusted to one of his own men than to her.

'They are all needed on deck.'

She knew that. Of course the men were all needed on deck—to man the oars in the hopes that rowing would lend the ship enough speed to get away before her father's men unleashed flaming arrows.

Isabella hoped a few of those arrows found their mark and set this flat-bottomed oak ship blazing. The single square-rigged sail alone wouldn't be enough power to get this cog away fast enough.

Maybe, if she were lucky and God saw fit, she along with these men would find themselves back on Warehaven's beach in a very short time.

'Get over here and help me or I will send you to your maker.'

'Then do it and be done with me!' She would rather die than make landfall at Dunstan.

The dagger in his hand wavered briefly before he tightened his grip on the weapon. As quick as a darting snake, he reached out with his free hand and grabbed her arm. 'You are far too eager. I'll not grant you such an escape from what Lord Dunstan has planned.'

'He murdered my father!' She tore her arm free. 'Do what you will.'

'Murdered? We were defending ourselves. Besides, you don't know if your sire is dead or not. He could simply be injured the same as Lord Dunstan.' He tipped his blade towards the man on the pallet. 'However, if his lordship dies you will belong to me instead.' He narrowed his eyes to mere slits. 'And rest assured, I will make every remaining moment of your life a living hell.'

Could her father still be alive? A tiny flicker of hope sprang to life. A flicker she quickly doused in fear that her relief would be short-lived. No. She'd seen the arrow pierce his chest. Had seen him sink lifeless on to the beach. Since he'd not been protected by chain mail—he'd been dressed for a celebration, not battle—he couldn't have survived. Isabella choked on a sob.

'Is that what you want?' The man leaned closer to her, crowding her in the already small confines of this cabin. 'Do you value your life so little?'

When she didn't answer, he warned, 'If the thought of becoming mine doesn't frighten you as it should, don't forget that there are over a dozen more men on this ship who would gladly make you suffer unimaginable horrors should Lord Dunstan die.'

The deadly earnest tone of his voice made her realise that his threat was not an idle warning. But it was the cheers from the men on the deck and the sound of oars scraping across wood as they were pulled into the ship that dashed her hopes of freedom. The sounds of a sail being hoisted and unfurled as it caught the wind to take her far from her home made his threat even more deadly.

Self-preservation overrode her desire to give in to uncontrollable tears and wailing, prompting her to join him near the bed built into the side of the ship.

Dunstan's man had used the dagger to remove his commander's clothing. She stared at the blood covering Dunstan's chest and bedclothes. Like her father, Dunstan hadn't worn armour either, making his body an easy target for the arrow to pierce. If they did nothing, the man would likely die from loss of blood.

The thought of his death did not bother her overmuch, since he deserved nothing less, but if he died while aboard this ship…what would happen to her?

No. She would not worry about that. Instead, she would assist Dunstan's man in caring for his overlord. The knave would heal. She would ensure that he'd soon be hale and hearty. Otherwise, how would she gain her own measure of revenge?

Swallowing the grief threatening to choke her, and willing her resolve to stand firm, she asked, 'What do you wish me to do?'

'I have already given him a sleeping potion.' The man wrapped his hand around the shaft of the arrow still lodged below Dunstan's shoulder. 'Now, I need you to hold him up.'

Isabella shivered. No matter how many times she'd watched her mother employ an arrow spoon to remove the tip, shove the arrow the rest of the way through one of Warehaven's men, or break the shaft leaving the arrow tip in place, the operation had never failed to make her ill.

Even though she knew the answer, Isabella asked, 'Can you not simply pull it free?'

The brief grunted response required no explanation. The arrow was nearly all the way through Dunstan's body. Without an implement to dig the tip out, they could try working the shaft free of the tip and leave the tip inside for now. The other option was to shove the arrow the rest of the way through his body, while hoping everything stayed intact, then either snap off the shaft or the tip at the tang and remove the weapon.

Either option meant someone was going to have

to hold him up and try to keep him from thrashing about if the pain seeped through the fog of his drugged sleep, while someone else worked the arrow free.

She doubted if she was strong enough to hold him, but she preferred that task over the other more gruesome one. Besides, there was no one to protect her and God only knew what the crew would do to her if she bungled the procedure enough that Dunstan died.

Isabella shivered and set aside the dark images forming in her mind. She took a deep breath and then knelt on the bed to support Dunstan's body. Between the two of them, they rolled Dunstan on to his side, his stomach and lower chest propped against her bent legs.

The man poured more liquid from a small bottle into Dunstan's mouth. If he was using the juice of poppies, he could very well send his master into a deep, permanent sleep. And the blame for his death would be placed on her.

'Are you ready?'

She nodded, then leaned over Dunstan's body to hold him in place and answered, 'Be quick about it.'

To her relief Dunstan jerked only once when his man took a firmer hold on the arrow's shaft. He immediately relaxed, as if he knew it would help make his man's task easier.

Isabella, however, couldn't relax. She tensed, fully expecting Dunstan to thrash about at any moment, fighting the pain he surely must suffer.

She hoped the pain was unbearable—hoped he suffered as much agony as she did. It would be so much less than what he deserved. After killing her father, nothing short of Dunstan's death would even the score.

But somehow, he managed to withstand the pain as his man shoved the arrow tip through, broke the shaft and pulled both parts of the weapon from his body. While she could feel his muscles tense and go lax beneath her, and could hear his ragged, uneven breaths, he offered no resistance. She was unable to determine if he slept, if the medicine was working this fast or if his self-control was stronger than most.

The procedure was over quickly, but as Isabella shifted to get off the bed, Dunstan's man stopped her. 'Stay there. I still have to sew the wound.'

She snatched the needle from his hand. 'Are you seeking to kill him?'

'He will bleed to death.'

Isabella studied Dunstan. She had originally thought the same thing, but the arrow had hit him high—just beneath his shoulder, closer to his arm than his chest or neck. Using the skirt of her undergown, she wiped at the blood covering him and then shook her head. 'The bleeding has slowed, so I doubt he will perish from loss of blood.' Pinning his man with a stare, she added, 'But if you close the wound now, it could fester and that very likely *will* bring about his death.'

'Then what do you suggest?'

She had a few suggestions—all of them uncharitable, so she kept those to herself. 'Do you have any wax?'

At the shake of his head, she stated, 'Surely you have some wine and yarrow or woundwort available. Some cloth would help, too.'

These were fighting men. Hopefully, more than one of them would carry yarrow or the wort in their pouch. Both were common ways to staunch the flow of blood from a wound and promote healing.

He left her side to rummage through a satchel in the corner of the cabin and returned with a skin of wine and a clean shirt.

Isabella hesitated. 'No herbs?'

He shrugged.

'You could go ask the others.'

Her comment provoked only a raised eyebrow from him. Isabella frowned a moment before the reason for his hesitation dawned on her.

'As much as I'd like to...' she nodded towards Dunstan '...I am not going to harm him.'

When the man didn't budge, she added, 'Besides, I would prefer he be whole and completely alert when I cut out his blackened heart with an old crooked spoon.'

Even though her words were true—to a point. When the time came, she would use his own sword, not a spoon—she'd been seeking to lighten the mood.

Her ploy wasn't very successful. While his lips did twitch, he only shook his head.

Now what would she do?

Isabella knew that her mother would use the wine to wash the blood from the wound and then make a wax tent to hold it open, allowing any further drainage to run free. Once there was no more seepage, she would remove the tent and then sew, or cauterise, the wound closed.

However, from the smell of the tallow burning in the lamp she should have realised that there wasn't any wax at hand. And she didn't know what else to use.

'What are you going to do?' Dunstan's man drew her back to the task at hand.

'The only thing I can do is bind his wound after I clean it. For that I need some water, please.' When the man reached for a pitcher on the small table, she amended her request. 'From over the side of the ship.'

She didn't know how they did things on Dunstan, but her mother preferred seawater when cleansing an injury, claiming it helped to heal and dry out the wound.

The man studied her carefully for a long moment, then left the cabin.

While he was gone, Isabella poured the wine over Dunstan's shoulder and used the clean shirt to wipe away the rest of the blood and the wine.

'Here.' A bucket hit the floor beside her. Ice-cold water sloshed over the sides, soaking through her already sodden shoes and making her shiver.

Once the skin around Dunstan's wounds were as clean as she could get them, she blew on her near-freezing fingers, asking, 'Is there another shirt or anything?'

'No.'

She glanced at the weapon now strapped to the man's side. 'Then I need your dagger.'

His eyes widened briefly before narrowing to mere slits. 'For what?'

She'd already told him of her plans to wait until Dunstan was healthy before killing him. Did he not believe her? Isabella sighed, then explained, 'I need to bind his wounds. To do that I need strips of cloth.' She plucked at the hem of her undergown. 'From this.'

Frowning, he hesitated, but finally, with obvious reluctance, slowly extended the weapon towards her.

Isabella rose and lifted her skirts, only to drop them at the man's gasp. She glared at him and ordered, 'Turn around.'

Satisfied that he did as she'd ordered, she paused. With his back to her, it would be an easy thing to run him through. Isabella sighed, knowing that the other men would hear the commotion and rush to his aid.

She gave up her brief dream, pulled the hem up and cut through the thin fabric. Wincing at what she was about to do to her finest chemise, Isabella took a deep breath, then tore a good length of cloth from the hem.

'Now, you hold him up for me.'

Once his man had him upright, Isabella crosswrapped the cloth around Dunstan's chest and back. 'I'm finished. All we can do now is wait.'

After placing him back on the bed, the man suggested, 'You might want to add prayer to the waiting.'

She shrugged. While it was true, for her own selfish reasons, she did want him hale and whole, praying for this man's health would seem more blasphemous than holy.

Isabella straightened, preparing to get off the pallet, but Dunstan wrapped a hand around her wrist and pulled her down next to him. She gasped at his unexpected strength. Nose to nose, she stared into the blue of his now open eyes. His pupils were huge, his eyes shimmering from the effect of the medicine he'd been given.

It was doubtful he knew what he was doing, or was even aware of doing anything, but when she tried to pull free, he only tightened his hold, trapping her hand between them, against his chest.

Behind her, she heard his man gathering up the discarded cloths and the bucket. 'I'll return shortly to check the wound.'

'Wait! You cannot leave me here alone with him like this.'

'It is not as if he can harm you. But if any further harm comes to him, you will be the one to suffer the consequence.' On his way towards the door, he paused to douse the lamp before leaving her alone on Dunstan's pallet in the dark.

The warmth of his breath brushed against her face. Even in the utter darkness of the room she could feel his stare.

'I cannot harm you.' His deep voice was low, his words slightly slurred.

His heart beat steady against her palm. The heat of his body against hers nearly took her breath away. She couldn't remain on this pallet with him. 'Please, let me go.'

'Too late.' Dunstan rested his forehead against hers. 'You had better be worth all this.'

Worth all what? Being wounded? Isabella opened her mouth to ask, but the steadiness of his light breathing let her know her questions would go unanswered.

She rolled as far on to her back as his hold would allow, stared up into the darkness of the cabin and tried to ignore the man so close to her side. Before she could stop it, a tear rolled down her cheek, followed by another and yet another. The need to cry, to sob aloud her grief at losing her father and being taken forcibly from her home was overwhelming.

No matter how hard she fought, her wayward mind always came back to worries and questions—each more heartrending than the last.

Who would assist her mother in the lonely, sad tasks that must now be completed to lay her father to rest? Who would stand by her side at the service, or lend a hand with those attending the wake? Who would be there in the middle of the night to soothe away the tears and the fears for the future?

Her sister? No. By now Beatrice would have locked herself into her chamber to give way to her own grief. It would be days before she'd think of their mother.

Jared? No, her brother would be too busy amassing a force to come after her—and the man who'd torn their family asunder.

While Jared's wife, Lea, would no doubt try her best, she was too new to the family to know that if she tried to do too much, in the mistaken belief that her mother-by-marriage would welcome the respite from duty, she would be unwittingly angering the Lady of Warehaven.

The first time Lea instructed a servant not to disturb the lady, or if she greeted a guest as the stand-in for the lady of the keep, she'd find her help met with near uncontrollable anger. Isabella knew how closely her mother oversaw every aspect of running Warehaven. It was her keep, her home, her domain and she'd not brook any interference, not even if it was offered in the most well-meaning of manners, lightly.

And what would now happen to Beatrice and her?

Beatrice was also of marriageable age. While she had her mind set on Charles of Wardham, Isabella knew her parents disliked him and would never permit Beatrice to wed the lout.

But would Jared let Beatrice have her way?

What about her? She hadn't had the opportunity to tell her parents about her decision not to wed Glenforde. Would her brother, who would now be the Lord of Warehaven, take it upon himself to sign the documents and force her into an unwanted marriage?

Under normal circumstances the answer to that question would be a resounding no. Her brother would never force her into anything.

However, these weren't normal circumstances. If he wasn't thinking clearly, there was no way for her to know exactly what he'd do.

Which meant Jared might either see her wed to Glenforde or someone else of his choosing.

His choosing. Another shudder racked her. Why had she not listened to her parents?

None of this would have happened had she not been so determined to always have her own way.

When her parents had first given her the rare gift of choice they'd done so only because they'd known full well that it would be easier than trying to force her into a betrothal she would fight no matter how perfect the man was for her.

An odd arrangement to be sure, but one her father

had chosen because of his own marriage. As one of old King Henry's bastards, her father had been forced to wed the daughter of a keep he'd conquered. And while, yes, her parents had learned to deeply care for and love one another over time, he wanted his children to at least know of love before they pledged their future to another. Even though it went against everything considered normal, he wanted them to have the choice.

She knew that—his wishes for his children had never been a secret. Just as she knew that had she simply gone to him about Glenforde the betrothal would have been called off.

Instead, she'd let anger at Glenforde's behaviour with the strumpet get the best of her and she had stormed from the keep.

And now...

Isabella clenched her jaw until it hurt, in an effort to keep a sob from escaping.

Now her father was dead and her mother alone.

Her chest and throat burned with the need to cry, but she'd not let the murdering lout next to her know the level of suffering and grief he'd caused her.

She'd sooner throw herself from this ship and drown in the depths of the black icy waters than give him the satisfaction of witnessing her pain.

If anyone was going to suffer it would be him.

Richard of Dunstan thought he'd steal her away from her home, kill her father and get away with it?

No. Not while she had breath in her body.

Oh, yes, she would ensure he recovered from his wound—and then he would learn the meaning of pain.

Chapter Three

The creaking of wood, the swaying beneath her and the sound of waves crashing nearby dragged Isabella from her fitful dreams. *Where was she? Why was her bed moving? What was that sound...?*

Consciousness swept over her like a racing storm, bringing her fully awake with a heart-pounding jolt. She was still aboard Dunstan's ship, heading towards his island stronghold. A keep that would become her future prison.

They'd been at sea for nearly three days now. She struggled to draw in enough breath to fill her chest. Three days—three of the longest days of her entire life. She'd done penances that hadn't seemed as arduous as this forced journey.

Sleep had been her only escape from the fears and worries chasing her, threatening to tear reason from her mind and send her screaming with misery and anger. She'd sought its comforting embrace as often as she could.

Isabella knew what caused her heart to race, her breathing to become laboured and her palms to perspire. She was well aware what brought about the darkness tormenting her.

It was more than just having been captured and witnessing her father's death. And it was more than the over-warm body next to her on the bed. She stared into the pitch blackness of the cabin. Even without the benefit of sight, she felt the walls closing around her, suffocating her, stealing her ability to think, to employ any rational measure of common sense.

This airless cabin was far too small, too confining and more of a cell than a cabin. It was a constant reminder of what she had to look forward to on Dunstan.

And the unconscious man next to her on the narrow bed didn't help lessen the feeling of being trapped in an ever-shrinking cage.

Isabella closed her eyes and conjured the image of her airy, open bedchamber at Warehaven. She concentrated, bringing the vision into sharper focus. When the memories of fresh-strewn herbs floated to her nose and the softness of her pillow cushioning her head, along with the warmth of her bedcovers surrounding her, she willed her pulse to slow.

She drew in a long, deep breath, filling her lungs near to bursting before letting it out ever so slowly, over and over until the trick her father had taught her so many years ago when she was a frightened child cleared her mind and calmed her spirit.

Once certain she could function with some semblance of reason, she sat up.

The door to the cabin opened, letting in a glimmer of evening light and air—icy-cold blasts of frigid air, along with Dunstan's man… Matthew, Sir Matthew as she'd discovered yesterday when she'd overheard the other men aboard the ship talking just outside the cabin.

'Are you hungry?' Without waiting for her answer, he handed her a hunk of dry, coarse bread and a skin filled with what she knew was wine so sour that it rivalled any verjuice she'd ever encountered.

Shivering, she frowned. It had been so hot beneath the covers that she'd been unprepared for such a cold, bracing wind.

No. Her heart nearly leapt from her chest.

Setting the offered meal on the floor, she turned towards Dunstan and jerked the covers from his chest.

'What is wrong?' Sir Matthew was at her side in

an instant, crowding her, hovering like a mother fretting over her sick child.

'I'm not sure.' She placed her palm against Dunstan's forehead and then his cheek. Biting back an oath at the unnatural warmth of his skin, she ordered, 'Bring the lamp over here.'

To her surprise he did as she'd requested and held the lamp over the pallet, allowing the light to fall on a flushed, sweat-soaked Dunstan.

Sir Matthew cursed, before asking, 'How long has he been like this?'

'He was fine when last I checked.'

'What are you going to do?' Tight concern tinged his question.

Isabella raised a hand. 'Give me a moment to think.'

'His wound is most likely infected.'

What she didn't require were statements of the obvious. The need to get Sir Matthew out of the cabin prompted her to make him useful. 'Get me a knife and have someone heat some water. Find something I can use for new bindings. And if no one aboard this ship has any healing herbs, then you must make port immediately.'

'We will be at Dunstan in another two or three days.'

She turned her head to glare at him. 'He could be dead by then.'

The man tossed her his dagger, placed the lamp on a stool near the pallet and then thankfully left without another word.

Isabella turned to the task at hand—making sure Dunstan lived so he could die by her hand at a time she deemed appropriate and in a manner that suited her. Kneeling over him, she slipped the dagger beneath the bandages, prepared to strip them from his body, then hesitated, fearful of what she might see. What if…?

'Can you not decide?'

Startled by hearing him speak for the first time in three days, she jumped, nicking the tip of the dagger against his chest.

Fingers closed around her wrist. 'I would prefer death by infection, thank you.'

Isabella lifted her gaze to Dunstan's face. 'You are awake.'

He stared at her with bloodshot eyes that never once wavered. And for a moment—the very briefest of moments—Isabella wished they might have met under different circumstances.

With his squared jawline, slightly crooked nose, even teeth and full lower lip, the man needed only a bath, a change of clothes and a razor to be what her sister, Beatrice, would call a very fine figure of a man. A description that would have drawn a soft, agreeing laugh from her.

Neither the fading bruise from the black eye she'd given him, nor the small gash running across his cheek from when he fell, lessened the more-than-pleasing appearance.

And his voice... Oh, how that deeply rugged voice brushed so easy across her ears before flowing deeper to touch her soul. Even the most pious of women would throw all thought of morals and chastity into the breeze just to hear another word fall from his mouth.

Dunstan's eyebrows arched as if he somehow sensed the direction of her thoughts and Isabella felt her cheeks flame with embarrassment, shame and not a small measure of self-loathing.

Sweet heavens, where had her mind flown?

The man was nothing more than a savage beast. He'd captured her, taken her from her home, from safety and caused her father's death. And here she sat like some besotted girl mooning over this murderer's looks and the sound of his voice?

'You are still here.'

Isabella blinked at his statement. 'Since Sir Matthew stopped me from jumping overboard, where else would I be?'

Instead of answering her, Dunstan tugged slightly at her arm. 'What is this?'

It was her arm. Was he seeing things? What did he think...oh...he meant the knife. 'I need to remove your bandages.'

He released her wrist, then nodded.

'Does that mean I should continue?'

'If you want.'

'Well, no. I don't *want* to do anything for you.' A quick glance towards the still-open door assured her Sir Matthew was not standing there. 'I wasn't given a choice.'

'No, of course you...'

His words trailed off and Isabella realised he'd once again fallen prey to the beckoning spell of the sleeping drug. It was to be expected since very few people could resist the siren's call of poppy juice.

She cut away at the bandages, peeling them back as she did so. Holding her breath, she focused on the wound left by the arrow.

To her relief, while it was an angry red and puffy, there weren't any telltale dark lines of advanced in-fection.

She'd need only to reopen the wounds front and back, let them drain and after cleaning them out, pack them with some herbs—if Sir Matthew found any. And if not, perhaps that verjuice they called wine would be strong enough to burn away any evil humours.

The bigger concern was his fever.

'What worries you so?'

And once again Dunstan was awake. As much as she'd like to rail at him for killing her father and kidnapping her, she knew that within moments he'd only fall asleep again and not hear a word she uttered.

In hopes that he might be alert enough to assist in his own recovery, she said, 'You have a fever and it seems there is nothing aboard this ship to help banish it.'

'Beneath my chainmail.'

She looked around the cabin. Not locating his mail, Isabella asked, 'And where is your armour?'

'Why would you want my lord's armour?' Sir Matthew asked, walking into the cabin carrying a bucket of steaming water, a length of linen and another skin of wine.

'He claims there are some herbs beneath it.'

Without voicing anything more than undecipherable grumbles to himself, Matthew put down the items he carried and headed out of the cabin once more.

In his absence, Isabella went to work on Dunstan's injuries. By the unevenness of his breathing, she assumed he was floating in that twilight region between sleep and wakefulness.

Hoping her assumption was correct, she pushed at his shoulder, asking, 'Can you roll on to your side?'

Thankfully, even though he groaned while doing so, he complied. By the time Sir Matthew returned, she was nearly finished.

He tossed a pouch on the pallet. 'Here. This is what I found.'

Isabella shook off a thin coating of sand before opening the small leather bag. She didn't need to ask about the sand since her father and brother stored their armour in barrels of sand when out to sea. Although, the herb pouch would have been in their cabin. The all-heal herbs inside were wrapped in waxed leather to keep them dry.

She tossed a pinch into a cup, then extended it to Dunstan's man. 'Could you pour a bit of the wine in here?'

While he did that, she put a larger pinch into a second cup and used the pommel of his dagger to grind the herb into a powder. Adding some of the still-warm seawater, she made a poultice, then applied it to his wounds, holding it in place with the bindings she'd made from the linen.

When they had Dunstan situated once again on his

back, with the covers over him, she tipped his head up to give him some of the herb-and-wine decoction.

'No more.' He tried to push the cup away, but was too weak to do much more than try. However, he was strong enough to tightly clamp his lips together.

Sir Matthew stayed Dunstan's hand. 'My lord, you need to drink this.'

'No more.'

She'd seen other scars, ones more gruesome than Warehaven's arrow would leave behind, on his body. So it wasn't as if he'd never been injured before. However, Isabella wondered if maybe this was the first time he'd been given poppy juice.

After her brother's first time, he'd refused to take the brew. He'd rather pass out from the pain than ever swallow the liquid again. Perhaps Dunstan had come to the same decision.

'It's not the sleeping draught,' Isabella explained. 'This is for your fever.'

He turned his head way. 'Stinks.'

'You will either take it like a man, or we will force it on you like a child, the choice is yours.'

He shook his head at her threat. 'No.'

'Listen to me, Dunstan.' She tightened her grasp on his head. 'You *will* take this medicine. You are not going to die until I decide it's time, do you hear me? And it's not yet time.'

'Very poor wife.'

His words might have been slightly slurred, but she clearly understood what he'd said. 'I am *not* your wife.'

'Will be soon.'

Isabella froze.

Cursing, Matthew grabbed Dunstan's face, forcing his lips apart, and poured the liquid into his mouth.

Will be soon? She released her hold on the back of his head as if he were suddenly made of fire and scrambled from the bed. Isabella staggered backwards until she hit the side of the ship.

Shaking with fear, dismay and anger, she clasped her hands to her chest, as if that would offer some measure of protection, and asked Sir Matthew, 'What does he mean?'

He remained silent, seemingly intent on settling his commander more firmly under the covers.

'Answer me!' Isabella shouted. 'After all that has been done to me, I have still helped save his miserable, worthless life. I deserve an answer. What did that miscreant scoundrel mean?'

Sir Matthew lowered his head, his chin nearly resting on his chest, he turned away from the bed and said, 'Dunstan's priest awaits his lordship's return—with his bride-to-be.'

Isabella's choked gasp nearly stuck in her throat.

'His bride-to-be?' She feared she knew the answer, but hoping she was wrong, asked, 'And who would that unlucky lady be?'

As he quickly headed for the door, Matthew answered, 'You.'

Chapter Four

Richard groaned as the surface beneath him heaved to and fro as if being pitched by a windswept wave. The motion let him know that he was aboard a ship. Hopefully, his own.

Outside of a strange dream about Warehaven's daughter leaning over him with a knife to his chest, the last thing he clearly remembered was vaulting into the small rowboat, grabbing a bow and turning to face Warehaven's men just as a hand grasped his leg. Distracted, he'd glanced down and fire had sliced through him, sending him head first against a cross-brace.

He raised his arm and half-swallowed a gasp at the pain lacing across his shoulder.

'Warehaven's archers rarely miss. You took an arrow.'

He opened his eyes, squinting against the flicker

of a lit lamp and stared up with relief at the crudely drawn map he'd nailed to the ceiling of his cabin.

'What a shame they hadn't taken aim at your heart.'

Richard raised a brow at the barely suppressed rage in her voice. If anyone should be angry, he should be. 'Then perhaps, instead of being vexed, I should be grateful for your timely distraction.'

'Distraction? I was kneeling on the hull.'

'Which didn't prevent you from grabbing my leg.'

'Should I have done nothing while you took aim at my father and his men?'

'They were aiming at me and my men.'

'I owe no loyalty to the men of Dunstan and had little concern about the arrows aimed at them.'

Valid as it was, he wasn't about to concede her point. 'You should be grateful the men of Dunstan didn't toss you overboard.' She didn't need to know that his men would never treat his bride-to-be so harshly.

She'd been pacing at the other side of the cabin, but changed direction and approached his bed. 'They would have, but you fell atop me.' With a toss of her head she turned to take a seat on a nearby stool, adding, 'So I've nothing to be thankful for.'

'I would think you might be thankful for your life.'

'As should you.'

Richard knew that she would find a contrary response to anything he said. At another time, under different circumstances, this verbal sparring might provide an entertaining moment or two. Right now, however, she was his captive, not his guest, and her contrariness did nothing but make his head throb even more.

Unmindful of his shoulder, he sat upright, shouting, 'Matthew!'

The man entered the quarters immediately. 'You are awake.'

'Could you find no other place for—?' Try as he might, he couldn't push through the fog still swirling about his mind to remember her given name. Richard settled his gaze on her long enough to say, 'I can refer to you as she, or her, or that woman, but a name would be easier.'

'Isabella.' She ground out the answer between clenched teeth. 'Isabella of Warehaven.'

Richard turned back to Matthew and asked, 'Could you find no other place for *her*?' Her hiss of displeasure whipped through the small cabin.

Matthew shrugged. 'Since she was caring for your injury, I thought it better she stayed in here, rather than on the deck with the men.'

'*She* cared for my injury?'

Her gasp and wide-eyed stare spoke of her surprise at his lack of memory. 'You remember nothing?' She looked at him, questioning, 'Who do you think cared for you?'

He ignored her to ask his man, 'What did you threaten her with?'

Matthew flashed him a crooked smile. 'My tender loving care, with the men's assistance, should you die.'

That she hadn't thrown herself overboard at such a threat was interesting. Most women would have done so or fallen dead of fright when confronted in such a manner by any of his men. They were an imposing lot who hadn't been selected for their good manners or refinement. Warehaven's daughter was either braver than most, or possessed not one ounce of common sense.

He did owe her his gratitude. 'I do thank you—'

'No need,' she interrupted him, but then frowned as if debating what to say next. Finally, after pursing and then unpursing her lips a time or two, announced, 'I am not going to marry you.'

Richard swung his gaze back to his man. Why had that information been divulged? Matthew tripped while making a hasty exit. Over his shoulder, he said, 'We'll be home within a day or so.'

A day or so? Depending on the winds, it was a five or six days journey back to Dunstan. That meant—

'Did you hear me?'

He shook his head, trying to clear his thoughts. If they were docking at the island in a day or two, that meant he'd been unconscious—

'You'll get my hand in marriage only if you remove it from my dead body first.'

Obviously she wasn't going to give him a moment of peace. Her acceptance—or lack of—hadn't been a consideration in his plans. He wasn't about to let her thwart his quest for vengeance.

'It is truly simple, Isabella of Warehaven, you'll do as you're told.'

'I…I will do what?' she sputtered, staring at him as if he'd gone mad. 'Killing my father does not grant you his place in my life.'

Richard paused at the bitterness of her voice. He frowned, thinking back to the day he'd taken Warehaven's whelp from her home. Scattered scenes rushed in swiftly filling in some of the holes of his faulty memory. Her father had taken an arrow on the beach. Since he'd also taken an arrow, why would she assume her sire had died?

'You don't know if he died or not. Like me, he might only have been injured.'

'I saw him fall to the beach with an arrow piercing his chest. He wore no armour for protection, so I…I can only believe he was killed.'

The catch in her voice warned him that she was already emotional, as was to be expected, but the last thing he wanted was for her to become hysterical over some imagined happening.

'Is believing the worst your attempt at logic?'

Her eyes widened briefly before narrowing into a fierce glare. Obviously his insincere question had the intended effect—she'd set aside the need to grieve a father who might or might not be dead for anger directed towards him.

'I guess we'll find out how valid my logic is when he or my brother come to pay you a visit.'

'That was the whole point of being seen. Otherwise they wouldn't know where to find you.'

She waved off his answer, to order, 'Turn this ship around.' Her eyes blazing, she informed him, 'They'll have no reason to find me as I am *not* marrying you, nor am I spending the winter on Dunstan.'

Since he had no intention of turning this ship about and every intention of marrying her within a matter of days, she would be spending much longer than just the winter on his island.

The crash of another wave sent the ship pitching dangerously. Without thinking, he quickly reached out and grasped Isabella's shoulders to keep her from being tossed from her seat on a stool to the floor.

She shrugged off his touch and leaned away. 'I can see to myself.'

He didn't get a chance to respond before the ship danced wildly once again, sending Isabella flying from the stool. The thin metal band confining her hair slipped from her head to spin like a top before it then clattered to the floor. On her hands and knees she glared at him as if daring him to give voice to the comments teasing his tongue.

To his relief, instead of trying to scramble back on to the stool, Isabella snatched her hair band from the floor, then crawled to a corner and wedged herself securely between the timbers.

From the ire evident on her face, she would be grateful if he took it upon himself to fall overboard. How high would her anger flame when she realised the depth of her predicament?

Isabella leaned forward and warned, 'You had better hope my family comes for me soon. Because I swear I will not be forced to marry you.'

'What makes you think you have a choice in this matter?'

'My family—'

'Is not here. The deed will be done long before they arrive.'

The blood appeared to drain from her face, leaving her pale and, from her trembling, more than a little shaken.

When she finally found her voice, she asked, 'Why would you wish to wed me?'

'*Wish* to wed you?' Richard shook his head. 'You misunderstand. I have no *wish* to wed anyone. You are merely a means to an end. One that our marriage will help ensure.'

One finely arched eyebrow winged higher. 'It matters not what petty grievance you seek to avenge. With my family's wealth, they will assume marriage was the reason for this madness of yours.'

Petty grievance? The murder of a small, defenceless child was far more than a simple grievance. Richard studied her carefully. The hazel eyes staring back at him appeared clear. Still, to be certain, he asked, 'Did you hit your head?'

'Are you asking if I have my wits about me?'

'Do you?'

'Of course I do.'

'That is up for debate if you think murder is nothing more than a petty grievance. I couldn't care less what your family thinks. They can rant and demand all they want, it will avail them not at all. My concerns are with Glenforde. I long for the day he comes to your rescue.'

Isabella frowned. 'You kidnapped me for some crime Glenforde committed?'

'What better way to get him to come to me on Dunstan than to kidnap and wed his bride-to-be on nearly the eve of his marriage?'

'You assume much since you can't be certain he will come.'

Richard slowly trailed his gaze from her wildly disordered, burnished gold hair, across the purely feminine features of her heart-shaped face, over the gentle swell of her breasts, past her bent legs, to the toes of her mud-stained shoes.

He dragged his gaze up to stare into her speckled hazel eyes. She quickly turned her head away, but not before he caught a glimpse of her flushed cheeks. 'Oh, rest assured, Isabella of Warehaven, he *will* come.' And when he did, Richard would be waiting.

'Brides are easily bought.' She leaned forward to wrap her arms round her knees. 'I am certain Wade of Glenforde will find another with little difficulty.'

Her pensive tone and response surprised him. Richard wondered what Glenforde had done, or said, to cause Isabella such doubt of her worth as a bride, or as a woman.

'Perhaps, but you forget what else he stands to gain in this union. Glenforde is greedy. He will not throw away the opportunity to secure his relation-ship with royal blood.'

Isabella shook her head. 'Now *you* forget, my father was never recognised. King Henry might have been his sire, but his mother was little more than a whore.'

'That's a fine way to speak of a blood relative.'

'Relative? She was a servant who sold herself for nothing more than a warm bed and a meal. Once my father was weaned she was never seen or heard from again. What would you call her if not a whore?'

She stared at his naked chest and then turned her flushed face away.

Richard retrieved a shirt from the clothes peg near his bed. 'A woman who sells herself for a warm bed and food isn't necessarily a whore.' He knew exactly what a whore was—a bed-hopping liar with not a trace of honour.

Something in the bitter tone of his voice caught her attention. What reason had he to sound so…resent-ful or cynical? Isabella turned to look at him. His shirt hung around his neck and he frowned down at it. He was no doubt trying to determine how to get dressed without using his injured shoulder.

As far as she was concerned she'd already helped him enough—more than enough. The obvious fact that he didn't seem to remember clearly was just as well. It was better for her if he had no reason to see her as anything but the enemy.

She didn't want Dunstan to think that she cared for his welfare—she didn't, not in the least.

It was imperative that he not misconstrue her actions. Because if he went through with this farce of a marriage, she would make his life miserable.

Not only would this marriage never be consummated—doing so would tie her to this knave for ever and she was not about to spend the rest of her life wed to a man she despised—but he would soon learn just how little his wife cared for him.

By the time her family came to rescue her, Dunstan would be glad to let her go.

Her family rarely used their connection to either royal—Stephen or Matilda—but in this matter she would use every advantage at her disposal to gain an annulment. However, freedom from this marriage would never be granted were she to let this man have his way with her.

No, she fully recognised the need to keep him at arm's length and to repel him at every turn.

Dunstan glanced in her direction and she held her breath, certain he was going to ask for help. Instead, he clenched his jaw and managed to get the shirt on by himself.

A sheen of sweat beaded his forehead, but she

refused to acknowledge his pain and weakness—not when his actions thus far would cause her much more than a moment or two of discomfort.

Her whole world would now be turned upside down. Her mother would be distraught with worry and fear. Her brother's rage would know no boundaries, his anger at her kidnapping and their father's death would surely make Dunstan's world tremble. But Glenforde was another story... Would her betrothed set aside their differences to come to find her, or would he think himself better off without her?

After all, there was another heiress still living at Warehaven—her sister, Beatrice. If Isabella's newly forming suspicions were right, Glenforde had formed no tender feelings for her. He was concerned more with the land, gold and regardless of what she'd told Dunstan, yes, Glenforde would also be concerned with the connections that would come with marrying a daughter of Warehaven. Once he learned that the daughters shared equally in Warehaven's wealth it was possible that either daughter would suffice.

The knowledge that she alone would pay the consequences for his actions with the whore that night at Warehaven made her head spin. How would she find the strength to do what she must to survive? And even when she did gain an annulment, would she be able to salvage anything of her dignity, her future or of her worth?

To take her mind off of the dark thoughts gathering in her mind, she asked, 'So, you think it is appropriate for a woman to sell herself for the necessities of life?'

Isabella truly didn't care what he thought. She just needed something to distract her.

He leaned forward, his elbows on his knees, his hard stare making her far more than uncomfortable. Her belly tightened at his single-minded focus.

It wasn't that he frightened her, even though a part of her mind whispered that she should be afraid. After all, her well-being was completely in his hands.

But had he wanted to cause her harm, would he not have already done so? There'd been nothing to stop him—except for the simple fact that he'd been drugged, unconscious and unable to cause anyone harm.

She swallowed. Perhaps questioning him on his thoughts about women of loose morals had been unwise. Especially considering the assessing look he'd given her when trying to convince her that Wade would come to her rescue for her features alone.

His smouldering stare had left little doubt in her mind that he found her physical form...pleasing.

His perusal then had sent a heated flush from her cheeks to her toes. Much like it did now.

Isabella shook off the unwanted warmth and mentally chastised herself. The narrowing of his eyes warned her that she'd held his stare far too long. He knew full well what his pointed gaze did to her and she'd just unintentionally made him more aware of her response.

'Appropriate?'

She pressed her back more firmly into the corner, but it did little to stop the tremor lacing down her spine. She should be afraid—needed to be very afraid of what the deep timbre of his one-word question did to her senses.

He had kidnapped her—stolen her away from her family and home, taken her from everything she knew and brought death to her father. It made no sense for her to note the blueness of his eyes, or the way his overlong ebony hair fell across his face.

It was wrong, near shameful to let the mere sound of his voice set heat racing along her spine and loosen tiny wings to flutter low in her belly.

The walls closed in around her, making her nearness to this man more acute, bringing their privacy more into focus. She raised a shaking hand to her chest, pressing it over her wildly pounding heart and struggled to draw in breath.

Oh, yes, she should be very afraid of him, but more so of herself.

One dark eyebrow hitched over a shimmering sapphire-hued eye, giving her the distinct impression that he somehow knew where her thoughts had flown. Horrified of what that might mean for her continued well-being, Isabella forced herself to look away.

'I cannot judge whether her actions were appropriate or not. People do what they must to stay alive.'

He rose and she felt his stare as he loomed over her. The very air around them crackled with tension. When she finally met his gaze, he suggested, 'That is something you might want to remember.'

It was on the tip of her tongue to ask if he was threatening her, but she held her words inside. She wasn't completely witless, of course he was threatening her, warning her that some day she, too, might need to do something dire to save herself. So she kept her thoughts and questions to herself, fearful of forcing his hand this soon.

'I need to see to my ship and men. You stay here.'

When she didn't respond, he nudged the toe of her ruined slipper with the side of his foot. 'Did you hear me?'

'I am not deaf, you lack-witted oaf. I heard you.' The moment the words were out, she winced. There was a time for mockery or name-calling, but this wasn't the time to give her tongue free rein.

He bent over. Then, unmindful of his shoulder, grasped her beneath her arms and hauled her up from the floor. When they were nose to nose, her feet dangling in the air, he asked, 'Do you think it wise to bait an enemy when you are the prey?'

'No.' Thinking quickly, she reminded him of his obligation as her captor. 'But as your hostage you need to keep me safe.'

'I will soon be your husband and while I may be honour bound to keep you alive, your tender feelings concern me not at all.' He dumped her on to his bed and came over her, resting most of his weight on his forearms. 'Keep your wits about you, Isabella of Warehaven. Not all injuries can be seen.'

While it was easy to ignore the beads of sweat on his brow attesting to the strain he'd placed on his body, it wasn't as easy to ignore the evident strength in the hard muscled thighs trapping her securely on the bed.

And even harder to ignore the implication of his threat.

'Honour? You killed my father, that proves you have little honour, Dunstan.' She turned her head away from the heat glimmering in his eyes.

He drew her head back so she faced him and Isabella fought the dread overtaking her shaking limbs.

His breath was hot against her cheek, his lips trailed flames across her skin. He paused, his mouth a hairsbreadth above her own, pinned her with his stare and asked, 'Why should I show you more honour than Glenforde did when last he visited Dunstan?'

Her chest tightened even more until her breaths were ragged gasps for air. His nearness, the physical contact of their bodies made thinking almost as impossible.

'I am not Glenforde.' It was the only answer that could find its way through the confusion and fear casting a fog over her thoughts.

He rose to stand over her. 'No you are not Glenforde. But you were to become his wife and you are here. Forget not your place, Isabella.'

Silently, she watched him exit the cabin. Relief washed through her, making her limp with near exhaustion.

Even though he'd told her that Glenforde had murdered someone on Dunstan—someone young, a child—she had no way of knowing if the crime was real or imagined. She couldn't help but wonder what had held Dunstan's temper in place. Had it been her reminder that she wasn't Glenforde? Or had he somehow sensed her confused fear and relented?

This was not a man to take for granted. He was more of a threat than she'd first thought. This man, above all others, seemed to have the power to reduce her to a mindless muddle with little more than a look.

She couldn't begin to imagine how she would have reacted had he carried through with his threat. Would she have fought him with every fibre of her being?

Or would she have followed the whispered longings of her traitorous body?

The only thing she knew for certain was that she needed to take charge of her wayward emotions before *she* became the greater threat to her well-being. Otherwise, she would bring about her own downfall.

Chapter Five

Richard leaned against a timber beam long enough to catch his breath before climbing the ladder to the open aft deck above. The hardest part of this venture was to have been the actual kidnapping and making a hasty retreat towards Dunstan unscathed.

His throbbing shoulder reminded him that he hadn't escaped unscathed. But at this moment, his injury was the least of his concerns. What bothered him was the uneasy feeling that there was more to his fragmented dreams than he could fathom.

He knew from the unquenchable dryness of his mouth that Matthew had drugged him. The lingering bitter taste meant the man had probably broken into their limited stores of opium. While the concoction was a pain reliever of miraculous proportion, it left the patient's mind foggy for days afterwards.

Still, the memory of a soft, warm body next to him on the pallet was too vivid to have been only a dream. Why would his mind have conjured gentle hands and a hushed soothing whisper to ease him when the pain grew close to unbearable?

His past experience with women hadn't led him to believe they were gentle or soothing with any except their offspring. Not for one heartbeat could he imagine Agnes easing anyone's pain but her own.

Yet in his dreams it had been a woman. There was only one woman aboard this ship—Isabella of Warehaven. Had she soothed him, gentled his need to rage against the agony chasing him?

Impossible.

None of it made any sense. And it was that unexplained senselessness that had him worried that marrying this woman would prove more difficult than the act of capturing her.

Why couldn't she be a few years younger or a great many years older? Either one would have made her less attractive in his mind, drugged or not.

Unfortunately, she was a woman full grown and too obviously aware of the untried desires teasing her body. Going into a battle without armour and weapons would be less dangerous than being in her company overlong.

When he'd loomed over her, threatening her, he'd hoped to see a glimmer of fear. Even though that had been his intent, it wasn't fear shimmering in her wary gaze—it had been an awareness of him, followed by curiosity and then confusion about what she felt.

Once he'd recognised her emotions, his body had threatened to betray him. The vision of their naked limbs entwined as he brought her across the threshold into womanhood had nearly been his undoing.

Nobody would have stopped him. They were soon to be wed. Had he been physically able, he could easily have taken her, shown her the pleasures of the flesh and then called it revenge for what her betrothed had done to his family. And no one would have faulted him.

But Isabella of Warehaven was not the object of his revenge. She was only the means to an end. He needed to remember that.

This desire, this unbidden lust for her was nothing more than a drug-induced torment that could and would fade with time. He would simply need to keep a tight rein on his desires until that time came.

Richard sighed and leaned on the rail for support. If he was this breathless and shaken from what little physical exertion he'd performed since rising from his bed, reining in his desires should prove an easy task.

Boisterous laughter from the men on the deck drew his attention. By the nods in his direction it was apparent that he was the focus of their conversation.

Richard straightened, squared his shoulders and then stepped away from the railing. Regardless of his injury he was not about to appear weak, or incapable of command, in front of his men.

He pinned a hard stare on Theodore, the largest in the group. When the guffaws ceased abruptly, he asked, 'What amuses you?'

Theodore shuffled his feet, batted at one of the other men, then answered, 'Nothing, my lord.'

At Richard's raised eyebrow, he added, 'We are simply glad to see you up and about.'

While they might be relieved to see him up, he resisted the urge to roll his eyes at the obvious attempt to garner his good graces. Richard doubted if his health had been the sole topic of their amusement.

If he knew anything about his men, it was that they enjoyed a good gossip almost as much as they enjoyed fighting. At times they were as bad—if not worse—than the women of Dunstan's village. There was little doubt in his mind they'd been making assumptions about him and Isabella.

Assumptions that might have been on target had he not been unconscious.

He bore her no ill will, but neither did he care overmuch about her feelings. For the most part she was unknown to him, he knew very little about her, something he needed to resolve since she would become his wife in a matter of days.

Richard frowned and gingerly moved his shoulder about. The men aboard this ship knew little about mixing potions or salves, meaning the woman had probably saved his life. Regardless of his hatred for her betrothed, he did owe her something.

His gaze settled south, towards the Continent for a moment, and then with a heavy sigh he climbed down the ladder to speak to his men before heading back into his cabin.

Isabella flicked her thumbnail at the dried mud on her slippers. They were ruined beyond repair, but she hoped the pearls could be salvaged.

Her father had given her and her sister a bag to share. Every night for a week she and Beatrice had painstakingly attached the small pearls to their slippers. She'd formed hers into the shape of a flower, while her sister had spiralled hers around the edges.

The stool beneath her shifted slightly, just enough to make her reach out to keep from falling on to the floor. The thin slivers of light came into the cabin from the port side of the ship. The sun had been behind them, meaning the ship had changed direction. A glimmer of hope sprang to her heart.

The cabin door banged against the wall, making her jump as Dunstan pushed through. He spared her a brief glance before dropping on to his bed to stare at the ceiling.

Eager to know if perhaps he'd changed his mind, she asked, 'Are we turning about?'

'No.'

Her newly borne spark of hope flickered out as quickly as it had formed. 'But the ship has changed direction.' She paused to get her bearings straight in her mind. Warehaven was off the south-east coast of England. Her little knowledge of Dunstan Isle was that it lay north-east towards Denmark. 'We are now headed south instead of further east.'

His soft chuckle grated on her patience. 'Don't think for a moment you are going anywhere but to Dunstan. I simply had the men adjust the course for home.'

She'd been aboard her father's and brother's ships enough to know how often the currents and the winds set them off course. 'Oh.'

'Tell me about yourself.'

Isabella blinked at the sudden request. 'What?'

Still staring at the ceiling, Dunstan repeated. 'Tell me about yourself.'

'Why?'

He turned his head and gave her a pleading look.

'Because I am injured, I don't feel well, I want a distraction.'

Dear heavens above, he was using the same tactic her father and brother had when they were unwell. That sad two-year-old's *feel sorry for me* gaze that always had her mother giving in to their whining with no more than a sigh. Well, she wasn't about to feel for sorry for him, not when he'd brought all of his misery on himself.

'Please.'

She crumpled the slipper in her hand and sighed. 'What do you wish to know?'

He stared back up at the ceiling. 'I should know something about you since you will soon be my wife.'

If he did anything that foolish, he would soon learn to rue the day he forced her into a marriage. However, between the lingering effect of the opium and the paleness of his face, arguing with him now would be pointless. If she read his features correctly, the drooping eyelids and downturned mouth signalled he would soon fall back to sleep.

To humour him in the meantime, she said, 'I have an older brother, a younger sister, a mother and no father.'

'And again you assume he is dead. Do you dislike your father so much that you secretly hope the worst?'

Isabella gasped at his insinuation that she would wish such foulness for her father. 'I love my parents dearly.'

'Love?' He shook his head. 'Of what use is love? I would think they'd rather have your respect and obedience.'

At this moment, he was most likely correct. Had she paid heed to her parents' warnings, she wouldn't be on this ship heading to Dunstan.

Although she found it interesting that he had such a lowly opinion of love. 'Did you not care for your parents?'

'I did not know my mother, she died when I was a babe. And my father did his duty by me.'

'Did his duty?'

'A roof over my head. Food in my belly and a suitable place to foster once I was old enough to hold a weapon.'

'Oh.' She felt no pity for the man, but found herself aching for the small boy. Had he had no one to offer him any gentleness? No welcoming arms to chase away the childish nightmares and hurts? She could not fathom such a life. She'd had both a mother and father who'd cared for their children dearly.

'You sound surprised. Did your brother not foster elsewhere?'

'Of course he did.' But he'd done so with their mother's family until he gained squire status and then he'd joined Matilda's court.

'What about you and your sister?'

'No.' Isabella wrinkled her nose, waiting for what would be disbelief on his part.

'No?' Dunstan turned his head to look at her. 'Surely you spent time at Glenforde's keep?'

She smoothed out her crushed slipper, brushing the caked mud on to the floor—busy work to keep from returning his gaze. 'No.'

'You expect me to believe that King Henry's granddaughter, Empress Matilda's niece, did not learn how to be a lady at the knee of her future mother-by-marriage?'

'My mother taught me how to be a lady. Regardless of acceptable convention, she would not surrender such a task to a stranger. Besides, I was betrothed to no one, so there was no future mother-by-marriage.'

He sat up on the bed and swung his legs over the side. 'Is there something wrong with you?'

Isabella paused. Since it would be normal for her and Beatrice to have been betrothed at a very young age, of course he would wonder at the reason for such a lack. She should lie and tell him that there was something drastically wrong with her.

It had to be something that would make him think twice about forcing a marriage between them. Something—gruesome. Some terrible thing that would make him shiver with dread. Perhaps something that would convince him to turn the ship about and return her to her family.

But what?

'Too late.' Dunstan leaned forward. 'It has taken far too long for you to answer.'

She narrowed her eyes and lifted her chin a notch. 'Perhaps my…condition is so severe I've no desire to sicken you with the details.'

'Other than a smart tongue and lack of common sense, there is nothing wrong with you.'

His smug certainty nipped at her temper. 'You can't be sure of that.'

'Actually—' he rose from the bed and stepped towards her '—I can.'

She held her slipper out like a shield, as if the scrap of fabric and pearls would protect her from his advance. 'What are you going to do?'

Dunstan snatched the slipper from her hands, tossed it across the cabin, then slowly circled her. He passed by her side, touching her ear as he kept walking. 'I know your ears are fine.'

He brushed a fingertip across her lips as he crossed before her, making her lips tingle. 'It is obvious you are capable of speech. And I know you can see, so nothing is wrong with your eyes.'

Isabella silently cursed her own stupidity. He'd accepted her statement as a dare—as a way to intentionally trap her in her own lie.

He stopped behind her and placed his hands on her shoulders. Isabella fought the urge to shiver beneath his touch.

Patting her shoulders, he lowered his hands, running them down to her wrists. Leaning over her, he commented softly, 'And if I am not mistaken, these two arms seem to be normal.'

He trailed his hands up to caress the back of her neck, asking, 'I wonder what else needs to be investigated?'

She tried unsuccessfully to pull away from him. 'Nothing.'

'No? Then how can I be certain you are whole?'

Isabella ground her teeth before answering, 'I am fine. There is nothing wrong with me.'

'Ah.' With his thumbs still on the back of her neck, he snaked his fingers to encircle her throat and with his fingertips beneath her chin tipped her head back, forcing her to look up at him.

While the placid expression on his face warned her

of no ill-conceived plans to choke the life from her, the gentle, deadly warmth of his hold silently threatened her in a way no brandished sword ever could.

This hold was more personal than the tip of cold metal against flesh. The heat of his fingers belied the damage he could cause.

'So, you were seeking to lie to me?'

She stared up at him. He knew full well she'd lied. He had only been mocking her, baiting her, and she'd stepped into his trap with little thought.

If she kept up this ruse, she knew he would follow through with his examination until she cried off. Unwilling to be humiliated any more than she already was, she whispered, 'Yes.'

'What?' He stroked the ridge of her throat. 'I didn't hear you.'

'Yes.' Isabella reached up and grasped his wrist. 'Yes, I lied.'

He slid his fingers lower to circle the base of her neck, but did not remove his hands. The less-threatening hold did nothing to ease the trembling of her limbs.

'You are being forced into a marriage you do not want. There is nothing you can do to prevent it.'

His hands, gently rubbing the tension from her neck, might be welcome another time, another place. Now, however, his caressing touch was an unwelcome reminder of what was to come. If they wed, and unless she could convince the priest on Dunstan to not perform the rites, it was becoming a certainty that they would, he would own her body and soul.

'Rest assured, Isabella, that I expect little from you as a wife.'

Her breath caught in her chest. Did that mean they would not share a bed? Once his business with Glenforde was complete, would she be able to petition for an annulment?

'We will wed. You will share my bedchamber.'

Isabella's heart sank. Sharing his bed would dash her hopes for an annulment. What would she do, how could…? She bit her lower lip to keep from crying out in surprise at the sudden clarity of the devious vision springing to life in her mind. If all else failed, her family could make her a widow.

'As long as you do not seek to lie to me, I will treat you well. Deal with me honestly and you will want for little.'

His statements gave her pause. He would not say such things unless someone, at some point in time, had deceived him. A woman most likely—a wife, or love interest, perhaps?

The irony of this moment was not lost on her. Now, as she plotted his imminent demise, he swore to treat her well if she did not lie to him.

A tiny pang of guilt grew deep in her belly, twisting its way towards her heart. Isabella swallowed a groan, refusing to let misgivings rule her future.

Dunstan stepped back. With his hands no longer on her, she was able to tamp down the guilt.

'I am weary and need rest.' He headed to the bed. 'Come.'

She stared at him in shocked dismay. 'I will not join you in that bed.'

'You have done so these past nights.'

'When you were incapable of doing anything more than sleep.'

'That is all I intend to do now.'

His intentions didn't matter, he was more than capable of doing whatever he wanted, should she agree or not. She shook her head. 'No.'

Dunstan sat on the edge of the bed. 'My bandages need to be changed.'

Isabella narrowed her eyes at his subterfuge. He was giving her that sad *oh, woe is me* look again. The same one her father had used on her mother when he wanted something he knew full well he didn't need.

She wasn't yet Dunstan's wife and she didn't care for him, his wants or his well-being in the least. 'Your man Matthew is quite capable of changing the bindings.'

'His touch isn't as gentle as yours.'

She shrugged. 'Then perhaps you need to speak nicer to him.'

'I rest easier with you at my side.'

Again, she shook her head. 'We are not wed yet. Until that day comes...' Because she held tightly to a slim thread of hope that Dunstan's priest would see reason, she silently added, *if it comes.* 'I will not share a bed with you.'

'Then where do you think you will sleep?'

She didn't know. But she was certain of one thing—she was not sharing his bed.

He'd been correct—she had done so these last few nights, but she hadn't felt threatened or in any danger. However, the situation had changed. Dunstan had already proven he was more than capable of forcing her to do his will.

Feeling his hard stare, she answered, 'Since I am not tired, it doesn't matter where I sleep.' At his frown, Isabella rose from the stool and plopped down into the corner of the cabin, wedging herself tightly against the hull's timbers. 'This will do fine.'

Dunstan shook his head and rose from the bed. 'It is cold. Permitting you to develop the chills and a fever will not suit my plans.'

His plans? What about the plans she'd had? 'What do I care about your plans?'

He ignored her question and motioned towards the bed. 'Join me of your own free will, like an adult, or I'll carry you like a child. The choice is yours.'

She clenched her jaw at having a version of her own words tossed back at her, but refused to move.

He rubbed his forehead as if seeking to ease the throbbing of an aching head. Then he shouted, 'Matthew!' When his man hastened into the cabin, he held out his hand. 'Give me your dagger.'

Matthew did so without question and, when waved away, left the cabin without a word.

Isabella gasped. He would kill her for not sharing his bed? She turned her face into the timber beam to avoid witnessing her own death.

'Oh, for the love of—' He broke off on a harshly snarled curse and grasped her wrist. 'If my intent had been to kill you, I would have done so at Warehaven. Open your hand.'

She did as he ordered, but kept her face averted.

'What is wrong with you? I thought a Warehaven would be braver than this.' When she turned her head to stare up at him, he slapped the dagger's handle on to her palm and tightly closed her fingers around it. 'Now, get in the bed.'

Chapter Six

Finally. After endless weeks of searching for Glenforde's whereabouts and these last six days at sea, this journey was nearly at an end.

A cold wind raced across Richard's face, bringing a chill to his cheeks and reminding him of the narrow margin in which they'd beaten the turn of the season. With the onset of winter at hand, this venture home had been a race against time. Another week at sea would have found them in dire straits. Strong winds, enormous waves and deathly cold water could have spelt doom for any foolish enough to set sail.

Yet he'd intentionally detoured this journey home by a day—long enough to set one of his trusted men ashore on the Continent with orders to return with the information he sought. The man would return to Dunstan on the last of his ships that would hopefully soon leave Domburg. Once that ship and this one reached Dunstan's harbour his entire fleet would be safely careened during the long winter for repairs and general maintenance.

Richard directed his attention towards the fast-approaching coastline. The quickly setting sun behind them cast shadows on the rock face of the cliffs. Soon, night would fall and they would be unable to safely enter the harbour until daylight.

A quick glance assured him that Matthew had the men and ship well under control. The sail slid down the mast as oars splashed into the water.

It was imperative that the ship be manually steered through the narrow inlet into Dunstan's harbour lest she be smashed to pieces against the jagged boulders hiding beneath the surface of the water on either side of the inlet.

Once again he looked shoreward, relieved to see the torches flare to life in the towers flanking the entrance to the harbour. It was necessary to have those lights as guideposts.

Richard positioned himself at the centre of the aft deck, noting that the bow of the ship was just off-centre of the torchlights.

'Hard to port!' he shouted down to the men on the rudder. When the bow pointed dead centre between the lights, he yelled, 'Hold!'

While steering the ship past the boulders, then

between the cliffs wasn't as easy as it might appear with a crew not as well trained as this one, he was grateful for the natural protection Dunstan's unwelcoming coastline provided.

Most of the island rose up from the sea like a rock-faced mountain and needed little protection from unlikely intruders. Those who were brave enough to try either gave up in frustration, or drowned after their ship broke apart against the boulders.

The short, narrow strip of beach on the other side of the island existed only at the whims of the tide and wind. If a ship anchored there, it risked being either blown against the cliff face, or left high and dry on the exposed sandbar.

The other danger, as he'd learned, was anchoring just off the beach, only to later watch his ship sail away without him when the tide unexpectedly turned and the anchor failed to hold against the rapidly rising water. Chasing the unmanned ship down had proven far easier than bearing his father's wrath.

Even with the dangers of anchoring at the beach, his grandfather had determined it the weakest point on the island. Which is why a stone-fortified keep had been built at the highest point above the beach.

If a force did manage to make landfall there, they would be unable to gain entrance to the keep without suffering the loss of many lives.

And still, even with all of this protection—natural and manmade—Glenforde had broken through Dunstan's defences. Richard knew the man had not done so unaided. Someone on the island had to have offered assistance.

Who? And why?

A sharp gasp caught his attention. He turned to see Isabella's head appear over the edge of the forecastle deck. 'Go back inside.'

But instead of doing as she was told, she scrambled the rest of the way up the ladder to stand beside him. After planting her feet for balance, she tipped her head back to look up at the sheer rock cliffs flanking them.

Richard swallowed his groan. When his wife had first witnessed this sight, she'd been terrified, claiming that he'd brought her to the entrance of hell. Agnes had hidden her face in her hands and cried with fear.

Since he'd expected the same reaction from Isabella of Warehaven he'd ordered her to stay below. Following orders was obviously not one of her strengths—a lack he would see remedied quickly.

From the way she easily fell into the rhythm of the slightly rolling deck, it was apparent that the Lord of Warehaven hadn't cosseted his daughters inside the keep on dry land. This one at least had been aboard a ship or two in her life.

Without looking at him, she said, 'The rocks are close enough to touch.'

'No. It only appears that way.' Although they were close enough that men were stationed along both sides of the ship with long, sturdy poles in hand just in case they did get too close to the cliffs.

'Has this always been here?'

Richard frowned. Did she think he built it? He could hardly imagine the feat. 'Yes. Of course.'

'Does it cut all the way across the island?'

'No. The cliffs will become lower and level out. After the curve ahead this inlet will open into the harbour. Beyond that is a small inland river that leads to the shipyard.'

'Oh.' So fascinated by the towering walls of rock, she barely glanced to the curve ahead. 'Is this the only way into the harbour?'

'Why?'

'I just wondered.'

He knew exactly what she wondered. Half-tempted to let her worry, he left her to stew a few moments before he finally relented. 'Your father and brother have both been here before. They know how to gain safe entrance to the inlet.'

'I thought perhaps…'

When her words trailed off, Richard laughed. 'You thought what? That I would lure your family here only to watch their ship crash against the rocks?' He shook his head, adding, 'Since their death is not what I am seeking, doing so would not serve my purpose.'

She closed her eyes, shivering a moment at the memory of watching an arrow find its mark in her father's chest, before asking, 'Then it is only Glenforde's death you seek?'

'As I said before—I am not interested in your family.'

He hadn't answered her question. 'I know you think Glenforde will come for me.' She shrugged her shoulders. 'I am still not certain.'

'And I say you are wrong.' He leaned closer to warn, 'You might want to pray that he does come.'

Isabella understood the unspoken warning—if Glenforde didn't come, she could very well bear the brunt of Dunstan's revenge. Instead of telling him the reasons Glenforde would never come, she stepped away, assuring Dunstan, 'I will.'

As the ship eased out from the gentle curve, the harbour opened up before them. She blinked at the sight before her.

An entire town seemed to appear from thin air. The harbour was alight with countless torches.

People—women, men and children—lined the full docks and streets. Some laughed, some cried, but all waved and shouted their welcomes to those aboard the ship.

Ropes were tossed to men waiting on the nearest dock and the ship swung easily about as it was wrapped and tied around the mooring post. Beyond were numerous, large storage buildings.

From the looks of it, Dunstan did more than kidnap unsuspecting women.

'You look surprised.'

She nodded, admitting, 'I am.'

'Did you think me nothing more than a brigand committed to mayhem on the high seas?'

Isabella couldn't help herself, she ran her gaze down his body. With his overlong near-black hair, dark looks and recent actions, how could she think him anything else? 'Apparently, looks are deceiving.'

He took her elbow and led her towards the ladder. 'This war for the crown makes pirates and thieves of us all. When in truth I am no different than your father or brother.'

But he *was* different. She shivered beneath his touch. So very different than either of them.

Richard easily picked Conal, his man-at-arms, out from the crowd of people on the quay. The big red-haired man looked grim, as if all were not well on

Dunstan. Since there was no show of force—neither friend nor foe—crowding the docks, things couldn't be too dire.

Certain that he would find out how Dunstan had fared in his absence soon enough, Richard turned his attention back to Isabella. 'Since you managed to climb up here, I assume you can get down, too?'

She peered over the edge of the deck and then took a step back. 'I can manage on my own, thank you.'

It was on the tip of his tongue to mention her mishap in his cabin a few days ago when she'd *managed* to be tossed to the floor.

Instead he descended to the deck below and waited for her to do the same before escorting her off the ship towards his waiting man-at-arms.

From the countless tears and seemingly overexcited cries of reunion, Isabella could only assume these men had been gone from Dunstan an unusually long time.

Extended absences were a normal way of life—especially for a community involved in sea trade. She'd been at the quay numerous times with her mother and sister when the ships had finally returned to harbour. Never did she remember witnessing such a display as this at any homecoming.

It struck her as odd. Had these men left under some cloud of doom? Had they been headed out to a known, or suspected, danger? Or did Dunstan's shipping schedules keep them from home often enough to cause this level of emotion?

If the size and number of the storage buildings were any indicator, Dunstan prospered well from his chosen method of commerce.

How much of it was legal would be anyone's guess. But then, less-than-legal goods had been stowed and transported on both her father's and brother's ships a time or two. Besides, with this never-ending battle for the crown, many not-so-legal activities occurred on a daily basis.

Her escort came to an abrupt stop. He released her elbow and pulled a flame-haired giant into his embrace.

Once the backslapping and greetings were completed, Dunstan scanned the harbour, asking, 'Has the *Lisette Reynolde* returned?' When his man shook his head, Dunstan frowned, then asked, 'Where is Father Paul?'

Shocked that Dunstan would so quickly seek the services of the priest, Isabella was speechless.

'He awaits you at the keep.' The red-haired man's gaze drifted to her and then back to Dunstan. 'I assume this is your intended?'

'I am *not* his intended.'

She waved off the man's assumption and turned to her captor. 'You plan to wed so quickly?'

'That is the plan, yes.' Dunstan glanced at his man. 'A plan everyone knew before I left.'

'Well, yes, but we hadn't expected it to happen the moment you stepped on land.' The man's voice rose, causing those around them to give the trio a wide berth. 'You don't think that perhaps a little… gentler handling…a bit of ceremony, or celebration might be in order?'

Dunstan grabbed his man's arm and turned him towards half-a-dozen waiting horses. 'Enough. I don't need you to tell me how to behave.' He spared little more than a glance at Isabella, ordering, 'Get over here. You'll ride with me.'

Only yesterday he'd commented on her less-than-brave behaviour. If he wanted her to thwart him, she'd be more than happy to oblige. 'Like hell I will.'

She grabbed the reins from his hands, tucked the long skirt of her gown into the girdle about her waist and then hauled herself up on to the saddle. Isabella put her heels to the horse's side, suggesting over her shoulder, 'You can walk, or use another beast.'

Catching up with Dunstan's man, who'd set off as soon as he'd mounted his horse, she asked, 'What do I call you and just where do I find this Father Paul?'

'Conal is my name and unless you have a taste for

becoming the next Lady of Dunstan this very night, you don't want to find the priest.'

In the end, she might not have a choice in the matter, but she'd prefer not to find herself tied to Dunstan before the moon fully rose. She'd rather swim back to Warehaven.

'Then would you—?'

Conal raised one hand, cutting off the rest of her request. 'Before you even ask, I'll not help you escape, nor will I naysay Lord Dunstan's wishes.' He cast a sidelong look at her. 'Have you considered that he may have had good reasons for what he did?'

'Oh, yes, I'm certain every knave has a good reason to steal a woman away from her home on the eve of her marriage.'

The ensuing bark of laughter didn't come from Conal. Nor did the hand grabbing the reins from her fingers belong to the man-at-arms.

Dunstan looped her reins to his own like lead strings, while saying, 'And I would think that a woman so eager to wed would have been at her betrothed's side instead of wandering around a dark bailey alone.'

'That still gave you no reason to spirit me away.'

He ignored her statement to warn, 'You take off like that on your own again and I'll make certain you rue the day you were born.'

She gasped at his obvious threat. 'You wouldn't.'

'Behave like a wayward child, my lady, and I'll treat you like one.'

She glared at him. 'You wouldn't dare.'

'I wouldn't dare what?'

Isabella was almost certain that he wouldn't lay a hand on her—damaging her wouldn't be in his best interest. So, what would he do? She felt the heat of her flushed cheeks as she remembered his earlier warning that some injuries couldn't be seen.

He leaned over on his saddle, closer to her, and answered his own question. 'I would lock you away in a tower chamber without much provocation.'

Even though his deep, sensual tone gave her a moment's pause, relief washed over her, making her response nothing more than a simple breathless, 'Oh.'

Dunstan sat upright and shook his head. 'I can only hazard a guess about the direction your mind took, my lady. But let me assure you that I would never force myself on you uninvited.'

Uninvited? 'And you think for one minute that I would ever—' The barely perceptible twitch of his lips told her that she'd once again fallen prey to his mindless prattle.

Chagrined that she'd so easily let herself be led into this absurd conversation, she lifted her chin a notch, gave a good jerk on her horse's reins to free them and urged the beast ahead of the men.

'Stay on this road. You'll end up at the keep.'

Richard watched her ride ahead of them. With the ocean on one side and ever-thickening brush on the other, she had no choice but to stay on the road. Thankfully, since the ship had returned, his men and some of the men from the village saw to it that the path to the keep was lit with torches.

'She is a high-born lady, my lord; you should not tease her so.'

'She is Warehaven's whelp through and through. Trust me, the lady is well able to take my jibes and hand out some of her own.'

'That may be so, but you aren't her father or brother.' Conal's bristling censure was evident in his words.

Richard ignored his man's attitude. Something had been bothering Conal before the ship had docked. 'No. I am not her father or brother. But I am soon to be her husband.'

Conal snorted before asking, 'Were you able to discover how that accursed dog, Glenforde, came to be involved with Warehaven?'

'No, I didn't. I still have no idea why the Lord of Warehaven gave his daughter to Glenforde, but he did.'

'Then it's a good thing you came to her rescue by kidnapping her.'

'She would never agree.'

'No. And from the looks of it, she'll agree with this marriage even less.'

Richard shrugged. 'Does it matter?'

'No. But over time she might be persuaded to change her mind.'

'You, my friend, are a hopeless sot when it comes to women.'

'Perhaps.' Conal nodded towards Isabella riding ahead. 'So, what if Glenforde doesn't come for her?'

That was the second time he'd heard that opinion voiced. 'He stands to lose too much if he doesn't.'

Conal's snort startled the horses. Once the beasts calmed down, he said, 'You'd better hope so. Otherwise you'll end up with a wife for no good reason.'

'I'm sure I can find some use for her.'

Conal laughed softly before commenting, 'Careful, you might find yourself wanting this wife.'

'Perish the thought.' Quickly changing the subject, Richard asked, 'How did you fare while I was away?'

The humour left Conal's face in a rush. He turned a hard glare on Richard. 'Next time, leave someone else in charge.'

'What happened?'

'The master of the inn is keeping company with the baker's wife. So the baker refuses to supply the inn with breads or cakes. The baker's wife tired of the bickering and has taken up residence with Marguerite.'

'That must make your visits…interesting.'

'My visits?'

'Do you think nobody has noticed?'

'I don't know what you're talking about.'

'Please, don't seek to fool me. Everyone on the island is well aware that you and Marguerite have been enjoying each other's company for at least three years now. I keep waiting for her to one day make an honest man of you. Although, I must admit, I am starting to give up hope.'

Conal ignored the jibe about his lady friend. As if Richard hadn't said a word, he added, 'Now the innkeeper is declaring his lover a whore and the baker is seeking restitution for his loss.'

'Ah.' Richard sighed. 'Well, good. Nothing has changed.'

Chapter Seven

Isabella paused before the gated entrance into Dunstan Keep. The men in the twin towers stared down at her a moment before shouting to their approaching lord, 'She yours?'

His? No, she was *not* his. If she belonged to anyone it was her father—her breath caught as she remembered her father's body falling to the beach. No. She would not slip into grief until she was safely back in her family's embrace. If she now belonged to anyone it was to her brother, Jared—or with hope and a trunk full of luck, eventually a husband of her choosing.

But most definitely *not* Dunstan.

However, on rare occasions, she did know when and how to hold her tongue. This seemed to be one of those times, so she waited for Dunstan and his man to join her.

Once they were alongside of her, she unclenched her jaw to say, 'I am *not* yours.'

He ignored her and waved up at the men as he passed beneath the arched gate. 'Yes, she's mine.'

It was all she could do not to scream. But his grin told her that he knew exactly what she felt and had goaded her on purpose. Instead of screaming, she forced a smile to her lips and followed him into the keep.

Once they were in the courtyard, Dunstan dismounted, then came to her side to assist her from the horse. She accepted his help, making certain to curl her fingers tightly into his shoulders—more to bring him pain than for support.

He rewarded her petty action by pulling her hard against his chest. She struggled to free herself from his hold.

'Keep fighting me, Isabella. I love nothing more than a good battle.'

She fell lax against him. 'Let me go.'

'Not until you apologise.'

Snow would douse the fires of hell before she did so. 'I did nothing that requires an apology.'

While keeping one arm securely around her, he grasped her wrist and placed her hand against the wound on his shoulder. The thickness of the padding beneath her palm made her stomach tumble with guilt.

She turned her face away and softly said, 'I am sorry. I didn't mean to irritate your wound.'

'I beg your pardon? I didn't hear you. What did you say?'

Isabella took a breath before repeating herself a little louder, 'I said I was sorry. I didn't mean to irritate your wound.' Glancing up at him, she added, 'But it was no less than what you deserved.'

'Perhaps.' He released her wrist and then grazed her chin with his thumb. 'But it would be wise for you to remember that I am your only protector here.'

He had a valid point. Had she done any serious harm, she would be at the mercy of his men. She had no way of knowing what manner of men inhabited this godforsaken isle.

She turned away from him and looked up at the keep atop the hill. Made of stone, with round towers at each corner, it was every bit as big as Warehaven.

He pushed past her. 'Come. Father Paul should be here soon.'

Good. At least then she would have someone on her side. The priest couldn't very well marry them once she voiced her objections to this union.

Following him up the steps cut into the earthen mound, she was more than a little surprised to find an entrance at the top of the hill. Confused, she asked, 'Isn't this dangerous?'

'Dangerous? How so?'

'A ground-level entrance?' Had this man spent so little time on land that he didn't know the first thing about defending his keep?

'Until the enemy can learn to fly, we are secure.'

If someone wanted possession of Dunstan badly enough, they would find a way. But she wasn't about to argue warfare with him.

He held the metal-studded door open and followed her inside. She'd expected to walk into a storage chamber at the ground level of the keep. Instead, she paused to discover they'd come through what she would consider a postern gate leading through a thick fortified wall that opened to a courtyard running the length of the keep and not directly into the building.

When she turned to ask why the gate was at the front of the keep, Dunstan hitched an eyebrow. 'Rather deceiving at first isn't it?' He glanced up at the wall to order, 'Drop it down.'

The men, who she hadn't seen at first, lowered a portcullis into place behind the studded door, effectively cutting off the entrance from the bailey.

Dunstan stared down at her. 'No one gets in.'

Before guiding her to the steps angling up against the wall, he added, 'And no one gets out.'

Isabella took his comment as a veiled threat—a warning that she'd be unable to escape. What would he do, or say, when she proved him wrong?

Although, as she trailed behind him along narrow courtyards, and up even narrower stairs, only to cross over walkways that had surely seen better days, Isabella wondered if his warning had been necessary. Escaping was one thing—simply remembering the way to get back to the outer yard would prove a challenge.

Finally, they entered the keep through a larger, heavily studded door. Her thoughts and concerns of escape vanished as the stale, rancid air of the Great Hall slammed against her face.

Isabella quickly covered her nose and mouth with the sleeve of her gown, but it did little to veil the stench of the ill-kept hall. She blinked as tears welled from her stinging eyes and prayed there wasn't some damp, musty tower cell awaiting her.

Dunstan shot her a dark frown that she couldn't decipher, but she wasn't going to uncover her face to question him.

It was all she could do not to gag when he led her across the filthy hall to a smaller chamber on the far side. While this room was in even worse condition than the Great Hall, at least it had two narrow window openings. Thankfully, he saw fit to open both shutters letting in fresh, albeit cold air.

'Your servants are lax in their duties.' She stated what she thought was obvious while gasping for breath.

'Lax?'

Isabella ran a fingertip across the thick layer of dust on the top of a chest. 'This didn't accumulate overnight.'

He turned his head to glance in her direction, his dark expression even more stormy. 'I've yet to see anyone perish of dust.'

She kicked at an obnoxious clump of mouldy strewing herbs, sending it rolling across the floor. 'It takes more than a few days for this to grow.'

'And is easily removed with a broom.'

'The lady of this keep should be ashamed.'

'Presently, there is no lady.'

'Then the housekeeper should be severely reprimanded.'

'There is no housekeeper. And before you ask, there are no chambermaids, scullery maids nor a cook.'

She'd assumed he had no wife, since he was so determined to give her that unwanted title. And he'd told her aboard the ship that his mother was deceased. But to do without any women in the keep was something she could barely imagine.

'It is just you and your men?'

He nodded in reply.

'What do you do for food?'

'The same thing men have always done.'

She knew that meant one of the lower-ranked men did the cooking or some of the village women acted as camp followers did during a march to battle and performed the duty.

Isabella looked slowly around the chamber. Besides the dust and mould, there were cobwebs thick enough to suffocate someone should they have the misfortune to walk into them. Sheaths of papers that had tumbled from the small table in the corner on to the floor were half-covered in rotting rushes. She didn't want to think about the vermin living undisturbed in the bedding.

This is what her father's and brother's chambers would have looked like without her mother's oversight. Well, at the very least her father's chambers would have looked the same, if not worse. Her brother Jared was a little more organised.

She doubted that Dunstan Keep had always been in this condition, not when the wharf and village appeared in order and inviting. *So, how had this happened?*

'And none of you see anything wrong with…' she waved an arm to encompass the chamber '…this?'

'We have managed quite well.'

'Yes, I can see that.'

'Enough!' He spun away from the window. 'I have no desire to listen to your complaints.'

His sudden movement, deep threatening tone and fierce scowl forced her back a step. 'Complaints?' The shrillness in her voice made her take a breath. Regardless of how threatened she felt, showing any sign of fear would be a mistake. To regain a semblance of self-control, she glanced pointedly around the chamber, asking in what she hoped was a milder tone, 'The sorry condition of your keep does not bother you?'

Dunstan stormed towards her, his hands clenched at his sides. 'The condition of *my* keep is none of your concern.'

She fought the urge to bolt from the chamber—where would she go? But it was impossible to stand firm in the face of his anger and it would be foolish to remain within arm's length of danger. Moving away quickly, she put the small table between them.

'Where I lay my head at night *is* my concern.'

'If this chamber isn't good enough for you, there is an empty cell available.'

If he was intentionally seeking to frighten her

more, he would have to do better than that. Besides, the cell might prove cleaner. Isabella squared her shoulders and stared at him. 'That would suit me fine, my lord.'

'I wonder.' His eyebrows arched. 'How would your bravado fare amongst the rats?'

Actually, if the closeness of the walls didn't take her bravado away and leave her near senseless, she'd be frantic at the first scurry of tiny feet, but he didn't need to know that. So, in an effort to retain her show of bravery, she shrugged in answer to his question.

'Do not tempt me, Isabella.'

He spoke her name slowly, deliberately drawing it out. She hated the way it rolled off his tongue. And she utterly despised the tremors it sent skittering down her spine.

'Lord Dunstan!'

Conal's voice broke through the closed chamber door a mere heartbeat before the man swung it open and entered. To her relief the priest followed in his wake.

Finally. She exhaled with a loud sigh, drawing the attention of all three men.

Dunstan motioned the men further into the chamber. 'Father Paul, is all ready?'

'Just as you requested.' The priest emptied the contents of the satchel he carried on to the table. 'I take it this is your intended bride?' the priest asked Dunstan.

'Yes.'

'No,' Isabella answered at the same time.

Ignoring her, the priest went about his business of unrolling and flattening a document, sharpening a quill and stirring the ink. He moved aside and waved Dunstan to the table. 'Your signature, my lord.'

Dunstan paused, holding the quill less than a breath above the document. The feathered end wavered slightly, a small drop of ink splashed down on to the vellum, spreading like a brackish-coloured droplet of blood.

An ominous omen of the future? Isabella's stomach clenched at the thought.

He scrawled his name at the bottom of the document, then extended the pen towards her, warning, 'Don't make this difficult.'

'No.' She stared at the quill before glaring at him across the table. 'You can't make me do this.'

'Yes, actually, I can and will.'

She gasped at the certainty in his words. Knowing there would be no reasoning with him, she turned to the priest. Surely he could be made to see how unwilling she was to wed Dunstan. 'I am being forced into this unholy alliance. It will not stand.'

The priest ignored her, seemingly content to gaze

around the chamber. His unconcerned air splashed an icy cold on the heated rage that had been building in her chest.

'Are you not a man of God? Do you not represent the Church in this matter?' Isabella swallowed hard in a desperate attempt to remain rational. 'I cannot be forced into this union.'

Father Paul looked down on her with the expression of a long-suffering parent dealing with an unreasonable child—the same type of look she'd endured countless times from Warehaven's priest when she'd railed against lessons she had no desire to learn.

'Child, it seems you do not fully understand the direness of your situation.'

The calmness of his voice had the opposite effect of what he'd most likely intended. Instead of soothing her, it set her teeth on edge. 'I am *not* a child.'

Dunstan snorted, before suggesting, 'Then stop acting like one.'

She ignored him, intent on making the priest see her side of this argument—and then agreeing with her. 'There is nothing about this situation that I do not understand. I was taken from my home. Saw an arrow pierce my father's chest as he came to my defence. I was made to tend my captor's injuries. And now—' she flicked her shaking fingers at the document on the table '—against everything that is just and right I am being forced to agree to a marriage that neither I, nor my family, would desire.'

The priest's eyebrows rose. 'I am certain your family would find it more desirable for you to wed someone you detest now, than to return to them next spring carrying a bastard.'

Next spring?

The floor heaved beneath her feet.

Dear Lord, she'd not taken the season, nor the weather, into consideration. Her brother and Glenforde would be unable to come to her rescue for months.

And the priest's concern over her carrying a bastard come spring made her ill. She drew in a long breath, hoping to calm the sudden queasiness of her stomach. There had to be a way out of this.

'Child.' Father Paul touched her arm. 'Surely now you see the sense in a marriage.'

'No.' Isabella shook her head. 'There will be no chance of creating a child.'

'You cannot know the future. You are here on Dunstan without any protection, with no suitable companion.' The priest shrugged. 'Even if Lord Richard was the most chivalrous knight of the realm and placed not one finger upon your person, nobody can say the same of every man on this island.'

She glared at Dunstan. 'You have so little control over the men in your command?'

When he said nothing, she crossed her arms against her chest and turned her attention back to the priest. 'Then lock me away in a cell.'

'Locks can be picked, cell doors can be broken.'

Would he thwart every idea she suggested? 'But—'

Dunstan cleared his throat, interrupting her. 'Enough. Your fate was sealed before I stepped foot on your father's land.' He tapped the quill beneath his signature on the document. 'Either sign this yourself, or I'll make your mark for you.'

'No!' She slapped both of her hands on the table. 'I will not do this. There has to be another option. One less…distasteful.'

Dunstan swirled the nib of the pen across the document, making a rather elaborate mark below his name. 'You will not do this?' He made a show of staring hard at the vellum on the table, before shrugging. 'It appears to me that you have already signed of your own free will.'

This could not be happening to her. In a hazy blur, Isabella saw Conal drop something into Dunstan's outstretched palm. Before she could make any sense of his intention, he grasped her left hand and slid a gold band on to her ring finger.

Instead of releasing her hand, he engulfed it in his

own. 'With this ring, I, Richard of Dunstan, wed Isabella of Warehaven.'

Her throat ached with the need to scream. She jerked free of his hold, asking in a choked whisper, 'What have you done?'

No answer was required, or forthcoming, as she knew exactly what he'd done. He'd planned this every step of the way.

He'd had some document drawn up that took Lord only knew what from her, placed his signature and hers on it with witnesses present who would swear she'd signed of her own free will. Then, he'd sealed the deed by placing his ring on her finger.

As far as anyone was concerned, she was wed to this knave. There was only one small…task…keeping them from being for ever joined in unholy matrimony.

While he might be able to forge her mark on a document, Dunstan would find bedding her much harder than he might think. Isabella clenched her hands into fists. Harder? No. She would make it impossible.

'My part here seems to be done.' Father Paul snatched the document from the table, rolled it up and tucked it back into his satchel. 'I'll take this. Should you have any desire to read it, you will find it safe in my care.'

He took a step back and paused. 'Lord, Lady Dunstan, if you wish a blessing on your union, you know where to find me.'

After the priest left the chamber, Dunstan crossed the room and pulled the sheet from his bed.

Isabella frowned. What was he doing now?

In the blink of an eye, he slid a dagger across the tip of a finger, splattered the blood on to the sheet and then tossed it to Conal. 'Lock this up somewhere safe.'

She stared in shock at Conal's back as he hastily left the chamber. Everything about this farce of a marriage—from the creation of the document, her forged signature and now to the evidence of the bloodied bedding—had been seen to in advance.

'You pig!' She turned her full attention to Dunstan. 'You dirty, filthy pig. I would like to see you gutted.' She paused to give her tremors a moment to subside before continuing, 'And your entrails slowly pulled from your body and fed to the dogs while you watched in dying agony.'

Dunstan unbuckled his belt and tossed it on to the narrow cot. 'Could we save all that for tomorrow?' He pulled his tunic over his head and dropped it atop his belt. 'Right now I'd rather sleep.'

'You do that.' She pulled his ring from her finger and threw it at him as she moved from behind the desk to march to the door intent on leaving this chamber, this keep and, if at all possible, somehow this island.

He grabbed her arm as she reached for the latch. 'And just where do you think you're going?'

Isabella tried to pull free of his hold, but he only tightened his grasp. 'Let me go.'

'Oh, my dear wife, you seem a bit upset.'

'Upset!' His mocking manner nearly made her spit with rage. 'I have never been so...so mistreated in my life.' She pried at his fingers. 'And do *not* call me wife.'

'Nobody has mistreated you.' He released his hold long enough to scoop her up in his arms. 'But perhaps someone should have done so once or twice.' He turned around and walked towards the far corner of the chamber.

'Put me down.' Isabella struggled against his overbearing hold.

As if she hadn't said a word, he continued, 'Had they done so, you might know how to deal with disappointment in a less strident manner.'

Disappointment? Is that what he considered these recent events? Nothing but a disappointment?

'Finding water in your goblet instead of wine is a disappointment. This is far more than that.'

She kicked her legs and to her relief, he lowered his arm, letting her feet hit the floor.

'I am certain you'll eventually find a way to come to terms with your future. But for now, it is time for bed.'

She glanced behind them at the narrow cot. 'I am not sleeping in that vermin-infested thing you call a bed.'

'No, you aren't.' While keeping one arm wrapped about her waist, he shoved aside a dusty tapestry hiding a door, which he opened and then pushed her into the darkness beyond. 'But neither am I.'

Chapter Eight

Richard nabbed a lit torch from the wall of the outer chamber before following Isabella into the room.

Standing with his back against the closed door, he held the torch high enough to illuminate the area around him before using it to light a brace of candles. He mounted the torch in a wall sconce, ignoring Isabella's gasp of dismay.

While a layer of dust had settled from weeks of non-use, this small chamber was serviceable and, as far as he was concerned, that was all that should matter. He crossed the room to slightly open one of the shutters just enough to allow in a breeze of fresh air.

He expected her to make some comment, but to his amazement, she held her tongue and simply glared at him.

The bed jutting out from the far wall looked more inviting that he'd imagined it would and he longed for nothing more than to crawl beneath the covers, drop his head on to a pillow and then sink into the overstuffed mattress.

However, he couldn't help but wonder if Isabella would plunge a knife into his heart while he slept.

Before he could formulate any plan to prevent such an undesirable occurrence, she asked, 'Where do you plan to sleep?'

'In my bed.'

Her brows winged over her hazel eyes. Light from the candles flickered in the speckled depths of her stare.

'And where then will I sleep?'

Even though there was little doubt his answer would be acceptable, he forged ahead. 'In my bed.'

'When boars grow teats.'

Richard wanted to laugh at her bald statement, but knew that would only encourage her. Instead, he asked, 'Did you learn your refined speech at Warehaven's docks?'

'My speech is none of your concern.'

'As your husband, it is of great concern to me. I'll not have you bandying coarse talk about the keep. You are well aware of the trouble it invites.'

'Are you once again saying you have no control of your people?'

She'd taken up that familiar arms-crossed-against-her-chest, rigid-spine, chin-up stance that he'd come to recognise as her ready-for-battle pose. He knew that she would refuse to see reason or agree with anything he said.

His patience was in short supply at the moment and suddenly the idea of locking her in a cell seemed a good one.

Richard sighed. Refusing her bait, he sat on the edge of the bed. 'If you want everyone to think you are nothing more than a trollop I pulled from the dregs, so be it.' He tugged at a boot. 'But don't come crying to me the first time one of the men decides to taste your wares.'

He tossed the boot across the room, drowning out her gasp of outrage. She could feign shock all she wanted. Right now he just wanted sleep.

'I do not have to stand here and listen to you.' Isabella headed towards the door.

Richard reached it first and hauled her over his shoulder. 'You are partially correct. You don't have to *stand* here.' He crossed the room in three strides and dropped her on to the bed. 'However, you will remain in this room, in this bed and listen to whatever I have to say.'

When she tried to get off the bed, he pushed her back on to the mattress. Holding her shoulders to the bed, he leaned closer. 'If you get up from here again, I will tie you to the bed.' Richard waited for her wide-eyed glare to ease into a frowning scowl to ask, 'Do you understand me?'

Oddly, instead of fighting him, arguing or making demands, she nodded. Her easy acquiescence now, along with her silence when he'd first pushed her into this chamber, made him wary. His concern that she might stab him in his sleep grew stronger.

Richard released her and backed off slowly, not certain she'd actually stay put. With one eye on her, he once again sat on the edge of the bed to remove his other boot and stockings, then turned to slide Isabella's shoes off.

'Don't.'

The tremor in her whispered command caught him unaware. Was she frightened, angry or tired like him? 'I was simply going to—'

'I know what you were going to do.' She drew her legs away. 'I can do it myself.'

'Then do so.'

Once she dropped her shoes and stockings to the floor alongside the bed, Richard stood and stared down at her. The look she returned was…timid… no, not quite timid, he doubted if there was a timid bone in her entire body—perhaps more worried or concerned than frightened. Her arrow-straight body, tense, poised for escape most likely, spoke louder than any words she might have said.

He jerked the covers and sheet from beneath her and drew them over her body. Her gaze followed him, he felt it burning a hole into his back, as he walked around the bed to the other side.

Sliding beneath the top cover, leaving the thinner blanket and sheet beneath him, he settled his head on to the pillow, unable to hold back a sigh.

The leather braces supporting the mattress creaked as she sat up. He opened one eye. 'What are you doing?'

'I can't sleep here.'

'You might want to give it a try before crying defeat.' He reached up, seeking to draw her back down. 'Close your eyes.'

She pushed his hold away. 'I can't sleep in this bed with you.'

He didn't need the candlelight to see the tenseness of her body—not when the tightness of her voice gave evidence to the anger roiling just beneath the surface.

'There is no reason we cannot share this bed.' Richard debated for a heartbeat, before reminding her, 'We are married.'

In a flurry of limbs and covers, she was up and out of the bed before he could stop her. From the other side of the chamber, she said, 'In name only and I'd prefer to keep it that way.'

'If you remember correctly, Conal left the chamber with proof that states this marriage is far more than name only.'

'That proof is nothing but a ruse.'

'Agreed. But who will attest to that in your defence?'

'I know the truth and that is enough.'

Richard knew any battle waged with words was lost, she would argue until the sun rose and beyond. 'This has become tiresome.' He sat up and dragged her side of the covers back, then patted the mattress. 'Get back in the bed and go to sleep. You will awaken in the morning as much a virgin as you are now.'

'What does that mean?'

He sighed. Apparently she was in the mood to argue every little thing he said. 'It means that if you do as I suggest, I will not touch a hair on your head…tonight.'

'And if I don't?'

Was she begging him for an all-out battle? He stared at her. 'What are you seeking to do, Isabella? Do you *want* me to force you?'

Ah, and once again her ready-for-battle pose—she stiffened her spine and crossed her arms in front of her against her chest. Why would this woman want to enrage him?

'You couldn't force me.'

'Haven't we already established the fact that I can? And I will?'

'You didn't force me to wed you. You simply forged my name on a document. I meant I would rather die than have you force yourself upon me.'

Force himself upon her? What the hell was she…? He frowned as her meaning dawned on him. They were talking about two different things. He'd only meant that he'd force her to sleep in the bed, nothing else. Yet she obviously thought he was talking about rape.

Outside of battle, he'd never in his life intentionally harmed any man smaller or weaker. He certainly wasn't about to start doing so with a woman now. He gritted his teeth at the ungodly thought, threw the covers off and rose from the bed. Without another word, he crossed the chamber.

Isabella backed away, reaching behind her for the door. 'Don't touch me.'

He again tossed her over his shoulder. 'Too late.'

This time, instead of arranging the covers to separate them, he dropped her on the bed and launched himself behind her. With one arm wrapped about her waist, he pulled her back tight against his chest, hooked a leg over hers and pulled the covers up.

'Now, close your eyes and go to sleep.'

When she struggled against his hold, he simply tightened his arm, hoping that eventually she'd wear herself out.

Once her struggles lessened, Richard closed his own eyes, certain that he'd have little trouble holding on to her if he fell asleep. After all, he'd long ago learned to remain alert even though he slept. Had he not, it was doubtful he'd be alive today.

Just as the hazy relaxing cloud of slumber rolled over him, Isabella reached for the edge of the bed. Her upper body followed her extended arms, while her soft rounded buttocks pressed against his groin, sweeping away any thought of sleep.

With a grumbled curse, Richard opened his eyes. While splaying his fingers low over her belly, he pulled the pillow from beneath her head and curled his arm in its place. He pressed his palm against her forehead, tipping her head back to ask hoarsely, 'Is it your intention to ensure neither of us sleeps this night?'

To lend emphasis to his question, he held her in place and thrust his hips forward. 'If so, you are succeeding.'

She froze immediately, gasping a strangled, 'No.'

The surprise in her voice only sent more blood rushing to his groin, making rational thought difficult. Richard groaned. What was it about this woman that enticed him so? She was nothing more than a means to an end—a pawn—someone to use to his advantage.

So why then did he keep having to remind himself of that simple fact? And why did he ache to touch her, to taste her, to take her and make her his wife in all ways?

Even through the layers of clothing separating them, the heat of her body swirled around him like a warm, beckoning caress. It was all he could do not to accept such a tempting invitation.

She tugged at his wrist, trying to move his arm. 'You need to release me.'

'No.' He snuggled impossibly closer. 'I find this rather comfortable.'

Finally, with an exasperated huff, Isabella fell still. After a few moments of blessed silence, Richard thought—hoped—she'd fallen asleep and he once again closed his eyes.

And once again, just as sleep promised to overtake him, Isabella broke through the fog. 'This will not work.'

Richard swallowed the growl rushing up his throat and asked, 'What will not work?'

She relaxed, easing down into the mattress and against his chest. 'If you think to seduce me with this sudden bout of gentleness, rest assured you cannot.'

Seduce her? The notion hadn't entered his mind—until now. He didn't know whether to laugh at her assumption, or curse at the ideas filling his head.

'I cannot? And why is that?'

'I am immune to your...charms.'

'Charms?'

She tapped his forearm. 'Yes, this holding me close and not attempting to force yourself on me.'

He choked on a laugh, then cleared his throat. 'The only reason I am holding you close is so you can't run a knife through my heart while I sleep.'

'No. I think you lie. If you were truly worried that I might murder you in your sleep, you would have gone elsewhere.'

'You don't think it would appear odd were I to sleep elsewhere on my wedding night?'

She shrugged. 'You gave your man bloodied sheets to flaunt before the others. As far as everyone is concerned you already...did your duty.'

Richard rolled his eyes. *Did his duty?*

Before he could say anything in response, she continued. 'So, the only reason for this...closeness...is an attempt at seduction. And just so there is no doubt in your mind, let me assure you, it will not succeed.'

Richard withdrew his arm from beneath her head, unhooked his leg from hers and rolled on to his back. He was torn between two immediately clear options—kiss her until she shut up, or lock her up somewhere and conveniently lose the key.

He sat up, grabbed a pillow and the top cover from the bed and tossed them to the far side of the chamber. Leaning over her, he stroked a fingertip along her cheek. 'Because I am too tired to think clearly or battle any further, you win this round, my lady. But to erase any doubt from *your* mind, let me assure *you* of one thing…' He paused until she turned her head and looked up at him. '…I have never in my life backed down from a challenge.'

'But I didn't—'

He cut off her denial by covering her lips with his own. It didn't matter what she'd said, she could lie to herself all she wanted, but her body didn't lie. He knew the truth the instant her mouth softened beneath his.

Chapter Nine

'My lady?'

Before Isabella could fully open her eyes the window shutters creaked open. Sunlight flooded the chamber, near blinding her and stripping away the last vestige of sleep.

She sat up on the bed and squinted at the older woman now bustling about the room while shaking her head and muttering in disapproval.

'What was his lordship thinking?' The woman tossed the linens from the makeshift pallet into a pile. 'Bringing a lady here with the keep in this condition is unforgivable.' She tossed some clothing atop the pile. 'And to keep you in this tiny room—he needs his ears boxed.'

Swooping up the pile, she stood alongside the bed. 'Never you fear, I'll see this set right. If you're hungry, I'm sure the cook has put something together by now.'

Isabella's stomach growled, supplying the answer before her lips could form the words.

'How thoughtless of me, of course you are hungry.' The woman headed towards the door, promising, 'I will return soon with some food.'

Her senses still muddled, Isabella called out, 'Wait. Who are you?'

'Hattie, my lady.' Still at the door, she added, 'His lordship came to the village at sunrise, on his way to the docks. After seeing to some matter at the bakery, he ordered his servants back to the keep and asked if I would see to your needs for a time. Now, with your permission I'll get you something to eat and then we can plan this day's activities.'

'Yes, thank you.' Rising from the bed, Isabella wiped her sleep-tousled hair from her face, wondering just what activities would be in store for her. Obviously a cook had been found—or retrieved— and perhaps a few servants would be on hand to help clean.

Actually, she hoped there were more than a few, because cleaning this keep would require an army just to make it presentable. She shook one of the bed curtains and coughed at the dust flying up into the air. Her mother would be horrified.

To her relief, the items needed for her morning ablution were stacked on top of the chest at the end of the bed. Noticing the ribbons to braid through her hair, she knew these necessities hadn't been provided by Dunstan.

Hattie returned with the promised food just as she finished adjusting her ornate girdle low around her waist.

Two men carrying a small table and benches followed the woman into the chamber. The younger man—little more than a boy—dipped his head, put the benches beside the table and left.

However, the older and much larger man wasn't as quick to take his leave. She'd seen this man before on the ship. He sauntered towards the door, then turned to face her. His bulk dwarfed the small chamber and he raked Isabella with a look that reminded her of a hungry wolf and made her feel somehow dirty. 'It's a shame Dunstan saw fit to leave you…unattended.'

Isabella guessed from his pointed hesitation that he meant defenceless, not unattended. She took a step away from him, noting the width of his shoulders, the size of his meaty arms and his two missing fingers with trepidation.

'I would never leave my *special* woman wanting for my attention.'

Special woman? What had Dunstan told his men? She moved towards the table, intent on arming herself with the knife sticking out of the round loaf of bread. The small weapon wouldn't do much damage against this oversized oaf, but it was all she saw readily available.

He came closer to tower over her. 'Come now, sweeting,' he drawled low and throaty as if that would tempt her to ignore his ale-laden breath and threatening manner. 'Wouldn't you rather have a real man keeping you safe and warm instead of a lad who uses you, then leaves you to fend for yourself?'

She swallowed the sour taste in her mouth as she reached for the knife. Hattie caught her attention and shook her head. For half a heartbeat Isabella feared the woman was working with the man and was silently warning her not to fight what would be a lost cause.

But a heavy thud and the man's gasp right before he dropped to the floor like a boulder at her feet dissolved that fear.

She drew her confused attention from the floor up to Dunstan's angry frown. 'Are you uninjured?'

After she nodded her reply, he shouted for Conal. When his man rushed into the chamber, he pointed at the moaning heap on the floor, ordering, 'Get him out of here. Confine him so I can deal with him later.'

Once Conal and his staggering charge left the

chamber, Hattie turned on Dunstan. 'Now will you listen to me instead of being so pig-headed?'

Taken aback by the way the older woman spoke to the lord of this keep, Isabella remained silent.

Dunstan sat down at the table, motioning for Isabella to join him before he answered Hattie, by asking, 'Which chamber would you prefer?'

'She is a lady.'

Isabella sat across from him and watched the by-play between this master and servant with interest.

'I am not opening either of those rooms.'

'Then she will take yours.'

'So be it.' He turned his attention to the food and Isabella. Without preamble, he explained, 'Hattie was my nursemaid and since then has become the island's chief busybody.'

The woman snatched the loaf of bread from his hands and tore it into two chunks—one for each of them. 'It's truly a sad thing that you still need a busybody to keep you from doing yourself harm.'

Isabella swallowed some water in an effort not to choke.

'It's more of a sad thing that you seem to constantly forget your place.'

Hattie's short bark of laughter was punctuated by a deeper frown from Dunstan. To break the tension she feared would escalate, Isabella asked the woman, 'Have you been on Dunstan Island long?'

'From before this one here was born, yes.'

Dunstan briefly pointed his eating knife towards Hattie. 'She came here with my mother and stayed on after I was born.'

'Someone needed to keep an eye on you.'

'I am no longer in need of a wet nurse.'

'And I am still waiting for you to prove that.'

'Enough!'

Isabella leaned back as Dunstan's face reddened. His eyes blazed. She wished she could somehow slide beneath the table before he completely lost his temper.

However, Hattie showed no signs of fear—or of relenting. Instead of making a quick escape, the woman patted Dunstan's shoulder. 'I tease you over-much at times and for that I do apologise. It is hard to remember you no longer need or want a mother figure.'

'Remember what you will, it makes no difference to me.'

Isabella cringed. His surly tone made it quite clear that he truly didn't care. However, Hattie's pursed lips and frown made Isabella wonder if Dunstan's current behaviour was out of the ordinary for him.

The older woman shook her head. 'Ack, I wonder how you've managed not to choke on your sour mood these last months.'

Dunstan shrugged in response, but from the smoothing of his brow, it appeared that his ire was fading as quickly as it had first appeared.

Dismayed by this odd exchange, and Dunstan's easy manner with this woman, Isabella tried to focus on her food. Obviously Hattie's relationship with his mother gave her added worth in Dunstan's eyes. While she wasn't quite family, neither did she appear to be a servant.

The older woman made the bed, asking, 'You will not be overwrought if I move Lady Isabella into your old chamber?'

'Aye, it will wound me deeply to have her housed elsewhere. Especially since I so enjoy sleeping with one eye open all night.'

'Warehaven would be a better place to *house* me,' Isabella interrupted his obvious sarcasm.

Dunstan rolled his eyes, but otherwise ignored her. 'I'm sure it will suit.'

'I have no doubts on that.' Hattie looked at Isabella, adding, 'But perhaps the lady would like to have the final say.'

Isabella nearly jumped at the chance to escape this small room. 'The lady would be happy to take a look.'

'No.' Dunstan shook his head. 'The lady and I have other matters to attend.'

After Hattie left the chamber, Isabella curled her fingers around the handle of the eating knife. At Dunstan's raised brow, she drew her hand away from the utensil. Not that the short blade could do much damage, but gripping it would have made her feel safer.

'What matters have we to attend?'

Yawning, he stretched his arms out, over his head and then brought them back down. 'There is still the matter of the bedding.'

'No. We—' Isabella pushed back from the table in a rush, knocking over the bench and choking on her reply.

Dunstan's eyes glimmered. But it was that familiar twitch of his lips that let her know he had once again intentionally led her mind astray.

He rested his elbows on the table. 'It is far too easy to unsettle you.'

She glared at him, wishing she could find words vile enough to describe what she thought of his amusement at her expense. While his action reminded her of Jared, this man was not her brother, he had no right to tease her in such a manner and she wanted to tell him so. But instead, she righted the bench and sat back down at the table. 'After all that has happened to me—at your doing—why would I not be unsettled?'

To her horror, she heard her voice waver. Her hands shook, stomach knotted and her throat grew tight enough to make swallowing difficult. Isabella knew that now, since she was dry, warm, had gained a night's worth of good sleep and had decent food in her belly, she was on the verge of losing the tight grip she'd kept on her grief thus far.

She could no more help it than she could stop the sun from rising. It was her way—she could forge through a crisis with her wits about her for the most part, but once all was calm and back to normal, she became inconsolable, weepy and unreasonable. It was a weakness, a fault her mother had brought to her attention more than once. Like a silly fool she'd actually thought she would be able to hold back the heavy sadness weighing on her heart until she returned to the arms of her family. She sniffed back the threatening tears.

Dunstan reached across the table and placed a hand over hers. 'Isabella, look at me.'

The unusual gentleness of his touch and his voice was nearly her undoing. She drew her lower lip between her teeth to keep it from trembling and lifted her head to stare at him.

'Do you remember when you thought I'd turned

the ship around to take you home and you knew we were heading south?'

Unable to reply, she only nodded.

'We did head south, just long enough for one of my men to depart the ship.'

'Why?' Her voice cracked and she wanted nothing more than to find a reason to grow angry and set her coming bout of sadness aside for a little while longer. Unfortunately, Dunstan's calm, easygoing manner, while unfamiliar, wasn't providing her an outlet for rage.

'Everyone knows that Warehaven is Matilda's half-brother and even though the empress is in Normandy, surely word of her brother's condition would have reached her. So, I gave my man orders to quickly find news of your father and to return on the *Lisette Reynolde*.' He stroked his thumb across her hand. 'The ship docked early this morning.'

Oh, no, she didn't want to hear this from his lips. No. It was not his place, not his right to tell her that her father had died at his hands and that she'd been forced to wed her sire's murderer.

She gasped at the pain lancing through her heart and tried desperately to blink away the tears blurring her vision. The rage she'd been seeking should have sprung to life, but it hadn't. Instead, fear—cold and empty—filled her with a dread she'd not known before this moment.

Dunstan's hand tightened over hers, as if offering comfort, and he reached up with his other hand to brush at the tears on her cheeks before cupping the side of her face. 'Isabella, he is not dead. Wounded, yes, and from what I hear, angry as a crazed boar, but your father is not dead.'

A roaring, like a gale-force wind, ripped through her ears, leaving her dizzy and muddling her mind. She shook her head, trying to clear the annoying howl. 'He lives?'

'Yes.'

She drew her hand from beneath his and rose. Quickly, before she lost the ability to speak, she said in a rush, 'I thank you for telling me. But if we're done here...'

As her words trailed off, Isabella felt his stare piercing her back, but she wasn't about to turn around to face him. She stood in front of the narrow window, her hands pressed tightly into her stomach and stared through a gathering of tears out at the windswept sea.

The scrape of the wooden bench moving across the floor let her know that he'd risen from the table. She closed her eyes tightly, praying he would just leave the chamber.

'Are you dismissing me?'

She nodded at his incredulous tone. Apparently it had been a long time since anyone had sent him away—verbally, or otherwise.

Thankfully, his heavy footsteps headed towards the door, which he slammed closed behind him.

Without waiting for more than half a heartbeat, she turned away from the window to throw herself across the bed, burying her face in her crossed arms. This ordeal was not yet over. So why was she suddenly falling into a such a muddled state now? Dear Lord, she'd not wanted this to happen, not now, not here, not until she was safely home, but she couldn't stop the tears, or the gasping breaths from escaping.

A firm hand on the small of her back surprised her until she realised it belonged to Dunstan. His nearness tore a strangled plea from her. 'Please, just leave me alone.'

Richard sighed and sat on the edge of the bed. 'That's not going to happen.'

Her odd behaviour moments ago had caught him off guard. It wasn't until he'd left the chamber and taken three steps away from the door when he'd realised what she was doing.

He'd heard her gasping sobs before he had come back into the chamber. The twisting of his gut had nearly kept him from pushing the door open, but he managed to swallow his unnerving response to her tears.

What was he supposed to do? Agnes's tears had fallen nearly every day, but he doubted that a single one of them had been anything other than a means of manipulation. However, it had taken him months to figure that out and in the meantime she'd made him suffer the pangs of misery.

For months he'd been left feeling confused, frustrated and consumed by guilt. It was hard to determine which gut-wrenching emotion unmanned him the most. Regardless, he had no intention of going through that again.

Richard drew his hand along Isabella's spine, knowing that whatever he did now would set the stage for their future. He didn't want more endless months of tears and guilt, but Isabella of Warehaven was not the type of woman who easily dissolved into tears for little reason. Quite the opposite, in truth. He'd seen her fight to hold them in more than once.

With a silent curse, and a fervent hope that she wasn't toying with him on purpose, he eased further on to the bed and pulled her up against his chest.

She stiffened, then tried to shove him away. 'What are you doing?'

Her broken words tore at his heart and he had no

desire to determine why that should be so. The only thing he wished to determine right this minute was how to make her stop crying.

He held her tightly against him, not permitting her to escape. 'Tell me what has upset you so. I thought word of your father's well-being would make you happy, not sad.'

'Of course I'm gladdened to know he is not dead,' she mumbled.

He stroked her hair, the silken strands curling around his fingers as if they wanted to cling to him, unlike their owner, who was doing all she could to avoid his touch. 'Then what reason have you to cry?'

Her sudden, loud intake of breath should have served as a warning. Instead, it was her shriek of rage that gave him his first clue to her anger.

'What reason do I have to cry?' She pummelled her fists against his chest, ordering, 'Release me this instant!'

Richard hesitated a second too long. She jerked back unexpectedly, slamming her head against his chin.

He loosened his hold and she bolted from the bed, shouting, 'What is wrong?'

Richard glared at her and swung his chin back and

forth to make sure she hadn't broken his jaw before saying, 'Obviously something is.'

She returned his hard stare. 'Need I recite the list of crimes committed against me?'

Again? He waved a hand at her. 'Oh, please do.'

'I was kidnapped from my home.'

'Guilty.' An act he was beginning to regret. He nodded. 'Continue.'

'Thrown on to your ship.' She paced the length of his chamber and while her expression remained tight and cold, her emotions were evident by the motions of her hands.

'I was then carried across the sea.' A deaf person could have kept track of the conversation by the way she punctuated each statement with a flurry of hand gestures.

'And I was forced to care for you.' Even she paused long enough to glance at the finger she'd pointed at him before quickly crossing her arms against her chest.

Richard leaned back against the pile of pillows at the head of the bed. 'Anything you forgot?'

She uncrossed her arms and stormed to the end of the bed with her fisted hands held tightly against her side. 'I was forced to marry you.' She took a breath before adding, 'Against my will.'

Oh, she was building a fine fit of rage. At least she

wasn't crying any more, which was an improvement. Instead of stopping her, he nodded and agreed with the obvious, 'Yes, well, forced usually does mean against one's will.'

'And then…then you made me sleep in your chamber.'

He shrugged. 'It would be deemed odd if my wife slept anywhere else.'

'Oh!' She turned away from the bed, only to swing back around and again exclaim, 'Oh!'

Apparently, she'd run out of crimes to list. 'Are you finished?'

When she nodded, he swung his legs over the side of the bed and rose. Like a hunter stalking his prey, he followed her as she backed away until the far corner of the chamber stopped her retreat. With both hands against the wall, he trapped her.

'We have had this conversation before, Isabella, and this will be the last time. Yes, I kidnapped you and forced your hand in marriage.'

In response to her mutinous glare, he took another step forward, pressing his thighs against hers. 'Not one hair on your head has been harmed. You are sheltered and fed.'

'Sheltered? In a pigsty.'

'It serves its purpose and, like it or not, this is your home now.' Agnes had hated Dunstan's keep.

It was too small, too plain, too far beneath her. He wasn't going to listen to another woman's complaints. 'You'd better get used to it, because this is where you'll live and this is where you'll some day die.'

At her wide-eyed look of horror, he added, 'You are a means to an end and I will do anything to see that Glenforde pays for what he has done.'

Instead of backing down, or cowering in submission like any rational person might, she stared up at him to ask, 'And I am to suffer for his sins?'

'Suffer?' He marvelled at her brashness. 'It does not appear to me that you are suffering. Oh, yes, you are angry that you did not get your way in this. But you are not suffering.'

'Who are you to decide if I am suffering or not? I am away from my family, bereft of all I hold dear—'

'Bereft?' He cut her off with a snort. 'Give over, Isabella. Had I not spirited you away from Warehaven, you would have soon wed Glenforde. It was unlikely that the two of you would reside in your father's keep. You'd have gone to Glenforde's home, alone, without your family to protect you. Trust me when I tell you that then you would have learned the meaning of the word suffer.'

'Oh, so I should be thankful you kidnapped me?'

'Yes, now that you mention it, perhaps you should be.'

'Phhpptt. You are mightily full of yourself, Dunstan. Does your arrogance know any bounds?'

'I may be full of myself. But you, my dear, are my wife and you are sorely trying my patience.'

'I feel so sorry for you.'

Richard closed his eyes for a moment. The urge to rail back at her was strong, but he stopped himself. Many months would pass before Warehaven landed on Dunstan and he had no intention of living in hell until then. Even when her father did come it would change nothing, they would still be married. He needed to somehow come to understand this woman's odd moods.

Why was she trying so hard to anger him? He peered down at her and noticed that her hands resting against his chest trembled slightly. Interesting. So, she did harbour some fear, some realisation of her current situation.

'What is all of this about, Isabella? Why the tears and the rage?'

'I've already told you.'

'No. I think you've led me on a merry chase to avoid whatever is truly bothering you.'

She lowered her hands and looked away, the pink

of her cheeks deepening. He bit back a smile at her flush. If nothing else, at least he hadn't been wrong. Something was chafing at her and whatever it was had little to do with the words coming out of her mouth.

To move this along, he stated, 'I have other matters to attend. I really don't have all day to stand here trying to coax answers from you.'

'Then go.' She tried unsuccessfully to shoulder past him. 'Just leave me alone.'

Richard sighed as he blocked her escape. And just like that, they were right back to where they'd started. 'I am not going to leave you alone.' He stroked her cheek. 'It is true, we are never going to be happy newlyweds, but most married couples aren't. Would it not be easier to at least try to find a way to get along?'

Her cheeks flushed again and he paused, frowning. What the...? Oh, dear Lord above, the woman was nervous in his presence. Her tears might have been from relief to discover her father lived. He could understand that. But her anger had flared far too quickly when he'd done nothing except seek to comfort her.

She *wanted* him to leave the chamber. She was intentionally trying to anger him enough so he'd storm out of here. Why? He studied her face. Her gaze darted everywhere but at him. And when he did finally catch her attention, his lips twitched at the liquid shimmer in her eyes.

'What do you find so amusing now?'

'You.' He slid his hand to the back of her head. 'I'm going to kiss you, Isabella. So don't say you weren't warned.'

She gasped. 'Don't you dare—'

He covered her mouth with his, cutting off her useless threat. When she tried to pull away, he tightened his hold, keeping her in place until she leaned against him, her lips softening, then parting beneath his. And when she hesitantly returned his kiss, he thought he would drown in the sweetness.

She reached up with one hand to caress his neck, while the other one twisted the fabric of his shirt, clinging to it as if she, too, were drowning.

His heart thudded heavy in his chest and he gathered her closer, resisting the urge to sweep her up in his arms and carry her to the bed.

This was nothing more than a stolen moment of discovery. He didn't doubt for one minute that when the spell wore off, she would once again find her anger.

But until then, he would savour the taste of her kiss, the silky slide of her tongue against his. He could wait, because he was certain that one day his fiery bride would want more than just a kiss.

She froze against him, her eyelashes brushing across his as she opened her eyes. Richard sighed with regret. He'd hoped the stolen moment would have lasted a little longer, but knowing it was over, he released her.

Isabella lifted her arm and he grasped her wrist as her opened hand headed towards his cheek. 'No.' He shook his head at her. 'That wouldn't be wise.'

'How dare you!'

'One day soon I'll dare much more.'

'Why you…you…' She stopped mid-sentence, seemingly speechless.

'You enjoyed that kiss as much as I did.' Richard dropped her wrist to place a finger beneath her chin, gently closing her mouth. 'So, don't play the offended maiden, Isabella.'

He stepped back, then turned to head towards the door. Without glancing back at her, he opened the door and said, 'I'll be at the wharf late and will probably remain in town tonight.'

He closed the door behind him and it was all he could do not to laugh when something bounced off the chamber door.

Chapter Ten

In the waning light of the day, Isabella stood beneath the archway of the alcove and surveyed the work they'd completed these last three days. This bedchamber on the upper floor was even larger than the master chamber at Warehaven. She didn't need this much space, but if her choice was this or Dunstan's current chamber, she'd stay here.

A shiver trickled down her spine at the mere thought of him…Dunstan…Richard…her husband. She wondered where he was and what business had kept him from returning for two nights. Not that she was complaining, or pining for his company. Even though, to her shocked dismay, she'd actually enjoyed his kiss, but she also enjoyed dropping into bed, with fresh mattress stuffing and clean covers, then falling into blissful sleep, knowing that she'd not have to lay awake, alert to his movements while worrying about what he intended to do.

Besides, with the lord absent it had been easier to step into being the lady of the keep. He had to have been blind not to realise how badly this place needed someone to take it firmly in hand. At least with him gone, the maids and women from the village didn't need to second guess her orders. Thankfully, only one of the men had seen fit to question her and she'd easily glared him down.

They might consider her young and possibly think her weak, but she'd been taught to command a keep by the best. As far as Isabella was concerned, no stronger woman existed than her mother. None would dare defy an order given by the Lady of Warehaven and come out of the confrontation unscathed. Isabella had no intention of being any less—to do so would only bring dishonour to her mother's teachings.

She shook off the idle thoughts chasing her to look around the bedchamber. Now that the cobwebs had been removed, the rushes replaced, everything scrubbed and the walls freshly whitewashed, this was the most liveable chamber in the entire keep—not counting the kitchens. Once the newly returned cook had taken charge of her kitchen and scullery maids, she'd set them cleaning with a vengeance. Isabella had never seen a fire pit so soot- and ash-free before—even the pots appeared clean enough to be new. The kitchens at Warehaven weren't as spotless as these.

One of the younger women that Hattie had coerced into helping them clean the chamber brushed an imaginary speck of dust from the freshly washed bed curtains. 'There you be, my lady. Is there anything else you'll be needing?'

While she would love to request hot water for a bath, Isabella wasn't about to risk being interrupted by Dunstan if he returned, or one of the guards. She would make do with the cold water and cloths she had on hand.

Besides, she didn't doubt that the woman was just as tired as she. They'd all worked non-stop to set this one chamber to rights. And they still had the rest of the keep to do. 'No, I think we've all done enough today. You should be heading to your home before it gets too dark.'

The woman nodded, then left the chamber. As she pushed open the door, Isabella briefly saw the man standing guard. It had been a different guard each day and night. For whatever reason, the lord of the keep wanted her under constant guard—or supervision, she wasn't certain which—but she wasn't going to question the men about their orders, she'd save that for the lord himself. She was just thankful that the guard on duty was never the man who'd tried to accost her.

However, that little bit of relief didn't stop her from wishing the door opened into the chamber and that there was a locking bar on her side. Whoever had installed the door must have been a drunken sot to have got it so backwards.

Just as she'd done the last two nights, she dragged a heavy bench over and placed it across the doorway. It wouldn't stop anyone from entering, but when they tripped over the bench, at least she'd know she was no longer alone.

Certain her privacy wouldn't be interrupted unexpectedly, Isabella moved the wash basin, bucket of water and cloths into the alcove off to the side of the chamber. She removed her gown, groaning at the damage done to the best piece of clothing she owned.

Isabella laughed at her thought. 'Best? More like only.' She draped it across a small table, hoping that tomorrow she would find time to somehow, at the very least, save some of the embroidery work at the hem.

Once they finished cleaning the keep, perhaps she'd be able to talk Dunstan into loaning her money to buy fabric for a gown or two. She'd see he was repaid when her family arrived in the spring, as they undoubtedly would once the weather cleared.

After washing, she stirred the coals in the brazier, climbed into the oversized bed, blew out the flame on the oil lamp and snuggled down under the covers.

Richard paused at the bottom of the stairs. It would likely be easier to turn around and seek the bed in his small chamber at the rear of the Great Hall. He hadn't slept above stairs in years—not since his first marriage had turned sour and he'd made avoiding Agnes his life's mission.

He heard the buzz of whispers behind him and felt the undercurrent of unease and curiosity ripple through those still gathered in the hall. If he turned away now all would assume this wife was no better than the last. And while he hadn't decided if that were true or not, he'd no wish for others to make that decision.

Besides, once the gossips on Dunstan Isle got started, there was no stopping them. Their tongues would wag until every last man, woman and child living here knew that Dunstan's lord had little use for his wife.

That was the last thing he wanted to happen. He'd had two long nights to think about it and had come to the conclusion that it was imperative everyone believe he cared for Isabella, and she for him, when Glenforde came to rescue her. He wanted that cur to suffer in every way imaginable and seeing that the man who'd kidnapped his betrothed was a good husband, and she a satisfied wife, would only be the beginning.

He headed up the steps, knowing full well that a battle of words would ensue the moment he walked into the chamber. The one night he'd planned on staying in town had turned into two and he'd not bothered to send word. Then again, she'd probably not even noticed his absence.

The guard at the top of the stairs nodded, then stepped aside, but the one outside the chamber was seated on the floor, his head resting against the wall, snoring. Is this how she'd been *guarded*?

Clearing his throat, Richard startled the guard. 'You're dismissed.'

The shame-faced man jumped to his feet, stuttering, 'My…my lord, I—'

In no mood for excuses, Richard ordered, 'Leave.'

He'd already lost a cherished daughter because he'd been so certain of her safety. That mistake would never be repeated.

Someone on this island was a traitor, they'd helped Glenforde and Richard had no way of knowing if that person was still on Dunstan or not. Until Glenforde was dispatched to his maker, along with his minion, Richard would not foolishly risk Isabella's life.

He was not completely lacking in wits—he knew that if anything happened to her, her father would see to not just his death, but to Dunstan's complete destruction.

Once the guard was gone from his sight, Richard cracked the door open slowly. Faint light from the glowing brazier lit the far corner of the room. The sound of gentle, even breathing coming from the bed assured him that his timing was near perfect— Isabella was sound asleep.

If he was quiet, perhaps he could slip into bed without her becoming aware of his presence. He opened the door as slowly as possible to ensure it didn't creak, then stepped into the room, slamming his kneecap directly into a solid object.

A blistering curse escaped his lips. His knee throbbed in sharp pain. Without thinking, he kicked a bench out of the way. Obviously she had little faith in her guards.

Even though she said nothing, Richard knew she had to have heard his not-so-graceful entrance into the chamber.

He limped over to the bed, unbuckled his sword

belt and propped the weapon alongside the bed before sitting down on the edge to remove his boots.

'What are you doing?'

'Going to bed.' Even to his ears the words sounded curt.

'You might try your own chamber.'

He tossed one boot on to the floor. Suddenly too tired to argue, he said simply, 'I am.' His other boot thudded next to the first.

She rolled on to her side, facing him. 'Oh, no you aren't.'

Richard pulled his tunic and shirt over his head in one swipe and dropped the clothing atop his boots. 'Go to sleep.'

The bed shifted as she sat up. 'Not here I won't.'

'I am in no mood to argue with you tonight. Just go to sleep.' He rose to finish undressing.

She said nothing, but, grabbing a cover from the bed, Isabella carried it to a chair near the brazier.

He stared at her. Unless he took charge of this situation he knew he'd get no sleep. Without giving warning, he crossed the room and pulled her up from the chair. 'You aren't sleeping here.'

'I am certainly not sleeping with you.' Her eyes widened as if she'd just realised his state of undress. 'You're...naked.'

Richard grasped the skirt of her chemise and

jerked the undergown over her head. 'And now so are you.' Before she could pull away, he picked her up and carried her over to the bed.

'Put me down.'

'Gladly.' He dropped her on to the mattress and quickly climbed in behind her. Not giving her time to escape, he pulled her tight against his chest while drawing the covers over them.

He wasn't certain what he noticed first—the warmth of her body against his, or the softness of her skin. Either way the combination was as intoxicating as any fine wine.

'Let me go, Dunstan.'

Her voice was low, the tone laced with warning. A warning he chose to ignore. With his lips against her ear, he whispered, 'Richard.'

'Let me go, *Richard*.'

Sadly for her, using his name didn't make any difference, he still wasn't going to release her. Instead, while keeping one arm slung around her, he propped up his head with the other and, to irritate her further, rested his chin on her shoulder.

She tried pulling his arm away from her body. 'Have you been drinking?'

'No, why do you ask?'

'You seem to have confused me with one of your whores.'

Whores? Her statement drew a laugh from him. 'I fear you are mistaken, wife. I don't have any whores, so I suppose…' He paused to trail his mouth along her shoulder before saying, 'You'll have to serve that purpose.'

His attention to the side of her neck made Isabella shiver. She wished she could find the will to be revolted by his actions as much as she was by his words. 'I am not serving as your whore.'

He paused, his chin once again resting on her shoulder. 'Nor would I want you to.'

'So, you don't desire me?' Isabella clamped her mouth shut. What had she been thinking to ask such a question? The whole idea was to somehow get through this entire winter without him turning into a rutting stallion. Otherwise, she'd never be granted an annulment.

'Desire you?' His voice was so deep, so near, that it threatened to take her breath away. 'Any man with half a brain would desire you.'

She rolled her eyes at that statement. Glenforde obviously hadn't.

'I desire you more than you could possibly imagine.'

Isabella tensed. Did that mean she was in imminent danger of losing her virtue?

A soft laugh brushed against her shoulder, a warm

rush of air that he chased with his lips. 'Fear not, my dear, you are quite safe this night.'

She relaxed slightly, but remained alert. Even when her eyes were impossibly heavy to hold open, she fought closing them, fearful he would change his mind. What would she do in that case? While she would fight him as hard as she could, she was no match against his strength, so in the end it wasn't as if she could physically stop him. Besides, from the odd warmth building low in her belly, she wasn't all that certain she possessed enough will to fight him for long.

Why did his arm slung across her, resting against her chest, feel so...right? Why did his steady breaths, brushing against the nape of her neck, beckon her to relax and fall asleep? The last two nights in this bed had started out so cold, she'd shivered herself to sleep each night. But now, the warmth along her back and all the way to her toes was welcome.

He shifted slightly in the bed and she was once again awake, tense and on guard. When he moved his arm to reach up and cup her chin, she held her breath.

'Just a kiss goodnight, Isabella. That is all.' His lips briefly met hers before he settled on his side in the bed. 'Go to sleep.'

Before she could determine why she found that

kiss so lacking, the sound of gentle snoring drew her out of her bewilderment. Perhaps he had spoken the truth—she was in no danger this night of attention she did not want.

However, as much as she longed to find sleep herself, she realised that she now shivered from the cold.

The gown she'd been wearing to bed was on the floor on the other side of the chamber. He would most certainly wake up if she rose from the bed. And the blankets, which had been plentiful the last two nights, were now mostly wrapped around him, leaving her with barely enough to cover her body.

A quick tug on the covers gained her nothing. They were tucked so tightly under his body that she wasn't going to get them free without rolling him off the bed. And as much as she'd like to do just that, he'd looked and sounded tired.

He probably was good and tired. Not because he'd spent the nights with some whore. She didn't truly think that was the case. She'd only accused him of doing so to see if it would anger him enough to leave the chamber. Unfortunately for her, it seemed that he found ignoring her barbs far too easy.

If he was anything like her father and brother, he'd likely spent so many long hours going over inventory and inspecting his ships that he hadn't had any ambition left to come back to the keep. She couldn't be certain, but felt fairly safe guessing there was a makeshift pallet in one of the warehouses. So, he probably needed a good night's sleep.

And since that meant she would be able to sleep without trying to keep one eye open, she was more than happy to leave him to his dreams. But she didn't wish to freeze in the meantime.

Isabella frowned, staring at him in the semi-darkness, and poked his arm, hoping it would irritate him enough that he'd roll over and free some of the covers. She quickly drew her hand back, waiting to see if she'd disturbed his sleep. But he didn't budge and, once again, the sound of his heavy breathing met her ears.

If he could sleep through the poking, then surely he'd not wake up if she moved closer to share the warmth of the covers. Easing closer, she snuggled against him and pulled the blankets over her shoulder.

Before she could made sense of what was happening, he'd rolled on to his back and she found herself resting halfway across his chest, encircled within his arm. Pushing against his chest gained her nothing except a tighter embrace.

'Let me go.'

He groaned softly and draped his other arm across

his body so his hand rested on her hip. 'You poked and prodded, tried to jerk the covers from me before seeking warmth. I am tired and obviously you were cold.' He patted her hip. 'Now, you aren't, but I am still tired.'

'I thought you were asleep.'

'I was.'

His voice was rough with sleep and his embrace was warm without being threatening. Yet her heart raced as if she'd been running in fear of losing her life. 'If you were asleep, how do you know what I did?' She was amazed at the breathlessness of her voice.

'Hmmm?'

She parted her lips to repeat her question, but closed them before doing so. Why risk waking him up all the way? Right now she was warm and while her body tingled wherever it touched his and hummed with curiosity, and unexpected anticipation, she too could easily fall asleep.

She snuggled closer against him, until his hand tightened on her hip, making breathing harder still. 'Please, stop.'

It sounded as if he'd spoken through clenched teeth and, unwilling to risk awakening him further, she closed her eyes.

Chapter Eleven

Richard slowly opened his eyes, quickly shutting them against the pounding in his head. He moved to get up from the bed and groaned at the stiff soreness of his limbs and back. What the hell had happened for him to ache so much?

The chamber door opened. 'Ah, you are finally awake, I see.'

He winced at Hattie's lively greeting.

'Where is my wife?'

The older woman answered with a 'tsk' and a shake of her head, before saying, 'Lady Isabella has been up and about for most of the day.'

Most of the day? He sat up slowly, biting back another groan. 'What time is it?'

'Vesper bells have just been rung.'

Vesper? It was nearly nightfall? He arched his back. No wonder he ached from head to toe. 'Why did no one think to wake me?'

'Lady Isabella tried twice. After that she gave orders to leave you asleep.'

'She what?' They'd been married less than a week, weren't even truly man and wife yet, and she was making decisions for his well-being? Richard knew his anger was foolish, there was no justifiable cause for it, but that didn't change the fact he was still outraged.

'Where is she?'

Hattie reared back at his snarling tone. 'Where is who?'

Knowing the woman was intentionally being obtuse, he glared at her. 'Where is Isabella?'

'Below.' She made a show of picking his clothes up from the floor with two fingers, holding them aloft a moment, before tossing them at him. 'Cleaning.'

Of course she was. Since he'd already informed her that the condition of his keep was none of her concern, she would naturally set about making it her concern. Probably just to spite him. He jerked on his clothing.

Hattie suggested, 'You might want to eat something before you go storming below.'

'Why would I eat now?' Richard pulled on his boots and rose. 'The evening meal will be served soon.'

'I was thinking more of your foul mood than your empty stomach.'

Before he could reply to her comment, Hattie left the chamber. Of course he was in a foul mood. After all, he…he…Richard sat back down on the edge of the bed. He felt like a raging bull. For no apparent reason other than his wife had let him sleep.

A weak defence even to his own ears.

No. He was the lord here. He could wake up in a foul mood any time he desired and no one could stop him. Although having a reason for such a foul mood made one appear less unbalanced.

Richard slapped a hand on the bed and rose. God's teeth, he was thinking in circles like an old woman. Out of habit, he started to strap on his sword, then changed his mind and tossed the belt, scabbard and weapon on the bed.

He strode towards the door, then spun about. Perhaps just a little something to take the edge off his grumbling stomach might be in order. Richard crossed the chamber to the alcove where Hattie had placed bread, cheese, slices of apple and a pitcher of water on the small table.

He frowned, noticing the slick shininess of the old tabletop, then studied the rest of the chamber. Cleaning? Is that what they called this? This chamber had been redone from ceiling to floor. It shone in a way it hadn't since he was a young lad.

Years of soot and grime had been stripped from the walls and they'd been repainted, the bedding and linen washed. He glanced behind him to find that even the old tapestry hanging on the back wall of the alcove had once again come to life. The colours of the threads appeared brilliant instead of dull with age. He'd nearly forgotten the details of the stitched hunting scene.

He intentionally crunched the rushes and strewing herbs beneath his foot, only to have the scents of lavender and rosemary waft up against his nose. The floorboards beneath gleamed as if they'd been freshly scrubbed and oiled.

A tour of the chamber brought other changes to light. The mattress had been restuffed and the covering cleaned, the skins on the narrow windows were obviously new since they were no longer brittle and cracking. The small tables alongside the bed also showed signs of a recent polishing cloth. The candles in the floor sconces were beeswax instead of tallow. Had he paid any attention last night he would have noticed that the telltale stench of rendered animal fat no longer permeated the room.

In a corner, near the alcove, a clothing chest had been placed beneath a row of wall pegs. Richard ran his fingers over the fur lining of his hooded mantle hanging on one of the pegs. From the fresh smell and softness of the fur, it too had found itself put through a rigorous cleaning. He opened the lid of the chest to find that all of his clothes had been washed, dried, folded and neatly stacked inside. Sachets of sandalwood and cedar at the bottom of the chest would keep the moths away while at the same time ensure the clothing retained a fresh scent.

The lid fell with a thud. Yes, she'd been busy these last couple of days. But Isabella couldn't have done all of this alone. She'd obviously had help. And he doubted if that help had come from the few women he'd sent back to the keep.

So not only was she seeing to the condition of the keep, she was ordering his men about to do so?

The door to the chamber opened and the town carpenter stopped in the doorway. He doffed his cap, twisting it in his hand, said, 'Forgive me, my lord, I thought you were elsewhere. I can come back later.'

'Why are you here?'

'The lady wants the door reversed. But I can—'

'No. Go ahead. I was just leaving.'

Even though she'd overstepped her bounds, he wasn't going to take that up with the carpenter. He'd seek out Isabella instead. Although the door should have been fixed years ago. The only reason it was on backwards was because when he was a small boy he'd picked up the habit of locking himself in the chamber and after his father had had to have the door removed to gain entrance more than once, he'd ordered it rehung to swing out into the passageway and lock from the outside.

Richard headed down to the Great Hall. He paused at the bottom of the steps. At least nothing had changed here. The boisterous shouts and laughter of his men scraped across his ears in a familiar manner, irritating him in the usual way.

Conal spied him and approached. 'I see you woke up just in time to eat and go to bed.'

Richard nodded towards the mostly drunken assembly. 'And I see you've made yourself useful in my absence.'

'Since I know the workload ahead of us, I thought we'd take advantage of a workless day.'

'That's rather obvious.' He glanced around the hall—most of these men would be near useless on the morrow. 'Where is my wife?'

'Last I saw her she was headed towards your chambers.'

Richard paused outside the door to his bedchamber. He took a deep breath, preparing himself for what he might find beyond the door. From what he'd gathered from a few of his men during his walk across the hall, she'd so far confined her cleaning to the chamber above.

If he ignored the fact that he'd told her not to concern herself with his keep, then what she'd done wasn't a terrible thing. He didn't like it, but it wasn't a crime worthy of punishment. However, there remained the fact that she'd taken it upon herself to employ the help of his people and men without consulting him first.

While he didn't want the people of Dunstan to hate her, he'd prefer they had nothing, or very little, to do with her until after his confrontation with Glenforde and her father.

Glenforde was going to die by his hand. Richard hadn't come this far to miss that opportunity. Every fibre of his being screamed for Glenforde's blood. The thought of revenge had been the only thing that kept him waking up every morning after the senseless slaughter on Dunstan, it had been the only thing that had dulled the pain. The passing of time had only tempered that thirst, making it stronger, hardening his resolve until it became as dear to him as breathing.

When that day finally arrived, he would not hesitate to kill anyone who physically came to Glenforde's aid. And that is what the people of Dunstan risked should they decide to support Isabella. He didn't doubt for one heartbeat that she would beg and plead for the life of the man she'd once been set to wed.

If, through some misplaced sense of loyalty, any of his people saw fit to answer her plea, he would send them to their grave. No one who stood in his way would be spared. So, it was safer for all if, for now, they kept their distance from her.

Of course he couldn't explain that to her. He didn't trust her not to use it against him. In truth, how could he blame her? She was a pawn, a mouse caught fast between two angry cats, and he'd put her in that position on purpose.

And until this matter was settled, that is where she would stay. Regardless of what he had to do, or how angry it made her.

He pushed open the chamber door. Isabella was hunkered over his open chest, holding something in her hand. A step closer to her brought the item in to view—a wooden doll, meticulously carved and painted by his hands.

Richard's heart seemed to stop. Time reversed itself until one fateful moment froze in his mind with horrifying detail. A single blonde curl rested against a too-pale cheek. Her head bent at a strange angle and blood had dried where it had pooled beneath her open mouth. Blue eyes, open wide as if in horror, stared at nothing. And the doll that never left the crook of her arm lay on the ground just beyond her reaching fingertips, as if, at the very moment of death, she'd still wanted her doll in her arms. But she'd been denied even that slim thread of comfort.

'No!' Without warning, he lunged to tear the doll and its final wrappings from Isabella's grasp. His hands shook as he carefully folded the embroidered scrap of fabric around the doll before placing it back in its fur-lined nest and slamming the lid of the chest closed.

He glared down at Isabella, trying to see her through the haze of rage and loss. 'Do not touch this chest again.'

Isabella's questions stuck in her throat at the look on his face. She scrambled backwards, away from the irrational anger reaching towards her, only to fall on to a pile of linens she'd removed from the chest. Raising her hands to ward off his approach, she choked out, 'I'm sorry. Richard, I'm sorry.'

His expression didn't waver and she wasn't all that certain he saw her. Isabella studied him. His unfocused glare seemed to slice through her, moving past her as if he was somewhere else, seeing someone else. She stayed where she was, not moving, and closed her eyes.

'How dare you touch her things!' He grabbed the

front of her gown and lifted her from the pile of linen. 'I will see you dead before allowing Glenforde's beloved to foul her memory.'

His nearly growled threat dried her throat so she could barely swallow. Isabella knew she should be afraid—any person with half their wits would know this was a moment to appear weak and submissive—and she was afraid, but she wasn't yet ready to die.

She reached out and wrapped one hand along the side of his neck, curled the fingers of her other hand over his shoulder, pulled her body against his, hooked her feet around his legs and hung on for all she was worth. Her reaction might appear foolish to another, but wrestling with a brother and sister had taught her to protect the soft parts of her body. If Richard's idea had been to beat her for going through his things, clinging to him would make that a little more difficult for him.

To her amazement, he tore his hands from her gown and when she thought he would pry her body away from him, he drew her harder against him in a tight embrace. With his face buried in her neck, he hoarsely whispered, 'Forgive me. I...'

His words trailed off as he released her. She loosened her hold on him. Not sure of his state of mind, she stepped out of his reach, but waved towards the bed, suggesting the only thing that came to her mind, 'Richard, you are exhausted. Rest awhile.'

His lack of response worried her. She wanted to get him off his feet before his shaking legs refused to support him any longer, but at the same time, she had no desire to get too close. Going to the opposite side of the bed, she patted the mattress. 'Just lay down awhile.'

He walked to the bed woodenly, like a man caught in the throes of a terrifying nightmare, and dropped on to the edge.

Uncertain what to do for him, she kept her wary gaze on him. His entire body still visibly shook and the hands he lifted to his face trembled so badly that fear for her own safety fled.

Friend or foe, this man was in agony and needed soothing. She would never turn her back on a stranger in need, how could she turn away from Richard?

She sat down near the head of the bed and reached across to place a hand on his shoulder. When he didn't shrug off her touch, she tugged gently, coaxing, 'Please. Rest.'

Slowly, he laid down on the bed, facing away from her on his side. That was fine, at least he hadn't tried to get his hands on her or bolted from the chamber. Isabella slid into the bed behind him and placed an arm across his waist. To her unexpected surprise, he turned over and drew her close.

He said nothing, but with his face buried in the side of her neck, he held on to her like she was a lifeline keeping him from going under. She, too, remained silent, stroking his back, running her fingers through his hair, waiting for the tremors to subside.

Once they finally did and he seemed to relax across her, she rested her cheek against his head. 'Richard, I may hate what you've done to me, what you've forced me to do, and while I might seek to annoy you in payment, I would never intentionally upset you in such a manner as this. Never. Please, tell me what I've done so I do not accidentally do so again.'

After one long, shuddering breath, he turned his head, so he rested on her shoulder, with one arm across her stomach. He shifted the arm beneath her so he could reach up to stroke light circles on the side of her neck. Gentle, teasing movements that suddenly made the muscular thigh resting between her softer ones more…noticeable, in ways that seemed inappropriate and far too welcome at the same time.

Isabella closed her eyes briefly, praying he couldn't feel the swift pounding of her heart.

'You didn't know.'

It took her a moment to make sense of his statement. She didn't know what? Oh, the trunk. 'Who
did the doll belong to?'

'Lisette.'

'Who was Lisette?'

'My daughter.'

Isabella frowned. He had once accused Glenforde
of killing a child and she hadn't believed him. Her
stomach tightened at the thought that he might not
have been making up stories to frighten her. Determined to find out what she could, she asked, 'Your
daughter?'

'Yes. A daughter born too soon.'

She sighed. This was going to be like picking nails
out of a board with her fingers. She reached up to
stroke his cheek and he jerked his head away from
her touch, but not before her fingertips brushed the
dampness on his face.

Isabella held her breath. This was not a man who
would shed a tear over something minor or imagined. This was serious and very real. She suspected
that he wasn't evading her questions, he was answering her as best he could under the circumstances.

Unsure how to proceed, since she was fairly certain she knew the answer, she chose the direct route.
'Richard, what happened to Lisette?'

The finger stroking circles on her neck stopped.

The arm draped across her stomach tightened. 'Your husband-to-be killed her.'

Every muscle in her body stiffened. She curled her toes in an effort to stop her legs from trembling. He hadn't been concocting stories.

'Why? Why would he do such a heinous thing?'

'Do you think I have not asked myself that very same question?'

When he made a motion to move away, Isabella tightened her hold on him. 'No, stay. Talk to me. Help me understand.'

In truth, it didn't matter whether she understood or not, but this ate at him, it was like a poison in his blood and she wanted to somehow lance it and let at least some of the vile humours drain away.

'Why? Your understanding doesn't change anything.'

No, it wouldn't change a thing. His daughter would still be dead and she'd still be here on Dunstan as bait for Glenforde. What would happen to her afterwards was anyone's guess. But right now, this moment, his talking about it might make things more bearable for him. Although she knew that if he were like most men of her acquaintance, his willingness to talk would soon pass. 'No, it'll change nothing. But it's part of your life and you are my husband. I want to know about the man I wed.'

He settled back into her embrace. 'It was all my fault.'

If she hadn't been confused before, she was now. 'What do you mean, your fault?'

'I wasn't here to protect them.'

She rolled her eyes at the ever god-like notions of men. 'Richard, are you not one of Stephen's men? Do you not own more than one merchant ship? Unless you are possessed of some inhuman power, you cannot be everywhere at once.'

'Perhaps not, but I should have been here.'

'Because you knew what was going to happen?' Isabella knew she could, and at some point probably would, cross an invisible line that would turn him from talkative to defensive.

'What? No.' There was a touch more life to his voice. 'Had a hint of what was to come reached me, I would have been here and none of this would have happened.'

'Or, you could be dead, too.'

'You think Glenforde could have beaten me?'

Ah, now his defensiveness was starting to kick in. Since she truly wanted to know what had happened, she needed to disabuse him of that notion. 'Heavens, no, Richard. The man is a weak coward who puffs up his own image by ill treatment of those deemed smaller.'

'Yes, well, he proved that well enough.'

'So, what happened? Did he attack Dunstan while you were away?' When he remained silent for a few moments, Isabella warned, 'If you don't tell me, I'll be forced to make up things in my mind.'

His heavy sigh brushed against her neck. 'He landed in the cove instead of the harbour. Nobody ever anchors a ship there, it isn't always safe. Someone from Dunstan, who knew the tides and currents, had to have told him when it would be safe to anchor there and how long he could stay before he would lose his ship.'

She knew she could be presuming much, but asked, 'The cove isn't patrolled during low tide?'

'Of course it is.'

'Then—'

'How did he make the landing?' He completed her question, then continued. 'That's what I haven't been able to determine. All I'm certain of is that he did and since three of the four men on guard there were also killed, he obviously had help from someone already on the island. The fourth man lived only long enough to identify Glenforde's ship, but didn't see his attacker.'

'Could he not have docked in the harbour to allow a man or two off his ship before leaving to sail into the cove and await some sort of signal?'

'Yes, he could have. But he didn't. The harbour master had no record of Glenforde's arrival at the docks.'

The Dunstans had been a seafaring family longer than her own, so she was certain he employed only the best men for the most important positions. But to make certain he'd considered every option, she had to ask, 'And you trust your harbour master?'

'Yes. Without reservation.'

'Then I'm sure you are right. Glenforde had to have had assistance. So, how did he come across your daughter? Wasn't she in the keep with her nursemaid?'

'That lying she-devil of a whore met him in one of the cottages and took Lisette along with her.'

'The nursemaid?'

'No. My whore wife.'

Stunned into silence, Isabella reminded herself to breathe. He was already married? Finally, after she could catch her breath, she hesitantly asked, 'Where…where is…your…wife?'

'Glenforde slit her throat.'

His short, blunt answer brought an icy fear to Isabella's heart. If Glenforde had treated Richard's wife and daughter so cruelly, and she had no reason to doubt him, what did that mean for her future? She knew she was here as bait, that had never been a secret. But what about afterwards?

Another thought shook her to the core. Dear Lord above, what if Glenforde turned his attention to her sister? For the first time since this all began back at Warehaven's bailey, she hoped Glenforde did come for her—and received all he deserved.

Richard released her and shoved himself off the bed. He stopped halfway to the door and turned back to look at her. 'Do you have what you need from the chamber?' He motioned towards the pile of linens. 'Is there anything else?'

'No, there's nothing else.' She sat up. 'I have no reason to come back here.'

'Good.' He turned back around and headed to the door.

'Richard.' He stopped with his hand on the door latch, but didn't look at her, so she asked, 'What happens to me after Glenforde pays for his crimes?'

'I don't know.' With that, he left the room.

Isabella stared at the door. His abrupt departure and even more abrupt change of mood confused her more than his rage and the aftermath. Since she didn't think he was normally given to such sudden changes, she could only surmise that after his family's deaths he had taken no time to mourn his loss, too intent on seeking revenge that he'd not given his soul time to grieve.

Other than her grandparents, she'd never experienced the loss of a family member. When her mother's mother had died, Isabella remembered being so sad that it physically hurt for days afterwards. And then there would be times when she'd be almost normal...until she remembered what had happened, bringing the sadness and pain back once again. But eventually, even though she'd have moments of near unbearable sadness, the pain started to fade until eventually she could think of her grandmother without feeling as if someone was trying to tear her heart from her chest.

Her mother had reacted in the same manner—only for longer periods of time.

But when King Henry died, her father spared one night for his pain at losing his father and, while he had still been sad for weeks afterwards, that one night had been his only display of grief.

Had Richard spared even one day for his loss? She didn't think so, not since he was still suffering bursts of outrage and utter sadness. His teasing didn't bother her overmuch, even though it did rankle at times. She could find a way to suffer through it until her father came. And his blustering barked orders, or demands, were easy enough to ignore—her brother acted in the same 'I am your lord' manner at times and she ignored him quite well.

But this anger, this blind rage that dragged him back to the horrors and left him shaken, needed to change. He had to somehow get beyond the nightmare and his need for vengeance. Otherwise his narrow focus on revenge might make him foolishly careless.

How? She frowned, wondering how she was going to help him without him realising what she was doing.

A niggling imp in the back of her mind asked, *Why?*

She shrugged. There was no way of knowing what was going to happen to her. Even though she dearly longed to return home to Warehaven and forget this entire kidnapping and marriage had happened, once her father found out she was married to Richard, he might very well make her stay.

A shiver prompted her to get up from the bed. As much as she hated to even think of that possibility, it did exist. After all, her parents were forced to wed and from listening to her aunt's telling of the story, many months passed before her mother and father could be in the same room without wanting to strangle one another.

So, God forbid, if it happened, it would be easier to live with a husband who didn't cringe at the sight of her.

Chapter Twelve

Richard took his seat at the head table and stared down the length of the Great Hall. The men had obviously spent most of the day drinking, they were sloppy, rowdy and loud. Yet they all sat before the table as if waiting for…what?

He leaned his head towards Conal on his left. 'Are we waiting for something?'

'I would guess Lady Isabella.'

Richard turned to look Conal in the eyes. 'Excuse me?'

'I've been with you in town.' Conal shrugged. 'So that's the only thing that makes sense to me. They did the same thing earlier—waited until she was seated before eating.'

'It is a welcome change, is it not, my lord?' Hattie set a pitcher on the table between the two men.

Welcome change? No. This wasn't supposed to be happening. Things were supposed to stay the same as they were. Richard silently cursed himself. He was supposed to discuss this with her, but seeing her with Lisette's doll had unexpectedly overwhelmed him and any thought of setting her straight flew out of his mind.

He held up his goblet for Hattie to fill, then took a much needed swallow of—water? 'What is this?'

Conal snorted and at the same moment Isabella took her seat next to him on the right, asking, 'What is what?'

'This.' He held the goblet to her nose.

'Water?' She dipped her fingers into the small washbowl near them on the table. While drying her hands, she asked, 'Do you think anyone here needs more wine or ale?'

'I do.'

'You do what? Need wine for yourself, or think someone else does?'

Richard narrowed his eyes. She was being difficult on purpose. He could tell by the bland expression on her face and devilish twinkle in her eyes. Fine. She wanted to play? Oh, she could play, but he'd damn well make sure she paid for it.

'May I please have some wine, my dearest wife?'

She shrugged. 'Entirely up to you, my lord. Hattie, wine with dinner, please.'

Hattie motioned the servers into action and retrieved the wine. Richard watched the servers. Their skills seemed newfound, but not one of them dropped a platter, or spilled a drop of food or drink as they placed their loads on the tables. It didn't require any thought to know who had taken them in hand.

Conal leaned over to whisper, 'She's been busy.'

Richard ignored him to put a generous portion of meat and a mix of vegetables on the trencher he shared with Isabella, while she poured wine into both of their goblets.

He finished his off in one long swallow before refilling his goblet. Her glare, had it been an actual flame, would have burned a hole through his head. Richard set the vessel down. 'Fear not, Wife, it would take much more than that to turn me into a fool.'

'Don't call me that.'

'What?' He leaned closer. 'Wife? Isn't that what you are?'

'Sometimes I feel more like a prisoner.'

Richard hooked a foot around the leg of her chair and dragged her closer so he could whisper in her ear, 'Do you want to be my prisoner, Isabella?'

A shiver rippled down her arms and a flush covered her cheeks as she stared at him in shock. He kept his smile of success to himself. He'd intentionally deepened his voice and made certain to let her name roll off his tongue because he knew she was unable to resist the seductive tone.

She broke his intent stare with a gasp and looked down at her food. 'No, I don't want to be your prisoner.'

'Pity.' He could envision her chained to a bed in a cell, helpless, and in desperate need of comforting. *From where had that thought come?*

'I just want to go home.'

He sat upright in his chair, more in an attempt to rid his mind of the erotic thoughts threatening to make this the shortest dinner in his life than anything else. 'You are home.'

'Warehaven.'

'That isn't going to happen.' He handed her the untouched goblet. 'Drink. I don't want you sulking.'

'Sulking!' Her voice rose and an odd silence descended down the tables.

Turning to look at her, he suggested, 'You could be louder, then everyone else wouldn't have to strain to hear us.'

The men at the tables turned their attention back to their food.

She lifted the goblet to her lips with a shaking hand and Richard wondered if she'd spill half of it down her gown. The sight of her gown gave him pause. It was the same one she'd been wearing when he'd taken her from Warehaven.

He refilled her empty glass and handed it back to her.

'No. Are you trying to get me inebriated?'

'Yes.' Actually he was, but not for the reason she thought.

She slammed the goblet back on to the table hard enough so some of the contents splashed out on to the white table covering, leaving behind a deep red stain. 'Why? So you can take advantage of me?'

He once again handed it back to her and lifted it to her lips. 'Oh, definitely, because I can't think of anything I'd rather do than have sex with a woman so full of wine that she'll pass out and not remember a thing. That certainly would make for an exciting evening.'

Her eyes narrowed to mere slits. 'You are a pig.'

'And sometimes you are a fool. Now drink.' Once she did as he bid, Richard slipped a hand behind her head and drew her closer. 'Trust me, Wife, the first time we make love, you won't be intoxicated from any drink and you will most definitely remember every touch, stroke and kiss for a very long time to come.'

When her lips parted for the gasp of shocked virginal outrage he fully expected, he covered her mouth with his own and swept his tongue across hers, then just as quickly released her and moved away.

This time the shiver tracing down her body was longer and lingering. He wondered if the deep flush on her cheeks burned.

'Oh! I never.'

Before taking a bite of meat, he agreed, 'I would hope not.'

She sat there for a while and just stared at her food. Richard had to give her credit because a few times he thought she was going to burst out in tears of rage and frustration. But she didn't. Somehow, after a few hard swallows, she managed to check the flow of tears.

He waited until she seemed more calm before pointing out, 'Your food is getting cold.'

'I'm not hungry.'

'Isabella, did your mother never tell you not to bait someone more experienced or stronger?'

'I never baited you.'

'Really?' He waved his eating knife towards the hall. 'What do you call this?'

'What?'

'I told you that my keep doesn't concern you, yet here we are, seated at a relatively polite dining table.'

He tapped the pitcher of water still on the table. 'With water as the main drink.'

'But—'

He raised a hand, cutting off her reply. 'I'm not finished. And what about the chamber above? Am I mistaken or has it not been cleaned, painted, rearranged and refurnished?'

'Yes, but—'

Again he raised a hand and she instantly stopped. 'Was that not a carpenter who was sent to reverse the door?'

'Yes.'

This time she didn't even attempt to add anything after her admission. So, he asked, 'You could not have accomplished all this without giving orders to my people. Am I right?'

'Yes.'

'Nobody gave you permission to do so.'

Her eyes widened and she stared at him speechless for about one heartbeat. 'As your wife, am I not the chatelaine of this keep?'

'No.' He fell silent to let that fact settle in her mind. The instant the disbelief filled her eyes, he added, 'Not until I say so.'

She placed her hands against the edge of the table and tried to push her chair away.

'Do you plan to run away now? Hasn't your past

experience with that tactic proven a mistake?' Her brows furrowed in question, so he reminded her by asking, 'Isn't that how I captured you to begin with?'

When she didn't answer, he stuck his foot behind the leg of her chair. 'You need to eat something. Then perhaps I'll permit you to leave the table.'

If she clenched her jaw any tighter, Richard was certain she'd break a tooth.

'You are…you are…'

'Yes, a pig. I know. That doesn't change the fact that you need to eat.'

'Fine.' She stabbed at the food in a manner that made him glad he wasn't on the trencher.

After a few mouthfuls, she said, 'This keep is filthy. It needs cleaning.'

He looked around. It didn't matter to him if it was filthy. But then it also didn't matter if it was clean. Either way made no difference to him. Which he found odd, but he just couldn't summon up the need to care. 'If cleaning makes you happy, be my guest.'

'And how am I supposed to do that without help?'

'You could try asking.'

'Who?'

'Me. You could try asking me.'

'Then can I have the use of a couple of your men to start on this hall tomorrow?'

He sighed. 'Surely you can do better than that.'

Again her jaw clenched, then unclenched. 'May I please use a couple of your men, my lord?'

'Oh, so polite and proper.' He set his knife down and turned to face her. 'But that isn't quite what I meant.' He leaned closer to whisper against her ear, 'Ask me nicely, Isabella.'

'Nicely? How nicely?'

He rested an arm along the back of her chair to toy with a lock of her hair. 'Why don't you just try asking and we'll see if it suffices?'

She stared down at her lap for a few moments, before raising her head to look everywhere but at him. 'Please, may I use some of your men tomorrow, Richard?'

He had to admit, she was a fast learner. Her imitation of his husky tone was worthy of any mummer. He stroked her cheek with his knuckle and this time felt her shiver trail along his touch.

It was cruel to play with her so. But Richard couldn't seem to help himself. She didn't dissolve into hysterics and usually handed his glibness right back to him. Verbal sparring with this woman was akin to foreplay, so he teased her on purpose—it seemed a harmless way to end the day.

Besides, he couldn't deny that he enjoyed the play of colour filling her cheeks, but could only imagine how the green specks in her eyes would darken if she looked at him.

Agnes would never succumb to his teasing. As soon as he would try to engage her in this way, she would turn around and leave.

Knowing Isabella waited for his response, yet not wanting this evening to end so early, he brushed his knuckle across her cheek again. 'You could try looking at me when you ask.'

She frowned for a moment, but to his amazement she finally met his gaze, batted her eyelashes, then leaned closer and placed a hand on his chest. 'My Lord Richard, ice will form at Satan's feet before I beg you for anything.'

Her words, spoken in a near breathless whisper, rushed against his chin like a lover's caress. His heart thudded and from the small half-smile playing about her lips—lips he could easily claim again with his own if he leaned forward just the slightest bit—she knew exactly what effect she was having on him.

Then the actual words she'd spoken filtered through the feelings they'd caused. He frowned. By the saints above, the woman excelled at handing him back a good measure of his own teasing.

One of the men cleared his throat. Another slammed a goblet on to the table and, from nearby,

Richard heard the distinct sound of a snort that seemed suspiciously like it came from Conal.

He didn't need to look out at the hall to know that everyone in attendance was watching and waiting to see what he would do.

He knew exactly what he wanted to do—pull her into his embrace and kiss that smug sliver of a smile from her lips. But he also knew that he wouldn't stop at a simple kiss. Unfortunately, there were too many prying eyes about for him to give into his urges.

Richard tilted his head down until his forehead nearly rested against hers. 'You play with fire, Isabella.'

'You started it.' She shrugged and leaned away.

'Perhaps. But to issue such a dare could prove to be a mistake on your part.'

'The mistake is yours. I issued no dare.'

He stared at her, slowly trailing his gaze from the top of her head, across her face and then down to her breasts before drawing his attention back to her face. 'You intentionally tempt a man to test your words and then deny it was a dare?'

Richard waited a moment for his meaning to put the flush back on her cheeks, before he mused, 'I wonder just what it would take to hear you beg me.'

The colour on her face deepened as she gasped, shoved back her chair and left the Great Hall.

He watched her until the ribald laughter from his men prompted him into action. However much he might enjoy exchanging quips with her, she would not be allowed to make him look a fool before his men. Richard followed her up the stairs two at a time. Catching up with her on the landing, he swept her up into his arms without missing a step.

She squeaked in surprise and tried pushing away to break free of his hold. 'Put me down.'

'I will.' He hit the latch on the bedchamber door, grateful it'd been reversed, shoved it open, stepped through, then kicked it closed and carried her to the bed where he dropped her on to the mattress.

She scrambled to the other side. 'What do you think you're doing? Get out of here.'

'No. Get undressed.'

Before he realised what she was reaching for, she freed the sword he'd tossed on the bed and grasped it with both hands to point it at him. 'I swear, I'll use this.'

He stared at her for a moment and blinked, not quite believing his wife was threatening him with the weapon. Had she any idea how to use the blade? Doubtful. He proved that by easily batting it out of her hold. 'It would take someone a lot stronger than you to use my own weapon on me.'

Richard grabbed the sword from the foot end of

the bed before she could regain possession, slid it back into the sheath and placed it under his side of the bed. 'Now, get undressed.'

With her head bowed and shoulders drooping, she sat on the edge of the bed to remove her slippers and stockings. Over her shoulder she shot him a mutinous glance before sliding beneath the covers to fumble with her gown. Pulling it free, she dropped it on to the floor.

It was all he could do not to sigh at her self-imposed fear. After quickly stoking the coals in the brazier and then undressing in the chilled night air of the chamber, he slid under the covers next to her and, before she could protest, pulled her against him. Her skin was like ice. 'You're cold.'

Isabella only nodded.

He gathered her closer, pulling her part way across his chest, with her head resting against his shoulder. He could feel her choked breaths warm against his neck.

'You can relax, I'm not going to hurt you.'

'I know what you're going to do and, yes, it will hurt.'

Richard stared up at the ceiling. He'd had no way of knowing whether Agnes had been a virgin on their wedding night. He'd been young, too young to have had enough experience with women to be able to tell and like a fool he'd not questioned her claim of virginity.

But the woman in his arms now was so nervous, so inexperienced, and so very certain of what was going to happen, that he knew she'd never slept with a man. From her hesitancy whenever he'd kissed her he doubted if she'd ever been truly kissed by a man before, let alone anything else.

He'd followed her from the hall with every intention of proving to her who was in command. Now that she was in his arms and he could feel her fear, all he wanted to do was to calm her nervousness and banish her worries. He kissed the top of her head. 'Isabella, I should have apologised earlier in my chamber. I am sorry for frightening you so.'

'And what about now?'

He smiled against her head, then reached over to stroke her hip. Ignoring her startled flinch, he asked, 'Should I apologise for wanting to touch the softness of your skin?' He buried his nose in her hair and breathed in deeply. 'Or for wanting to savour the scent of a beautiful woman?'

She rolled over on her back, claiming, 'Now you should apologise for being so silly.'

Richard shifted on to his side, propping up on his forearm. When she immediately tried to shift away, he put his arm across her and caressed her side, not letting her escape.

Again, he said, 'Relax, Isabella. I am not going to hurt you.'

She wouldn't even look at him. With her eyes tightly closed, she asked, 'Then what are you doing?'

Drowning in your innocence. 'Relishing the feel of a woman next to me.' He splayed his fingers across her belly, feeling the sudden contracting of muscles beneath his hand. He kept his movements slow, barely brushing his fingertips across her smooth flesh.

She grasped his hand. 'I don't think this is going to help me relax.'

Richard captured her hand beneath his and threaded his fingers between her own, then once again lightly stroked across her belly and over her ribs with their hands joined. He leaned his head down to softly ask, 'Do you feel how soft and smooth your skin is? Can you feel the warmth against your fingers?'

Once she nodded, he brought her hand to his stomach and mimicked the same movements, asking, 'Do you find the difference as interesting as I do? Where your skin was soft and pliant, mine is tougher and the muscles beneath hard and less giving.'

'Not so tough.' She adjusted her fingertips to

trail along a scar. 'It is smoother than I thought it might be.'

He was surprised to discover she actually thought about it at all. Allowing her to guide the direction of their exploration, he sucked in a breath when she drew their hands up his ribcage and wandered across his chest. She slowed their movement to lightly trace a circle around one now hardening nipple, before trailing her touch down the line of hair to his waist.

But he wasn't at all surprised when she stopped there, her hand trembling lightly beneath his. To take her mind off what she feared to find, he moved their hands back to her stomach, where he then traced the same path she had, up her ribs and between her breasts.

Richard closed his eyes. He longed to tear his hand free to cup her breast, to feel the warmth, the softness and weight against his palm. With an effort he reminded himself that this wasn't about him.

So, he slid their hands to circle along the side, then beneath the fullness. Back and forth, slowly edging a little higher with each pass until she breathlessly gasped. Not wanting her nervous anticipation to get the best of her, he drew his fingertips around, then over her hardening nipple.

'Oh!'

Richard shivered. He couldn't remember ever having heard such a softly issued exclamation before. The obvious surprise and wonder in her hushed voice nearly made him groan with desire.

She turned her face towards his. 'Does it feel like that for you, too?'

'Probably not as much.' He turned his lips to hers, capturing her with a kiss to stop her questions and distract her on purpose.

She opened her lips to accept his kiss and soon followed his lead. When she moaned, he reluctantly drew their hands away from her breasts, stroking down the length of her ribs and stomach, along the curve of her hip and down her leg as far as her arm would reach.

He deepened their kiss, drawing her curiosity and wonder deeper into the play of their lips and tongues. She leaned up towards him, close enough that he could feel the pounding of her heart against his chest.

Isabella was so focused on meeting the demands of his mouth, that she didn't seem to notice he'd skimmed their hands up the inside of her silken thigh. There was no change in her breathing, or her focus, when he lingered over the patch of tight curls to knead the soft flesh beneath.

Richard fought to restrain himself from giving into his urge to roll her on to her back and settle himself between her legs. He couldn't remember the last time he'd so intensely wanted to claim a woman.

Instead, he dipped a finger between the swollen folds of flesh. Surprised and emboldened by the hot, slick dampness already evident, he teased the nub with his fingertip. She curled the fingers of her hand resting against his chest, digging her fingernails into his flesh and angled her hips as if to get closer to his touch.

Richard swallowed a smile. *Oh, not just yet, sweeting.* There was still at least one body part he wanted her to discover before taking this any further. He withdrew his touch to slide their still-clasped hands to his belly.

He once again let her take the lead and without coaxing, she brushed over the thicker thatch of curls covering his groin to draw one fingertip along the length of his erection and around the rim towards the tip. His heart thudded inside his chest.

Richard gave her but a few moments of tantalising exploration before he took back control of their movements to curl her fingers around his shaft and then grasped her wrist to move her hand up and down the length.

As he'd already gathered, she was a fast learner and shook off his hold, giving him the freedom to do some exploring of his own. Which from the pounding of his own heart and the difficulty he was having in keeping his breaths even, he either needed to do quickly or expend more concentration on reining in his lust.

Certain she was intent on discovering his reactions, he focused his attention on teaching her about pleasure.

She didn't reject his touch between her thighs, instead she let her legs go lax, giving him the freedom to cup her, kneading, stroking until she hastily broke their kiss to raggedly question, 'Richard, what—?'

'Shhh.' He soothed her, then coaxed, 'Trust me in this, Isabella.'

She nodded, then buried her face against his chest.

He felt her confusion and uncertainty in the sudden tensing of her legs. Before she could change her mind and pull away, he delved between the padded folds of flesh to once again feel the hot slickness of her more-than-ready body. Teasing, stroking until her breath was nothing but ragged pants and she released her hold on his shaft to curl her fingers into his back.

With ease he slid a finger into her, drawing in a deep shuddering breath at the slick, hot flesh wrapping around him. He could barely imagine what it would feel like to bury himself in that lush warmth.

Her soft gasp of surprise urged him on and he imitated the strokes that he hoped one day soon to make with more than just the touch of his hand.

Richard gritted his teeth at the sound of her building climax. The heavy throbbing in his groin wanted more than just a touch.

No, he silently whispered. It was more important to disabuse her notion of pain and fear than it was to satisfy his needs. Sweat beaded on his forehead from his shaken control over his body.

Soon, her moans of pleasure turned to a frozen gasp as she arched her back. He felt her toes slide, then curl against his leg. The hot, wet flesh surrounding his touch pulsed as if trying to draw him in further.

Just when he thought he could no longer deny himself, her legs fell lax, the pulsing eased and she withdrew her fingernails from his skin.

Richard withdrew his hand and wrapped his arms around her, pulling her into a tight embrace as he rolled on to his back, bringing her along with him.

Even though his heart still thudded heavy in his chest, hers eased and she pushed up on his chest to gaze down at him with an embarrassing, to him, look of awe. 'I don't think I'll be needing any of your men tomorrow. I have other plans.'

Humour teased at him. 'What might those plans be?'

'I need to gather ice for Satan and learn how to beg.'

He knew exactly what she was saying. At the dinner table she'd sworn that ice would form in hell at Satan's feet before she begged him for anything. And now…she was so willing to beg for more of his touch that she herself would provide the ice for Satan. It was completely inappropriate, but there was no helping it—he burst out in laughter.

Chapter Thirteen

Slowly stretching awake, Isabella sighed. She hadn't felt this well rested since being taken from Warehaven.

She yawned and threw back the covers, only to have her hand come in contact with a solid object. A quick glance brought her wide awake. Richard sat beside her on the bed, fully clothed.

Her cheeks flamed as her mind whirled, remembering last night. She jerked the covers back up over her body and then sank down beneath them.

'I need to go back to the warehouse today.'

His tone was non-committal, flat. *Where had the teasing man from last night gone?* Unwilling to answer, she simply nodded. It wasn't as if she required him for anything. Although she did wonder at the tweak of disappointment building in her heart.

'We need to go over your plans for today.'

Confused, she asked, 'Why?'

'I need to know how many men you'll need and what tasks you wish them to perform, so I can give them their orders.'

So, he had been serious at dinner last night. She was not permitted to perform her duties as the keep's lady. 'I have nothing planned for today. You can keep your men.'

His glare could have lighted the cold charcoals in the brazier, but she didn't care.

'Now you're going to be contrary.'

He hadn't asked a question, so she didn't respond.

'Why? Because you can't get your way?' When she remained stubbornly silent, he continued, 'I am not going to give you control over men you know nothing about.'

Isabella turned her head away from him. She knew she was being petty and that it could possibly come to hurt her in the end, but if she let him take complete charge of what was supposed to be her position, one she had trained for her entire life, where would that leave her?

He grasped her chin and forced her head back to face him. When she closed her eyes, he tightened his hold. 'Look at me.'

She ignored him, afraid of losing her will in the deep blue depths of his gaze.

'God's teeth, woman, I am not giving in on this. You will do as I say.'

At what sounded like a threat, she did look at him. 'Or what?'

He stared at her for a few long heartbeats, then released her chin and with a vile oath rose from the bed. 'You have no need of any men today?'

'No.'

'Have it your way, then.' He strode briskly to the door, pausing to ask, 'Are you certain?'

'Very.'

'Do not leave the keep.'

His unexplained order and the slamming of the door behind him brought her flying from the bed. She was an idiot, a stubborn, witless fool. Perhaps if she gave in to him now, after a while he would relent. She needed to stop him. Her hand on the door latch, she opened her mouth and heard Conal's voice float through the still-closed door, making her pause to listen.

'Did you bother to explain it to her?'

'Explain what? That someone left a missive stating Lady Dunstan is in danger? We don't know who left it, nor do we know what the danger might be. Besides, she was being so contrary that she wouldn't have heard me if I had tried to explain.' The anger in Richard's reply made her cringe.

'Still—'

'No.' Her husband stopped his man from saying anything else on the matter, and then continued. 'She'll wallow in her self-righteous anger for a few days. But as soon as boredom overwhelms her, she'll give in.'

Self-righteous anger? If he wasn't so close to the truth, she'd throw open the door and rage at him.

'And if she doesn't?'

Isabella knew she would likely give in long before he expected her to—the thought of doing nothing for even a single day made her stomach churn.

'She will. But in truth, she's safer sitting in her chamber than anywhere else while I'm not here.'

Conal's snort of reply made her frown. *Safer? Was she in some danger?*

Richard's man asked, 'Have you been able to determine who issued the threat?'

Threat? What threat? As far as she knew the only person who'd ever posed a threat was her husband.

'I've narrowed it down to a few people. We'll discuss it on the way to Marguerite's.'

'And why would we go there?' Conal's voice held a note of surprise.

She heard what sounded like a heavy slap—as if maybe Richard had slapped Conal's shoulder, or back. 'Because you stop there every morning to visit with your lady love before going to the warehouses—why would today be any different?'

Conal's grumbled reply faded beneath their departing footsteps.

Isabella leaned against the door. What was going on? And who was Conal's lady love, Marguerite?

If Richard was seeking to protect her from something, why didn't he just explain that to her? The thought that he was intentionally keeping her in the dark rankled. Why would someone threaten her safety?

She wandered back to the bed and sat on the edge. She hated secrets, just hated them. Mostly because she could never figure out the correct scenario.

Isabella dropped back on to the mattress, her head coming to rest on a pile of soft fur. She sat up and looked behind her. Someone—most likely her husband—had draped a gown, chemise, a pair of plain slippers, soft boots and a fur-lined mantle on the end of the bed.

She ran her fingers through the silken fur and sighed with pleasure at such a wonderful gift. Apparently he truly wasn't as displeased with her as he'd led her to think.

If she couldn't successfully figure out secrets, how would she ever figure out the man she'd been forced to wed?

She picked up the deep forest-green gown and rose to dress. There would be an entire day of nothing to do but devise a plan to coax Richard into telling her what was going on. That way, tonight after dinner, and after they'd climbed into bed, she could set her plan in motion.

Isabella pulled the fur-lined mantle tighter about her in an attempt to shield herself from the biting wind. She stood on the wall surrounding Dunstan and stared out across the stormy windswept sea.

'My lady?' Another one of Richard's ever-present guards braved the weather to try coaxing her back inside.

She turned to glare at him. This one was much younger than the last, perhaps they thought she'd feel sorry for him. If so, they were wrong.

'I am fine. Go back inside.'

'But his lordship—'

A curt wave of her hand stopped his words. 'Is at the wharf and won't know I'm disobeying him if you don't tell him.'

The guard's sigh as he turned to stomp back to the ladder would have been laughable if she wasn't so angry at his lord.

Nearly a month ago Richard had carted her off to her chamber and taught her such a wondrous lesson about being in bed with a man. She still shivered with desire every time she thought about it. But since then he'd been distant and cold, ignoring her whenever possible. She'd never been able to coax him into their bed, let alone get him to explain what was happening. The one time she'd tried had ended with him leaving the chamber, never to return.

A blast of wind pushed the hood of her cloak from her head. She pulled it back up, sinking her fingers into the luxurious lining. She had been quite pleased to find such treasured gifts then, especially after she'd forgotten to ask him for enough gold to purchase fabric to make a gown. But now they felt more like some sort of payment—a compensation.

Which, as far as she was concerned, was fair considering the work she'd accomplished in the Great Hall without the help of his men. While he'd told her she couldn't order his men about, he'd never said she wasn't permitted to put the women to work.

And she had. It hadn't been that difficult, not after she'd stooped low enough to explain the circumstances to the women of Dunstan. Her mother would be horrified to learn she'd used such a sneaky trick, but her mother wasn't here. And while Isabella wasn't going to argue this with Richard any further, she wasn't about to live in a pig's sty.

So, with help from Hattie, the women servants

and a dozen more women from the village, the only thing they had left to finish was the floor. Everything else was cleaned, repaired or painted.

She knew full well that Richard had noticed. Every night when he returned from the wharf, he'd paused to look around the Great Hall, his expression growing darker each passing day. Isabella wasn't going to say a word until he asked. Of course, she knew that asking would come with pointed glares and angry accusations.

Right now, though, his shouting would be a welcome change from his one-word answers and silence.

She knew that men could be moody creatures at times, but this... Isabella shook her head. Something was wrong with him. Something she was not at all familiar with. Granted, there was some sort of secret danger that she'd not been able to discover anything about, but why would that make him ignore her? She posed no danger to him, or Dunstan. So, his off-putting manner had to be due to something else.

She leaned her shoulder against the wall and gazed down towards the snow-covered village. Surely there was someone here on Dunstan who could answer her questions. Someone who knew her husband better, on a more personal level that his men did.

Never would she question his men. Not only had he basically forbidden her contact with them, it would be foolish and wrong of her. He needed their respect, needed them to follow his orders, not be his friend, nor a confidant to his wife.

She'd tried asking Hattie, but the woman seemed unwilling to divulge much in the way of useful information. Oh, yes, the older woman had told her stories about when Richard was a babe and young lad. Perhaps if she asked again, explaining why she wanted to know, Hattie might be more forthcoming.

Isabella knew she really didn't have many choices. Maybe a midwife? They were usually privy to every snippet of gossip. Or the priest? She'd not seen him since the evening he'd so willingly helped to seal her fate.

No. Her best source would be Hattie. She just needed to figure out how to gain the woman's trust enough to talk to her.

A movement on the road leading up to the keep caught her attention. She leaned away from the wall. Richard and Conal were returning. And they were closer than she'd like. If she didn't want her jaunts up here to the wall forbidden to her, she needed to get back inside before he saw her.

She grabbed the edge of her mantle, so she wouldn't trip over it as she raced down the ladder to the inner yard. Thankfully, she'd been able to get one of the women to show her an easy way out of the keep and into the bailey. Unfortunately, the quickest way back inside would take her right across the middle of the open bailey where he'd be likely to see her.

A quick glance towards the gates assured her that he wasn't quite yet entering the yard. Still holding on to her garments, she took off at a decidedly unladylike run, hoping to reach the postern gate before Richard and Conal passed through the main one.

'My lady!'

Isabella cursed, looked over her shoulder to see which guard was now hailing her and tripped, slipping on a patch of ice. Her knees hit the frozen ground hard enough to bring tears to her eyes and she fell forward, landing on one arm.

She wanted to scream in frustration and pain, but before she had time to clear her mind a horse stopped alongside of her. There was no need to look up at the rider, she knew who she'd see. So, she relaxed as best she could, giving in to the throbbing of her knees and burning of her elbow, letting the sharp pains roll over her until she was able to take a deep breath.

'Get up.'

'Richard, the woman is injured.' Conal's tone was filled with censure.

'This is none of your affair.' Isabella winced at Richard's cold, unforgiving voice.

He repeated, 'I said, get up.'

She pushed herself up on to her knees with her good arm and then struggled to her feet. 'I am fine.'

To prove it, she took a step, prepared to return to the warmth of the Great Hall with as much dignity as she could muster, and then cried out in pain as her ankle crumpled beneath her weight, sending her right back down to her knees on the cold ground.

Before she could catch her breath, Richard dismounted and came to her side. He pulled her up from the ground and swung her into his arms, holding her against his chest.

She wrapped her arms around his neck and buried her face in the lining of his mantle. 'I am sorry.'

'Be still.' His voice was gruff and he headed towards the side gate, shouting orders over his shoulder, 'Conal, bring Marguerite. Someone find Mistress Hattie. Now.'

Once inside, he took the stairs to her chamber two at a time as if he held nothing heavier than a tankard of ale. The only sign that he'd exerted himself at all was a slightly faster beating of his heart.

Isabella held back a smile when this time he deposited her on the bed gently instead of dropping her on to the mattress as he had in the past.

He sat next to her and unpinned the brooch holding the front of her cloak together. It fell from her shoulders and he pulled it from beneath her.

To her amazement, instead of tossing it on the floor, he went and hung it on a peg. His own followed before he came back to the bed to push the skirts of her gown and chemise up to her knees.

'What are you doing?'

'Trying to decide how to get your boots off.'

She sat up. 'I can do that.'

He batted her hands away. 'Just lie back.'

Isabella frowned—why in the name of heaven did his voice shake? And why was he acting like a mother hen when she'd expected him to be angry?

Before she could question him, he returned to sit next to her, the boots forgotten, and pulled her tight against his chest. 'When you first fell, I thought someone had killed you.'

Why would he think such a horrible…? Oh, Lord, was that the threat he'd talked to Conal about? Someone had threatened to kill her? And she was out in the open, an easy target, without any hint, or warning, of danger?

She shoved hard against his shoulders, pushing

him away. 'That was the threat? Someone plots to kill me?'

At least he had the decency to look sheepish when he nodded and answered, 'Yes.'

'And instead of simply telling me, you thought somehow I'd be able to guess what was going on just because you held a conversation with Conal outside this chamber door where you knew I'd hear?'

'You were smart enough to deduce why the conversation was held within your earshot. I thought—'

'For the love of God, Richard, the only thing you said was that Lady Dunstan was in danger. How was I to make sense of that? I may be able to guess at a few of your moods, but I cannot read your mind.'

His sheepish look vanished. He narrowed his eyes to glare at her. 'Had you done as I ordered, there would never have been any danger.'

'I may concede that point, but still, a better warning was warranted.'

'At least now you understand why you need to stay within the keep.'

'No. I don't understand. Nobody harmed me. I was distracted and fell on some ice. I will not become a prisoner in what should be my own home because of some vague threat. No.' Isabella gaped at him. He couldn't be serious. She shook her head. 'No. What I understand is that you need to find the miscreant and take care of this. You are the lord here. And while I may have been brought to Dunstan as bait, I am now your wife. Your *wife*, Richard, not some unnamed captive. I am not about to suffer further for another person's actions.'

'Oh, so once again you are suffering?'

'And don't you start with that again.' When his lips thinned to a hard line and his eyes seemed to blaze, she shook a finger at him. 'Don't you dare try to avoid this issue by feigning outrage. You know exactly what I meant. Without question, *you* are responsible for me being here. So, you are now responsible for me being in danger.' She lowered her arm. 'You need to see to this, Richard. Immediately.'

He leaned away to stare at her. 'Apparently, fear for your life steals your common sense.'

'And you think that is why? Because I dare take you to task? Did you think I was going to cower and cry? Or that I would hide in a dark corner wringing my hands?'

'I think that because you sound like a shrew.'

'A shrew?' She grasped the front of his tunic in both hands. 'I do not know whether I fear for my life or not. But I do know that I am in pain. And I am so angry with you right now that I could spit.'

He lifted one eyebrow, then shoved her arms away, pushed her down on to the bed and came over her to whisper a warning against her lips. 'Stop talking before you say something you regret.'

She knew exactly what he was going to do. Against all common reason, she urged him on by parting her lips as if to speak. His mouth covered hers and he gathered her into an embrace that he most likely thought harsh. But she found it warm and comforting enough to want to sigh with relief.

His kiss was near ruthless and she welcomed it gladly. He plundered and took, leaving her to do little else than slide her hand up to caress the back of his head, holding him close as he swept her away.

'My lord?'

Richard broke their kiss on a groan and sat up at Hattie's entrance into the chamber, her arms laden with enough supplies to heal an army.

Isabella sighed with regret at the loss of his warmth and touch. She looked at the older woman's array of items and laughed. 'Hattie, I may have twisted my ankle and bruised an elbow, but I assure you that I am not at death's door.'

Hattie sat her goods on the floor near the bed and shrugged. 'Nobody knew what was wrong, they said you were hurt and that I needed to get up here.' She looked at Richard, adding, 'Now.'

At that moment another breathless woman loaded

down with more supplies rushed into the chamber. 'Hattie, what happened?'

Isabella rolled her eyes. She pointed at her left foot. 'Twisted ankle.' And then to her right elbow. 'Bruised elbow.'

The new woman joined Hattie in glaring at Richard. 'And *this* is the life-or-death situation I need to attend?'

Richard stood and backed towards the door, holding his hands up before him as if to ward off an attack. 'I know when to retreat. And since I am outnumbered, this seems a good time.'

He lowered his arms and in three long strides returned quickly to the bed, to cup the back of Isabella's head, lean down for a quick, mind-robbing kiss and then whisper, 'I will return, later, after your troops have thinned out.'

Before her lips could cease tingling, he was gone from the room. She blinked twice, then turned her fuzzy attention to the other women. They, of course, had their heads together, twittering behind their hands.

Isabella swallowed hard to banish the heat of embarrassment flooding her cheeks, before addressing the woman she didn't know. 'Obviously I'm Richard's wife, Isabella. And you are?'

'Marguerite, my lady. Dunstan's midwife.'

Sitting up straighter on the bed, Isabella smiled at her sudden stroke of good fortune. 'Oh, it is so nice to meet you, Mistress Marguerite.'

The woman flipped her auburn braids over her shoulders while coming closer to the bed. 'I recognise that tone. What are you looking to discover, Lady Dunstan?'

'Isabella, please. Whatever I can about my husband.'

Marguerite glanced at Hattie, who had started mixing a poultice together on the table near the window. 'You were right, subterfuge is not one of her strengths.'

'If you prefer, I could chatter merrily on about the beauty of the snow and then complain about Richard's lack of manners.'

Marguerite grasped her boot. 'Go on, tell me all about the snow.'

Isabella frowned. 'Is there a reason for distracting me?'

The woman easily stripped the boot and stocking off her right foot, then began tugging on the left boot.

Isabella winced. Naturally her ankle had already begun to swell, making the distraction welcome. 'Yes, well, the snow is white. And cold. Very cold.' She curled her fingers into the covers beneath her as a decidedly painful jolt shot up her leg at Marguerite's not-so-gentle tugging. 'Yes, very cold. And I don't think it'll ever end.'

She paused to take a deep breath. 'And I'm fairly certain—' When Marguerite gave one final jerk, pulling off the boot and stocking at once, Isabella jumped, gasping out, 'Damn, that hurts.'

Marguerite swung the boot on the tip of one finger before tossing it and the stocking next to their mates on the floor. 'Didn't seem fair to prolong the inevitable.'

Isabella glared at her. 'I wager you're a joy during childbirth.'

'And I wager you'll sound like a guttersnipe during the birth of your own child.'

'Yes, well, that's something we have no need to worry about.'

Marguerite's eyes widened in surprise. 'Really now?'

'How odd.' Hattie joined them to hand Marguerite the poultice she'd made. 'Everyone in the keep is already placing wagers on the date of your first child's arrival.'

'When it doesn't happen within the next nine months, do I get the money?' Isabella slapped a hand over her mouth to stop herself from saying anything further on the subject. What was she thinking to be sharing this type of information with these women?

'Blunt and entertaining.' Marguerite spread the poultice over her ankle. 'We'll become fast friends.'

Isabella offered no comment since that remained to be seen. She did ask, 'Comfrey root?'

'Of course. I'll wrap the ankle and, as long as you stay off of it for a day or two, it should be good as new.'

Hattie handed Isabella a goblet of odd-smelling wine. 'I don't think that will be an issue tonight.'

Isabella wrinkled her nose at the warmed, overly sweet-smelling wine. 'What is in this?'

'Never you mind.' Hattie pushed the vessel to Isabella's lips. 'Just drink it.'

Marguerite stayed Hattie's hand with a shake of her head. 'A little lavender, lemon balm and lovage, with just a touch of rosemary for the swelling and honey to make it palatable.'

Sceptical and more than a little leery, Isabella asked, 'Nothing to dull the pain?'

'Pain?' Marguerite made a show of studying Isabella's foot as she wrapped the ankle. 'Did you cut off your foot, or just twist your ankle?' Without waiting for an answer to the obvious, she added, 'I just want you to rest tonight, not addle your wits.'

The thought sounded good. However, she had responsibilities to attend to before the day was done. 'But the evening meal should be just about ready. If someone would assist me down the stairs, I'll be fine.'

Marguerite pulled the covers from beneath her, then drew them up and tucked the ends under Isabella. 'I will stay to assist Hattie with the meal. After all, it will be nice to enjoy a meal I didn't have to make and it will give me a chance to discover why Lord Richard has been so inattentive to his new bride.'

Isabella gasped, horrified at the idea of Marguerite questioning Richard on something so personal. She tugged at the covers encasing her like a cocoon so she could swing her legs off the bed, but the midwife stopped her with a laugh.

'Good heavens, I was but teasing you. Never would I think to so boldly divulge something you said in private. Stay in bed, drink your wine. I'll send your husband up with some food. You, Hattie and I can have a fine chat tomorrow.'

Chapter Fourteen

Richard felt the tick in his cheek twitch faster the third time the midwife asked, 'Yes or no? Are you going to take this food up, or should I find someone else?'

Seated between him and Conal, Mistress Marguerite surveyed those gathered in the Great Hall for the evening meal, settling her gaze on one of the finer-looking younger men at the far end. She nodded towards her selection. 'Perhaps he would be inclined.'

Richard unclenched his jaw long enough to order, 'Enough.'

The woman pointedly turned her attention to Conal. 'Do you not agree that it would be best if Lady Dunstan was offered some food and drink?'

'You need stay out of this, Marguerite.' Conal leaned away from her, shaking his head. 'He's already had his fill of your harping.'

'I am not harping in the least. I am only suggesting what might be best for his *wife*.'

'Concern yourself with her ankle and leave the rest to me.' When the good, albeit oddly intrusive, mistress made a noise that sounded suspiciously like disapproval, Richard tightened his grip on the knife in his hand. This is exactly what he had feared. Once the people of Dunstan started interacting with Isabella they would find themselves defending her at the most inopportune times.

How could they not? It wasn't as if she was an evil or unlikeable person. She possessed a quick wit, cared for others, knew how to control the running of a keep without letting anyone realise she was in fact also controlling them.

He let his narrowed stare roam the Great Hall once again. How had she accomplished so much with no men to help?

Each evening for the last month, he'd return from the warehouse to find more progress completed on the reordering of his keep. And each night he tried to fathom how she'd accomplished such feats.

He could understand the scrubbing of the furniture, fire pit and such. But the tapestries hanging high on the walls had somehow been cleaned, along with the decorated shields belonging to his family that were perched above the tapestries. They had been removed, cleaned and returned to their rightful spots. And the fresh coat of paint on the walls didn't miraculously apply itself.

Someone was helping her. The question was, who? He'd intentionally made certain that every man, excluding whichever three he had left behind to guard her, was put to work in the warehouses or on ship repairs. And the guards swore they'd not lifted a finger to help the women.

He couldn't believe for one heartbeat that the women were doing this alone. The idea of Hattie, or any of the maids, scurrying up and down a ladder was absurd. He should have followed his gut instinct and not hesitated. Instead of waiting until the evening to return to the keep, he should have dragged himself back here some time during the day to catch the culprits acting behind his back.

The only thing that had kept him from doing so was simple, to him at least. He actually didn't want to catch any of the men in the act of disobeying his orders. He didn't want to have to discipline them for helping the lady of the keep. They wouldn't understand his actions, which would only breed resentment. And in the end, he'd look like a fool for marrying a woman he appeared to despise and not trust.

He should never have married her. He should have

taken her as a hostage and held her captive in a cell. It would have been much easier to do so. As long as he didn't take his conscience into consideration.

At the time she'd done nothing to him. Nothing. He'd had no reason to harm her, or treat her poorly. She was never his target for revenge. So, he'd mistakenly believed that marrying her would not only save her reputation, but that it would make controlling her easier, and would also ensure her a measure of safety from the other men on Dunstan.

Granted, it had preserved her reputation. But what had possessed him to believe either of the other two was true?

He could no more control her than he could the falling snow. And there was a poorly written missive in his private chamber that threatened her life.

What bothered him right now more than anything else was the fact that when he'd seen her fall in the bailey and had thought someone had struck her dead, he'd felt as if not just his heart, but his entire world, had stopped.

He'd been angered when he'd found Agnes's body. He hadn't cared for the woman, but she hadn't deserved to die in such a vile manner. And he'd been nearly torn asunder when he'd happened on Lisette's small form. His chest had tightened—and hadn't yet relaxed. He'd seen red—a blood-red rage that did nothing but grow stronger with each passing hour.

But today had been different. When Isabella had fallen to the ground, he wanted to die with her. His first response had not been anger, or even fear. It had not been a terrible thirst for revenge. Truth be told, he hadn't even looked for the man who had let loose the arrow, or rock, that had taken her life. Instead, it had been all he could do not to throw himself from his horse, race to her side and plunge a knife into his own heart so he'd not be without her.

That dire vision of taking his own life had enraged him. It wasn't as if she was his life, she wasn't even his love. She was nothing more than a means to an end. That was all. His only hope had been that once Glenforde was dead, that he and Isabella could somehow find a way to be…friends. Companions who could work together for the good of Dunstan.

So why then the ungodly urge to take his own life? And why then did he sit here now, in the Great Hall, not touching his food and dreading his return to her chamber?

'Richard.' Conal grasped his wrist and slapped a tankard of ale into his hand. 'Go talk to her. Tell her what is happening, so this doesn't occur again.'

Richard shook the fog from his vision and turned to look at Conal. To his surprise, Mistress Marguerite was no longer sitting between them. He spied her helping Hattie and the other servants to clear the tables.

'So what doesn't occur again?'

Conal snorted. 'You can lie to yourself. You can lie to her. You can even lie to God if you so desire. But you can't lie to me. You care more for that sharp-tongued wife of yours than you'll admit.'

If he couldn't figure out what he felt about Isabella, or why, then how could Conal? 'You are seeing things that aren't there, my friend.'

'Perhaps. But after the way you reacted in the bailey, I don't think I'm wrong. Never have I witnessed such a look of horror on your face before.'

'Why wouldn't I react with horror? If anything happens to his spawn, Warehaven will descend on Dunstan, sparing nothing in his path.'

'Again, that whole lying to everyone else is fine. But rest assured it is not going to work with me. If Warehaven descends with the intent of waging war, we fight with the advantage of defending our homes and loved ones. In the end, he will return to Warehaven a little worse for wear.'

Richard shoved back from the table and rose. 'Conal. Have I recently told you what an ass you can be at times? Like now?'

'Probably, but I hear it so often that it no longer

sinks in.' He tapped the platter of food the women had prepared for Isabella. 'In your haste to escape, don't forget to take this to her.'

Richard set down the ale, grabbed the plate and left.

Isabella picked at the edge of the top cover. Her head spun from the wine, steadily revolving faster with the passing of time.

Apparently she'd been forgotten. That didn't surprise her considering how little she mattered to anyone here at Dunstan.

Her mother wouldn't have forgotten her. Neither would her father or sister. Jared might have, but her brother usually had so many things on his mind that he always ended up forgetting some thing or another. But the others would have brought her food and drink. They'd have come into her chamber more often than she'd liked just to check on her, to see if she wanted or needed anything. They'd have come simply to keep her company.

But she wasn't home at Warehaven. She was here at Dunstan where nobody cared about her.

She sighed, dropped the cover and crossed her arms over it against her chest. Thankfully she had earlier realised this melancholy settling over her was caused by the herb-laced wine, otherwise she knew she'd have dissolved into tears of self-pity and homesickness by now.

The door to the chamber opened and she sat up, eager to see who had come and if they'd brought something to eat. Richard walked through the doorway, with a heavily loaded platter in his hand.

She took one look at his face and leaned back against the pillows she'd piled up at the head of the bed. He didn't look angry, but neither did he look pleased. Actually, if anything, his expression was bland, as if bored. She felt her eagerness fade, knowing he'd be less than cheerful company.

He hooked a foot around the leg of a bench and dragged it over to the bed to use as a table. Setting the platter down, he said, 'I know it's a little much, but they thought you'd want a selection to pick and choose from.'

Even his voice sounded bored.

'It doesn't matter.' She sniffed. 'I'm not hungry.'

He stared down at her. 'Are you in pain?'

'No.' Isabella swiped at her watering eyes and silently cursed.

'Then what are you crying about?'

'I have no idea.'

Richard frowned, then looked around the chamber until he ended his search on the empty goblet tipped on to its side on the table next to the bed. 'What was in that goblet?'

'Wine.'

'And what?'

Unable to remember everything in it, she shrugged. 'Some herbs and stuff.'

'Stuff?'

'Yes, stuff.'

'Oh, well, yes, if they put *stuff* in it, I'd probably be crying, too.' He sat on the edge of the bed and pushed her over. 'Make room.'

She wiggled over far enough so he had enough space to sit beside her.

Richard adjusted the pillows, took off his boots, then swung his legs up on the bed. 'So, what dark thoughts have you in such a morose state?'

Isabella leaned against his arm. 'Everyone forgot about me.'

He hooked his arm across her shoulders and pulled her against him. 'That would be impossible.'

'Everyone left and I was alone.'

'Ah, yes, I know. For almost an entire hour.'

She shook her head. 'No, it was much longer than that.'

'Not really.' He handed her a hunk of bread. 'Eat this.'

She nibbled at a corner, but couldn't swallow past

the thick dryness of her throat. 'Can I have something to drink?'

'No. All I brought with me is wine and you don't need any more.'

'But I'm thirsty.'

He took the bread from her. 'How about some broth instead?'

'Fine.' Somewhere in the back of her muddled mind Isabella knew she sounded and was acting like some spoiled child. But at the moment, she was unable to find the will to care. What she wanted most of all was for the bed to stop spinning like a top.

He held the bowl of broth to her mouth. When she reached for it, he said, 'I've got it, just take a sip.'

She did and felt some dribble down the front of her gown. With a shudder, she pushed the bowl away. 'Richard, I think I am intoxicated.'

He wiped a rag across her chest. 'Isabella, I know you are.'

She tried to slide down on to the mattress. 'I need to sleep.'

'No.' He dragged her back up against the pillows. 'You need to eat something first.'

Her stomach lurched at the thought of food. 'I don't think that's a good idea right now.'

'Are you going to be sick?'

'Sick? I am a lady.'

'Ah, yes, how foolish of me to forget that ladies never vomit.'

Isabella wanted to laugh, but the best she could do was to bat at his leg. 'You, Lord Dunstan, are vulgar.'

'I think I've been told that a time or two before.' He eased his arm from her shoulders and swung off the bed. 'I'll find you something to drink.'

'You are leaving me?' To her horror, her lower lip quivered and her eyes welled with tears.

'Isabella, I will be right back.'

'You won't. I will sit here all alone.' She choked on her words. 'For ever.' God's teeth, what was wrong with her? Every time she opened her mouth, something more foolish spewed forth. Isabella waved towards the door as she slid sideways off her pillows on to the bed. 'Go. Leave me.'

She vaguely heard Richard's grumbled curses over the sound of him stomping across the chamber to open the door and shout for Hattie.

Everything seemed to be coming at her through a thick, hazy fog. Her heart pounded so hard and fast that her pulse sounded like roaring waves in her ears. She curled her fingers tightly around the bedcovers. 'Richard?'

He came back to the bed and pulled her upright. 'I am here.'

'Some…thing…something is…wrong… I…'

With a sigh she closed her eyes and sank into the welcoming embrace of a warm, dark void.

'Isabella!'

Richard's shout, followed by a stinging slap across her cheek, jerked her back to the murkiness of her spinning and now oddly bouncing chamber.

He had lifted her into his arms and asked questions she couldn't understand. Unable to form words, she grunted in reply to his undecipherable queries.

People shouting, and what sounded like countless items hitting the floor, made her wonder if Dunstan was under attack.

A hand grasped her chin. Hard, unforgiving fingers pressed into her cheeks, forcing her lips apart. She flailed her arms at the rough treatment, but her pleas to be left alone were cut off when someone poured a foul-tasting liquid in her mouth, clamped her mouth shut and stroked her throat, forcing her to swallow.

The arms holding her placed her on a hard, solid object. It wasn't cold enough to be the floor. But she couldn't imagine what it might be instead because she was trying to focus on what she swore sounded like Richard apologising for something.

Isabella groaned. There were too many things to try making sense of when all she knew for certain was that her head throbbed horribly and her stomach cramped in the most painful manner possible.

Yet, when she tried to curl into a ball to ease the cramping, hands pushed and prodded her on to her stomach and dragged her until her head hung over the edge of this hard, unyielding bed.

She stared down at what appeared to be the floor. Even though it rippled and undulated like a wave, it still looked like a floor.

A hard, dirt-packed floor that made her mouth water profusely and swallowing only made it water more. When her stomach gurgled Isabella gagged and gripped the edge of her uncomfortable bed, realising then that she'd been placed on a table.

Richard combed his fingers through her hair, dragging the mass to the back of her head where he held it in one hand, while he rubbed her back with the other one. His infernal massaging made her feel worse, but before she could tell him to stop, her throat and stomach convulsed at the same time.

After what seemed like hours, her bruised-feeling stomach settled, permitting her to groan in exhaustion and rest her forehead on the table. Her throat felt raw, her face wet and she shivered uncontrollably. But the room had stopped spinning, her heart had slowed its riotous pounding and her head no longer hammered in agony.

She turned her head and opened her eyes to see Richard place a fur-lined bedcover over her before he sat down on a bench, clasping one of her hands in his own. He brushed her hair from her face and cupped her cheek.

He looked terrible and rather pale, making her wonder what had happened to upset him so. The hushed sounds of people talking prompted her to tip her head back far enough to see what had to be half of Dunstan's citizens gathered around them.

Humiliated to be seen in such a state, she swung her focus back to Richard, to hoarsely beg, 'Please, get me out of here.'

She struggled to rise, only to have Richard place a hand on her shoulder blades. 'Stay still, let me.'

He slid his arms beneath her and rolled her into his embrace. Marguerite tucked the hanging edge of the cover around her, and pressed the back of her hand to Isabella's cheek. With a nod, she said, 'Go, I will be right behind you.'

Once in her chamber, the most wondrous sight met her—a huge, oversized tub with rose-scented steam rolling from it had been set up in the alcove. Never had she seen such a large, more inviting-looking bath.

Richard set her down on a small bench facing the

tub. When she swayed, he steadied her with a hand on her shoulder.

Isabella sighed. If she couldn't sit upright by herself, how was she going to take advantage of the bath? And she so wanted to soak in that lovely tub. It was calling to her, inviting her to relax in the warmth of the water and let the troubles from this day fade away with the steam.

Her lip trembled and when she couldn't stop it or the cursed tears from building, she closed her eyes and turned her head away to hide her unwarranted distress. She couldn't believe she was going to start crying about nothing again. How could she be any more foolish than she'd already been this evening?

A calloused hand wiped away the tears from her cheek, then rested there. 'It will soon be better, I promise, Isabella.'

She leaned into his caress. 'I am a silly fool.'

'No, you aren't. You are a woman who had a terrible reaction to either the herbs, or the wine.'

'And one who is blessed to be alive,' Marguerite interjected from the doorway. She carried a pitcher, a cup and at least a dozen drying cloths over to the bath before joining them at the bench to pull the cover off Isabella's shoulders. 'Come on, into the bath with you. I want you to sweat the rest of the poison from your body.'

Shivering, Isabella gripped the edge of the bench. 'I can't even sit upright, how am I going to sit in that tub without drowning?'

Deftly untying the laces of her gown, Marguerite nodded towards Richard. 'I am sure your husband will see to it that you don't drown.'

Isabella gasped. That meant he was going to be there for her bath—a thought that made her burst into tears. 'Have I not embarrassed myself enough in his presence today?'

He chucked her lightly under the chin. 'Sweeting, feel free to cry all you want. Hell, if you have the strength, you can scream and fight me. But you'll not win this one.' He leaned over to wrap his hands on either side of her waist and lifted her from the bench far enough for Marguerite to pull her gown and chemise free. Then he lowered her back to the bench, adding, 'You may as well resign yourself to my presence. I'm not going anywhere.'

Her cheeks flamed, making him laugh before he started to remove his own clothing. By the time he was down to nothing but his braies, Marguerite had managed to strip her mostly naked, too. The only part of her body still covered by cloth was her ankle.

Isabella squeezed her eyes closed, hoping when she opened them that all of this would have been nothing but some odd, drugged dream. She peeked out of one eye to see Richard reaching for a bucket of steaming water next to the tub. She inhaled sharply at the play of muscle across his back and arms as he hefted the bucket.

Marguerite's soft laugh made Isabella more self-conscious and nervous than she'd already been at seeing Richard's almost naked and completely healthy body.

'Like I said, I'm sure he'll keep you from drowning. Come on, up with you.' The woman tugged on Isabella's arms, pulling her from the bench and helping her over to the side of the tub.

Without so much as a by your leave, Richard swooped her off her feet from behind and, holding her against his chest, stepped into the tub, still wearing his undergarment. There was no stool to sit on and she couldn't figure out how this was going to work in the high-rimmed tub until he bent his knees and plopped down into the water, bringing her along to sit on his lap.

Water sloshed out of the tub, flooding on to the floor. Marguerite unfolded and dropped a few of the towels on the floor to soak up the water before attaching a pole to the outside of the tub behind Richard. She then draped a cloth over the pole and fluffed it out to surround them, with the edge of the cloth hanging just past the top rim of the tub. Not only did it provide them privacy, but it kept most of the steam trapped inside with them.

Isabella couldn't see them through the makeshift tent, but she heard heavier footsteps approach and jumped when two more buckets of hot water were poured into the bath at her feet.

Once the footsteps faded out of the chamber, Marguerite stuck her head inside the tent to address Richard. 'I put the bench with cool water and a cup to your right. There will be two guards outside the door. More water is already heating. Call out when you want it added, or need anything, and make sure she drinks all the water in that pitcher.'

'Consider it done,' Richard replied over her head.

Marguerite briefly touched Isabella's shoulder. 'Relax. Let your husband care for you. He owes you that much.'

The chamber door closed and a heavy silence fell over the room. Richard's heart thudded against her back and hers fell into the same rhythm.

Isabella struggled to breathe and leaned forward, only to be stayed by an arm wrapping beneath her breasts and pulling her back. 'There's nothing here you haven't already touched and stroked. Be still, Isabella, be still.'

Would she ever be able to resist that deep gravelly tone? Or not welcome that firm yet gentle hold?

She took a long breath, let it out slowly, then leaned her head back against his shoulder.

Chapter Fifteen

Richard leaned his head back against the rim of the tub. He wasn't tired and didn't fear falling asleep, not with such a soft, curvaceous woman stretched out on top of him. But he did long for a few moments of respite to wipe the memories of the last few hours from his mind.

This wife of his had probably frightened a good ten years off his life. And in return, he'd probably frightened at least that many off the lives of his men. He could only imagine how he'd looked when he had bolted down the stairs, carrying her in his arms, her head lolling about as if she was dead and him shouting at the top of his voice for Marguerite and Hattie.

Conal had never moved so fast in his life, clearing the table of platters, trenchers, goblets, utensils and bowls with one swipe of his giant arm. The rest of his men had instantly jumped into action, Matthew leading half of them to draw their swords and guard the studded double doors at the entrance to the Great Hall, Conal leading the other half to clear Richard's path, shoving benches, stools, people out of the way.

His earlier concern about the people of Dunstan coming to care for his wife was obviously a moot point. Their actions made it plain that they already saw her as their lady and that was something he was never going to be able to change. He wouldn't know where to begin.

The deep lines of fear and worry on Mistress Marguerite's face had nearly caused his heart to stop beating. She'd not expected such a reaction to the herbs she'd given Isabella. For far too many moments, the woman had been convinced she'd killed Dunstan's lady. To be honest, so had he.

Thankfully, they had both been wrong.

'I am sorry.'

'Hmm?' Apparently his stolen moments of respite were over. He nearly laughed at his wish for her to return to normal. It wasn't that long ago when he'd wished she was meeker and much more quiet. Now, he would so much rather she rail at him, than simper and cry. Her anger set his blood boiling, but her tears? He sighed. Her tears raked across his heart like a whip, making it bleed.

'I said I am sorry.'

He dragged his fingers through her hair, trying to free the tangles. 'For what?'

'For acting like such a witless nit.' Her shoulders rose and fell with a huge sigh. 'And for embarrassing you in front of your men.'

Richard wondered which misconception to address first, since one was as incorrect as the other.

'A witless nit for crying?' He placed a palm against her forehead, tipped her head back and looked down at her. 'Had you been sleeping when I came up here, I never would have known anything was wrong with you until it was too late. Your tears and babbling were what warned me that you were in dire trouble. So don't apologise for them. They saved your life.'

'Perhaps, but I did embarrass you along with myself. I don't think anyone other than maybe my father has ever seen my mother be ill. Doing so in public the way I did was shameful.'

'Surely you are jesting?' He shook his head in disbelief. 'Isabella, if you drank overmuch and became ill on a regular basis, that might pose a problem and we would have to consider watering your wine. But this had nothing to do with over-imbibing of your own free will.' He stroked his fingers down her cheek to her chin and turned her head to face him. 'Do you understand that you nearly died tonight?'

'I am sure my parents will be relieved to know I didn't.'

He released her chin and frowned. Was this more senseless babbling or was she regaining a bit of her wayward tongue? It was too soon for her to have regained all of her wits, so this had to be more of the malaise that had affected her earlier.

'Yes, I am sure they will be.' *But so was he.*

A sudden bout of sniffing made him want to cut off his tongue. He shifted her so she was more sideways than straight across his legs. Her liquid gaze gave away her losing battle with yet more tears. 'And so am I, Isabella, so am I.'

She rested her cheek against his shoulder. 'I can't help myself.'

'I know.' He wrapped his arms around her, suggesting, 'We could distract you.'

'I doubt that anything could distract me from this infuriating *oh, poor sad me* mood that has captured me fast in its clutches.'

'Oh, ye of so little faith.'

They were in a tub together and she was naked. Distracting her would take little effort. He lowered the arm he'd draped across her chest and placed his hand on her thigh.

'Well, yes, that might distract me somewhat.'

'Somewhat?' He caressed her leg, stroking a lazy

path from knee to hip and down again. 'Just some-what?'

She shrugged and said nothing. But the quickness of her breaths told him that he'd already surpassed distracting her *somewhat*.

'While you're *somewhat* distracted, you need to drink.' He reached under the tent for the pitcher of water and the cup, which he handed to her. 'Hold this.' After filling it with the water he nudged the bottom of the cup, then waited for her to finish it off before returning the items to the stool.

Settling back against the tub, he casually rested his hand on her stomach, asking, 'Now, where was I?'

Isabella picked up his hand and placed it on her thigh. 'I believe you were here.'

'But I remember being here.' He moved his touch to caress the soft skin covering her ribcage.

'I think your memory is faulty.'

'My mistake. I was here.' He cupped her breast, teasing the pebbled nipple with his thumb and tight-ening his arm across her shoulder when she jumped in surprise.

'No, you're wrong.' She turned slightly in his arms to breathe against his neck. 'I would have remem-bered that.'

'Are you certain?' The sound of her quick breaths

coaxed him to tease a little more. 'After all, you were drugged. That might have confused your memories.'

'Maybe.' She gripped his shoulder. 'I might have been remembering someone else.'

Richard laughed, knowing she was but teasing him. 'My lady's humour is returning.'

She trailed her hand along the side of his neck, up to his cheek and turned her face up to his. 'Humour is not what I'm feeling.'

He placed a quick kiss on her lips, then reached once again for the water and cup. 'What you're feeling is called thirst.'

Isabella briefly pressed her fingernails into his shoulder before taking the cup. 'What you're feeling is plain mean.'

'Drink.'

When she finished, he once again put the items back on the stool. 'So, I'm feeling mean, am I?'

She squirmed on his lap, making him gasp as his lust leapt from wanting, to clawing need. Richard breathed deeply to calm the riotous pounding of his heart. He wasn't turning this leisurely bath into anything other than what it was—a means of helping her relax and rid her body of the poisons that had made her sick.

'Yes, you are being mean. You tease and tempt, but do nothing to ease my torment.'

He stared at her, wishing there was enough light inside the dark confines of this bathing tent to see her face. Did her eyes shimmer with desire, or were they still glassy from the herbs?

When she started to move around again on his lap, he grasped her hip. 'Stop it.'

'Why, my Lord Dunstan, you sound...distracted.' She ran a hand down his chest, coming to rest low on his belly.

'Cease.'

She inched her fingers lower, sliding them beneath the soaked fabric of his braies.

'Isabella, you need to choose.' He caught her wrist. 'You can either sit here with me in this bath. Or you can sit here alone.'

'But I yearn for you and I'm willing—'

'I'm not.'

She jerked as if he'd slapped her. 'You don't desire me?'

From the waver in her voice he knew she was still at least partly caught in the drugged fog. 'Not desire you? Have you lost your wits completely?'

Still holding on to her wrist, he pushed her hand to his groin, closing his eyes with a groan when she wrapped her fingers around him through the thin fabric. Before he lost control, he pulled her hand to his chest, placing her palm over his heart. 'Can you feel the pounding of my heart? I don't just desire you. I lust for you.'

'Then—'

He didn't know whether to laugh or rage at himself. He'd started this, so his building frustration, and hers, was his fault for trying to distract her with teasing. 'Woman, you have not the strength to stand on your own two feet, or even sit upright on a bench. I may be a black-hearted knave, but I am not low enough to take advantage of a woman in such a manner. No. Not tonight.'

She sniffled against his chest. 'Now what are you crying about?'

Of course losing his patience only made her sniffle more. Richard released her hand to grip the edge of the tub, fighting to get himself under control. He closed his eyes tightly and breathed.

Once he was certain he could talk, move, think without wanting to either lose his temper, or satisfy baser urges, he wrapped her in a tight embrace. 'I'm sorry. Tell me, what's wrong?'

'Nothing.' She wiped at her nose.

Richard stretched an arm over the edge of the tub, reaching for one of the towels. Using the corner of it, he ran it over her face. 'No. Come on, tell me.'

'You'll think me foolish.'

'Probably.'

'You are not a black-hearted knave.' Her sniffs had turned to earnest cries. 'You are the kindest, most gentle man I know.'

Richard was…speechless…and not a little bit frightened. Kindest? Gentle? She thought him kind? And gentle? He'd gone too far with this helping her feel better. He should have left her in the capable hands of Marguerite and Hattie.

Now, instead of seeing him as the brute who'd kidnapped her, forced her to wed him and plotted to kill her former betrothed, she saw him as kind and gentle? That did not bode well for the future.

He needed to disabuse her of that notion before she did something truly foolish.

'Isabella…' He cleared his throat and began again, 'Isabella, listen to me. The wine and herbs are making you imagine things are different than what they are. Nothing has changed here. You are still bait to draw Glenforde out and he will still die by my hand. There isn't anything about me or my motives that you could consider kind, or gentle.'

He waited for her to say something—anything to show him that she understood.

She rubbed her fingertips across his shoulder. He felt her mouth working against his chest as if she were mulling over his words and debating how to respond. Finally, she sighed softly, then asked, 'I am never going to have the kind of love my parents share, am I?'

She confirmed his worst fears. This tenderness he had shown her made her long for things that he would never be able to give her. He couldn't lie, he wouldn't lie to her. That would be unfair and would only lead to broken false promises down the road. He knew the type of pain that created and he wasn't going to be the one who caused her to suffer like that. 'I am sorry, but, no.'

She pushed against his chest and sat up to grasp the edge of the tub. He watched her struggle to rise before she let her arms fall to her sides. 'I want to go to bed.'

Richard swallowed hard against the tightness in his throat. He hadn't wanted this night to end this way, but there was nothing he could say, nothing he could do to ease the disappointment she now felt.

He rose from the water, pulling her up with him. It was better this way. The hurt she felt now was minor compared to what it would feel like later if he had lied and led her to believe there was hope for some grand love in their future. Perhaps eventually she would learn that love was a myth, or something couples envisioned in their minds, and she would come to accept a comfortable companionship as something worthwhile.

For now, however, he didn't want to argue with her or fight over this. She was weak and not herself, it wouldn't be fair.

He stepped out of the water and quickly wrapped her in an oversized drying cloth before sitting her down on the stool next to the tub, so she could hold on to the edge if need be.

Briskly rubbing another towel over her limbs and hair, he dried her off, then unwrapped the cloth strips binding her ankle. Marguerite could replace them shortly.

He took a towel to his own body and once he'd squeezed as much water as possible from his braies, he reached for his clothes.

'What are you doing?'

Confused, Richard left the clothes on the floor and turned to look at her. She leaned against the tub, staring at him.

'I'm going to get dressed, tuck you in bed and leave. I'll send Marguerite or Hattie up to stay with you.'

Isabella shook her head. 'No.'

'What do you mean, no?'

'You are coming to bed with me.'

'I beg your pardon?'

'You heard me.'

Richard rubbed the towel over his head, trying

to give himself enough time to figure out what thoughts were running around in her mind. 'Don't you think we've gone beyond repairing this night?'

She pushed herself to her feet, still gripping the tub, and let the towel fall. She closed her eyes for half a heartbeat and then stared at him hard. 'My lord husband, you have sentenced me to a loveless marriage, with no chance of escape. Since you saw fit to wed me and confine me to this island, I have no options before me but to accept that as my life, as my future. But I will not live without someone to love and cherish. And since it will not be you, then you owe me someone as a replacement.'

He dropped his towel to the floor and crossed his arms against his chest. 'A replacement?'

'I want a child.'

'A child?' He studied her face. She was still a little pale, but her gaze seemed totally focused—on him.

'Yes. You owe me at least that much.'

'I owe you?'

Her cheeks blazed with colour. 'You have taken everything from me and now, even my future.' She lifted her chin. 'I demand my marital rights as your wife.'

He clenched his teeth together to keep his jaw from falling open. Not certain he could speak without sputtering, he asked, 'You demand?'

She tilted her head slightly to the side and lifted one finely arched brow. 'Did you lie?' She stroked a hand down the curve of one hip. 'Is my skin not soft and pliable beneath your touch?'

Her hand slowly roamed up over her stomach and ribs to cup a breast. Keeping her stare locked on his, she brushed her thumb across the peaked nipple. 'Do you not find these enticing?'

She stroked a trail to her parted lips to trace them with a fingertip. 'Do you not enjoy my lips against yours, or the taste of my kiss?

'You do not want my heart, or my love. So be it.' Isabella leaned a hip against the tub and spread both arms wide. 'Does that mean you want nothing? Not any part of me?'

He'd thought her a quick learner. She was obviously far more than that. She'd taken his few lessons and created an entire curriculum on seduction.

God forgive him, but in her anger, her hurt, her rage, she was breathtaking. Her boldness captivated him. Her demand stole his mind. Oh, yes, he wanted her. And if she couldn't see the proof of that standing out before him, then she was blind.

He freed his tongue from the roof of his suddenly dry mouth, to warn, 'This will change nothing between us.'

'It will change everything. I will be your wife in more than just name.'

He took one step towards her. 'If I take you to that bed, there will be no turning back.'

'I may hate you at this moment, but, Richard, I burn for your touch.'

That declaration grabbed hold of his lingering reservations about her being weak and tossed them out the window. He peeled the still-damp fabric from his body, cleared the distance between them in two steps, swept her into his arms and, without breaking stride, placed her on the bed.

He released her, intending to stretch out by her side, but she dug her fingernails into his shoulders and pulled him down on top of her. 'Don't try to be nice. Don't think to make me swoon and forget what is truly happening here. I don't want your love play, Richard, it's a lie. I just want your child.'

Oh, no. No. He wasn't going to play this sort of game with her. She wasn't some cheap whore that he was going to use to gain his release and then toss aside. Regardless of anything else, she was his wife and he wasn't about to spend a lifetime not taking full advantage of what pleasures could be shared with her.

He shrugged out of her grasp and grabbed her hands, pinning them to the bed. 'I'll give you the child you so desire, but we're doing this my way, not yours. Do you understand me?'

When she nodded, he released her hands. He knew she was nervous, it would have been odd for her not to be. And he knew just how to distract her from her worries.

His lips against her ear, he whispered, 'I told you once that you'd have to beg me for this. Are you ready to beg, Isabella?' He drew out her name intentionally, knowing how it made her shiver.

'I'm not going to beg.'

'Ah, and there's that challenge again.'

Isabella closed her eyes, wondering if she had made a mistake—a huge mistake, one that was too late to correct.

He brushed his lips across hers, running his tongue along the seam before delving inside to sweep her into his kiss. This is what she'd wanted to avoid, this mind-robbing wave of pleasure that she was unable to resist.

She raised her arms to wrap him in her embrace, and he broke their kiss, to sharply order, 'No. Don't.'

When she dropped them back to the bed, he once again stole her breath with a kiss. The moment she thought she would drown, he trailed his lips to the soft spot where her neck met her shoulder, kissing, sucking the sensitive skin until her toes curled.

His low husky laugh should have been a warning, but when he eased down her body to cup a breast, then tease the tip with his tongue before closing his warm mouth around it, her breath caught on a gasp of surprise.

While he gave full attention to one breast with his mouth, his hand sought the other. Isabella clamped her lips tightly together to hold back a moan of pleasure as her pulse quickened and the need he was so artfully building rippled down her stomach. The need grew warmer, hotter, spreading until she swore she could feel her heart beating low in her belly, coaxing her moan to escape.

A deeper laugh made her wonder what pleasure-filled torture he intended to inflict now in his quest to make her beg. She was uncertain she'd be able to withstand much more.

Keeping a hand on one breast, he stroked the other along her side and over her hip as he eased further down her body until he manoeuvred his shoulders beneath her thighs.

She held her breath, her legs hooked over his shoulders trembling, uncertain what to expect.

He caressed her breast one more time before sliding his hand to her stomach, resting his palm flat against her as if to hold her in place. 'Breathe, Isabella.'

She sighed, trying to ignore the rapid beating of her heart, and took a breath. Only to have it catch in her chest at a kiss so intimate she thought at first she was imagining the rush of wonder and unadulterated lust-filled need washing over her.

This is what riding a white-capped wave would feel like. She was certain of it. Weightless, having no control as the strength of the water carried her up, then cresting, pulling away to let her fall breathlessly before once again catching her to push her towards another crest. Isabella curled her fingers into the covers beneath her.

He paused, slowing his onslaught, and she fought to catch her breath. The moment her shaking legs stilled, he renewed his relentless need to break her, to hear her beg as he'd promised she would. Isabella closed her eyes, knowing he was right and that soon she'd not be able to stop herself from crying out mindlessly, begging him to fulfil her.

The exquisite stroking, circling of his tongue against her fevered flesh had her panting, gasping for each breath. Her belly contracted and when the crashing wave carried her higher and higher her body tensed, then pulsed madly around the touch of his finger inside her.

Isabella released the covers and reached for his shoulders, crying out, 'Richard, please, I beg of you.'

Before she could finish her cry, he was over her, angling her hips with one hand beneath her as he eased himself into her.

She moaned at his gentleness, wanting more, needing more, and pushed her hips harder against his.

He cupped her cheek, teasing her lips with his. 'Easy. Take it easy.'

'No.' She curled her fingers into his shoulders. 'It doesn't hurt.'

She gasped as her release beckoned. 'Please, Richard, please.'

He picked up the tempo, quickly finding the pace that made her toes curl. She wrapped her arms around him, holding him tightly, clinging to him as she felt herself fall, spiralling down to claim the release she so desperately needed.

Before her ragged breaths could ease, Richard stiffened, his body shaking as his own ragged groan raced against her cheek.

Isabella ran her fingers through his hair, whispering a teasing dare she hoped he'd not be able to ignore, 'You will never be able to make me beg again.'

His shoulders shook with laughter and he rolled on to his side. 'Wife, you are quite the bawdy temptress, aren't you?'

She snuggled against him, not yet willing to let the inevitable distance come between them just yet.

Richard sighed and patted her hip. 'I should go. You need to sleep.'

'No.' She reached up to place her hand against the side of his head. 'Don't leave me. Stay.'

'But—'

Isabella placed a finger over his lips. 'If this is all we are to share, then can we not share it fully? There is no reason for you to sleep elsewhere.' At his raised brow, she continued, 'I know what this is. I know full well that it is not a sharing of hearts. But, Richard, it is something, it connects us and is that not at least a thing to treasure?'

He clasped her hand and brought it to his lips. 'Isabella, I fear your tender heart is going to suffer mightily for this, but I will stay with you...this night.'

Chapter Sixteen

As the aromatic scent of cinnamon, cloves and nutmeg in the mince pies baking in the kitchen filled the keep Isabella couldn't help but wonder if her family would celebrate Christmas in her absence this year. She hoped they would. And she prayed they'd be merry and thankful in honour of the season.

'What do you think he'll say?' Isabella helped Hattie wrap another garland of pine boughs around one of the support beams in the Great Hall.

The older woman shrugged. 'Once the deed is done, will it matter?'

'I suppose not.'

It wasn't as if he hadn't seen the piles of freshly cut evergreen, ivy and holly stacked in the hall as he'd left this morning. She'd had the men put the piles near the door intentionally so Richard would see them. That way, if he had any complaints, he could voice them before she placed them about the keep. He hadn't said a word, hadn't confronted her about her plans, so surely he'd not been averse to her decking the keep with the greenery.

Marguerite's laughter as she trapped Conal beneath a sprig of mistletoe hanging from ribbons over the archway of a small alcove at the far side of the hall made Isabella smile.

It was nice seeing the two of them so at ease and so obviously enjoying each other's company. She couldn't help the twinge of jealousy over what they shared, especially knowing she would never have the type of marriage she'd longed for. Richard had made that quite clear.

'Child.' Hattie touched her arm. 'It isn't my place, but it needs saying. He has been through much. Give him time.'

Isabella turned her attention back to the evergreens. 'An entire life would not be enough time for him.'

Hattie snorted and shook her head. 'My lady, do not be blind.'

'It has nothing to do with not seeing. He has made it perfectly clear that I am little more than bait.'

'There was a puppy once.'

Uncertain where the older woman was headed

with this sudden turn in the conversation, Isabella asked, 'A puppy?'

'Hmm, yes. A deep dark-brown, floppy-eared puppy that the young master so badly wanted as his own. He would sneak out to the stables every chance he had to hold and play with the pup. She was his entire life. To him the sun rose and set on that gangly-legged ball of fur. I don't remember how many times I had to go out there, intending to chase him in for the evening meal, only to find him fast asleep with the puppy in his arms.'

Having had many litters of puppies at Warehaven, Isabella understood the young boy's devotion to the playful animal. There was nothing easier to fall in love with than a soft, warm puppy.

'His father made certain to give that puppy away first.'

'No.' Isabella groaned at the heartlessness of such an action—by his own father no less. 'That was cruel.'

'Yes, it was, but his lordship would not listen to reason. He was determined to teach the boy a hard lesson about life. The boy cried himself to sleep for countless nights afterwards.'

'The only lesson he could have learned from that was not to care overmuch for something.' Her heart ached for the little boy he'd been.

Hattie stopped, a branch of evergreen clutched in her hands, to stare at her. 'Exactly, my lady.'

Isabella frowned. Could that explain his reluctance to let himself care for her?

'It was a lesson reinforced by his first wife and then again by losing Lisette.'

'But, Hattie, I am going nowhere.'

'You can't be certain of that, can you? What happens when your family comes for you, Lady Isabella?' The woman turned back to hanging the evergreens, adding softly, 'And what happens to him?'

Isabella could not say what her father would do when he arrived. He might consider the marriage binding and be content to leave her at Dunstan. But he might also still be angry enough to take offence to the entire situation—the kidnapping, the marriage—and escort her back to Warehaven.

What *would* happen to Richard then?

She gazed around the Great Hall. Dunstan Keep was by no means a large dwelling. It would fit inside Warehaven with room to spare. There were no decorative paintings on the walls, just a simple lime-wash. Even the tapestries were worn. The furniture was serviceable, not cushioned for comfort.

But it was a sturdy keep, built to last many generations. When she'd first arrived it had been immediately obvious that it cried out for a caring touch. And now it was a dwelling to be proud of, a safe harbour in which to raise a family.

What would happen to it if she left? Would Richard let it fall into ruin? And if he had no one to argue with him, no one to set his temper flaring, would he let himself fall into ruin, too?

No. She couldn't imagine Richard moping about the keep alone. He would direct his full attention to his ships and warehouses. After all, isn't that what her father did whenever her mother went to visit her family without him?

She frowned, confused by her own questions and her inability to answer them. Even though her father became rather morose during her mother's absence and he spent far too much time at the docks, he had always known that his wife would soon return to him.

'What dark thoughts are swirling round inside your head, Isabella?'

Ice-cold fingers stroked the side of her neck, making her jump. Surprised to see him back at the keep so early, she looked up at Richard to ask, 'What brings you back from the warehouses so soon?'

'The warehouses?' He turned to point towards the doors. 'What good is a pile of greenery without a Yule log?'

She peered around him to see a good-sized oak tree trunk resting alongside her piles. 'Ah. You didn't have to do that.'

'I know I didn't have to, but I am not such a black-hearted knave that I wish to ignore Christmas.'

'Please, Richard, that is not what I meant.' She rested a hand on his chest. 'I didn't think that of you.'

'Even armies pause for Christmas, Isabella. There is no need to be so serious.' He covered her hand with his own. 'I was but teasing you.'

His heart beat steady beneath her palm. The heat of his gaze flowed into her, bringing to life memories of the night three long weeks ago when he'd truly made her his wife. Suddenly shy and embarrassed for no obvious reason other than the visions her mind created, she looked away.

He leaned closer to whisper against her ear, 'Isabella, it is easy to tell where your mind has now flown.'

She shivered with longing from the warmth of his breath and the deep, raspy tone of his voice. Uncertain how to respond, she reluctantly pulled her hand free, took a deep breath and stepped away.

His soft chuckle at her withdrawal only flustered her more.

'My lady, do you think you and your husband can finish this?'

Relieved by Hattie's timely interruption, Isabella took the greenery the older woman held out to her and looked at Richard. 'If he agrees to lend me a hand, I'm sure we can.'

At his nod, Hattie sighed. 'Good. I want to see if they need a hand in the kitchen.'

Isabella knew Hattie was making up an excuse to give her and Richard time together. They didn't require any additional help in the kitchen. She and the cook had spent many hours going over the menus for the holiday feasting. More than enough extra help had been put to work days ago.

But she appreciated the woman's gift of time with her husband and without a word watched her leave the Great Hall.

Richard climbed the ladder to wrap the upper portion of the support beam with the evergreen, while she went and retrieved some more branches and ribbons to hold them in place.

When he finished, he climbed down from the ladder, only to watch as the rope of evergreens slid down the beam.

Isabella laughed and sprinted up the ladder, teasing him, 'If you only knew how to tie a ribbon, my lord, the decorations might stay in place better.'

He handed her the end of the greenery, shaking his head. 'Well, that answers that question.'

Busy securing some holly into the ribbon, she asked, 'And what question would that be?'

As she reached up as high as she could, he grasped her legs to keep her steady on the ladder. 'Now I know who painted the hall.'

She looked down at him. 'Who did you think did it?'

'I wasn't certain.' He slid his hands beneath the skirt of her gown to wrap his fingers around her thighs. 'But now I know it was someone with soft skin.' He brushed a thumb across the back of her leg, making her gasp, before sliding one hand higher. 'And the most enticing pair of legs I've ever had the pleasure of caressing.'

She lost her balance on the ladder and, with an undecipherable squeak, fell into his waiting arms.

'Richard!' Isabella batted at his shoulder. 'Are you trying to kill me?'

He nuzzled her ear. 'No. Just distracting you.'

She heard the twitters and laughs of amusement from the others in the Great Hall and batted at him again. 'Put me down.'

To her surprise he did so without arguing. Straightening out the skirt of her gown, she reminded him,

'There is much to be done before the Angel's Mass tonight.'

'Yes, there is.' He nodded in agreement. 'We need to eat.'

Of course he would think of that before all else.

'Then I need to find the remains of last year's Yule log so we can light the new one later.'

She was actually a little surprised that he thought of that considering how miserable the months in between had been for him.

He glanced around the hall. 'Tables and benches still need to be arranged for tomorrow's feast. And you will need time to get dressed before we head down to the church.' He paused, then asked, 'Did I forget anything?'

'Richard, catch.' Conal tossed something at him.

Richard caught it and smiled. 'Oh, yes, I see that I did forget something.'

He held a beribboned sprig of mistletoe over her head and graced her with a familiar half-smile that never failed to set her heart fluttering. 'My lady?'

She leaned against him and tipped her head back for his kiss, sighing when his lips covered hers.

When their kiss ended, he kept his arms around her, holding her against his chest. Content to remain in the circle of his embrace, Isabella closed her eyes. She had no mistaken notion that this easiness between them would last beyond the holy season. But she was determined to enjoy it for as long as possible.

His embrace tightened around her and he kissed the top of her head, before releasing her. 'I have a log to find and the men should be here soon, they can help you with the tables and benches.'

While Isabella had found the three holy masses comforting, she was glad they were done traipsing back and forth to the church in the village. The walk at midnight for the Angel's Mass had been cold, but the sky had been clear and myriad stars had twinkled brightly. The warmth of her husband's hand clasped securely around hers had made the frigid air less biting. After being kept awake by Richard's undivided attention most of the night, the dawn trip for the Shepherd's Mass had been exhausting. The church bells had called them to the Mass of the Divine Word just as she'd been directing the placement of the last trestle table for the Christmas feast.

Everyone on Dunstan had gathered at the keep after the last church service to partake in the Christmas feast. With so many people in the Great Hall, at times the din was near deafening.

But she was pleased that everyone seemed to be enjoying the merriment. The cook and her helpers had outdone themselves. Everything, from the deer, half-a-dozen geese roasted in butter and saffron until golden, partridges and a spitted pig, were done to perfection. To Richard's amusement, Isabella had moaned in pleasure when the meats seemed to melt in her mouth. A perfect blend of shredded meat, fruit and spices, the mince pie had been as near to heaven as she could imagine.

One long side table, laden with other baked goods and sweets, supplied by Dunstan's baker, and wheels of cheese brought up from a warehouse near the wharf, was so overflowing with food that Isabella feared the wooden legs would snap beneath the weight.

Ale and wine flowed freely, but she'd confined her choice of drink to the contents of the wassail bowl. The spiced and sweetened ale was warm and gentled her normal dislike of noisy, crowded places.

At Warehaven she was free to bolt when it seemed the walls were closing in around her. But not here. Not now. As odd as it still sounded to her ears, she was Dunstan's lady and she'd not shame herself, or Richard, by running from her duties.

With the meal now over, the men had helped clear the tables and rearranged them for games now taking place. While some took chances dicing, others played chess and all appeared to be enjoying the company of their friends and neighbours.

She leaned back in her chair, which had been placed near the burning Yule log. After much searching, Richard had found the leftover piece of log from last year's fire buried under the small bed in his private chamber. They'd used it to start this year's fire, which from the size of the current log would easily last until the twelfth night.

A giggle from Marguerite seated nearby, next to Conal, caught Isabella's attention. She smiled softly at the couple. They were lost in each other's company.

Richard leaned closer as he took a seat next to her, to ask, 'What are you smiling about?'

She nodded towards Marguerite and Conal. 'How long have they been together?'

Richard reached over to clasp his hand over hers, laughing softly at her curiosity. 'Ever since Conal was old enough to realise she was a girl.'

'And this arrangement is fine with Marguerite?'

'You don't approve?'

She shook her head. 'I didn't say that. I simply wonder if he knows what a good woman he has.'

'I've never asked.'

'Oh.'

Richard squeezed her hand. 'He's not just my

friend. Conal is my right arm on this island. I'm not going to risk that by asking questions that are none of my business.'

She understood his position, because right now, there were many questions she wanted to ask him about Conal, about Richard's father, about her husband's life growing up, but wished not to risk losing his good mood. So she bit her tongue to keep them from spilling forth.

'Go ahead.'

She looked at him. 'Go ahead, what?'

'From the pensive frown on your face, you want to ask me something. So, go ahead.'

'No, it's nothing important.'

His long, drawn-out, exaggerated sigh made her want to laugh. Instead, she explained, 'You have made this day very pleasant for me and I simply wish not to ruin it. My questions will wait.'

'They're that bad that you feel it needful to wait until I haven't made your day a pleasant one?'

'That's not what I meant.'

'Then, ask.'

Obviously he wasn't going to let this go. So, Isabella chose what she hoped would be the least dangerous one to ask. 'Do you think Conal cares enough for Marguerite to marry her?'

'Are you asking me if he loves her?'

Well, yes, she was, but she knew Richard's thoughts on that subject. 'No. Just wondering if he cares for her.'

'Of course he cares for her. Isn't that obvious?'

'To who? Not to me. I wasn't certain they had any relationship until yesterday when they helped me decorate the hall.'

'You haven't heard any of the island's gossip?'

She rolled her eyes. 'In case you've forgotten, I, too, have spent my entire life on an island. I learned long ago not to listen to gossip.'

'Oh, I haven't forgotten. I don't know how it works on Warehaven, but the only way to know what's going on here is through gossip.'

'Are you serious?'

'Quite serious. For example, how much gold will you gain if a child isn't born before summer?'

Isabella felt the burn of embarrassment rush to her cheeks. How had he heard about the off handed wager she'd made with Hattie the day she'd sprained her ankle? It wasn't even a serious one. After hearing about those in the keep placing wagers on how soon a child would be born, she'd simply made a sarcastic comment about winning the wager herself if she proved everyone wrong.

'Or, were you aware—?'

'Enough.' Isabella cut him off. 'I see your point.'

He released her hand, dragged her chair closer and slung his arm across her shoulders. 'Listen to the gossip. Just remember that while most of it is pure fabrication, there might be a grain of truth buried beneath. You'll have to determine what's worth re-membering and what's not.'

She groaned. 'I am not very good at that.'

'You'll learn.'

'I suppose I will have to.'

A group of men called out for Richard to join them. 'I am slated to challenge the winner of this round of chess.'

'Go.' She waved him away. 'Enjoy your game.'

He rose and then leaned over to quickly kiss her cheek, whispering, 'I'll be back soon.'

A shiver rippled down her spine at his hushed promise and she watched him take his place at the table, unashamedly hoping his king quickly got checked and checkmated, ensuring a speedy return to her side.

Chapter Seventeen

Christmas, Epiphany and now Candlemas had come and gone. And as she'd expected, so had the comfortable easiness between her and Richard. She watched him from across the Great Hall and fought to ignore the constant longing that burned deep in her belly. While he had shared their bed Christmas Eve and again Christmas night, he'd not returned since then. Nearly six long weeks had passed since she'd felt the warmth of his body next to hers and she wondered if anyone else could see the desperate hunger in her eyes.

She knew what he was doing, or she was fairly certain she did. He had claimed that he feared her tender heart being broken, but she had to wonder if he might also be concerned for his own. Did he believe that he could spare either of them by keeping his distance?

Foolish man.

Little did he realise that he was just fanning the fires for an all-out battle between them.

He turned his head and caught her staring at him. Isabella felt the heat creep up her cheeks as he smiled. That slow, deliciously sensual half-smile that was reserved only for her never failed to make her shiver.

She looked away and then spun back to stare at his hair. His face. His clothes. Who was this clean-cut, freshly shaven, well-dressed courtier who possessed her husband's face? And when had this change taken place? How had she not noticed?

One of the serving girls walked up to the group Richard was standing with, to offer the men wine or ale. She swayed back and forth, playing with her hair while talking, laughing and flirting with one of the younger guards. But it was Richard's gaze that trailed after her when she left.

Isabella frowned. This would not do. She'd often overhead her father's men make off-hand comments about being married, not dead, and she'd seen how her mother dealt with her father when his eyes wandered. She highly doubted that her father had ever taken another woman after marrying her mother, but even after all the years they'd been married, he was not above trying to make her jealous.

And her mother was not above threatening to castrate him with a dull knife.

Although she didn't think that tactic would work well with Richard. He might be tempted to push her just to see how far she would go. Thankfully, she'd never have to test that theory, since she had no liking for that type of game.

The only game she wished to play with her husband involved much less clothing and a bed. However, she needed to find a way to coax him back to her chamber before she could even think of getting him into the bed.

Isabella leaned against one of the support beams on the far side of the hall to study her husband. Even though they'd shared nothing more than a passing word, a brief touch, a meal now and then of late, she'd noticed small changes. He seemed less angry, less willing to burst into unreasonable fits of rage. And on an occasion or two, like now, he'd taken time to talk, jest and even laugh with his men.

She didn't think for one heartbeat that he'd given up his quest for revenge—there were times when an unsettling darkness fell over him and she knew without a doubt the direction his thought had drifted—but it didn't seem to consume his every waking moment.

And there were times, other moments, when she'd

catch a glimpse of his face and see such overwhelming sadness that she ached to hold him and to chase away the terrors haunting him.

Oh, Richard, do you not see what is right before you?

Isabella sighed. If she stood here any longer, she would sink into the same depressing malaise that afflicted him at times. She pushed away from the timber to cross the Great Hall.

Her husband had moved away from the group of men to talk with Conal in private. Their conversation ceased when she joined them.

'Are you looking for something?' Richard slid his arm around her as if he hadn't just spent the last endless weeks avoiding her.

Unwilling to lose the warmth of his touch, Isabella bit her tongue. Instead, she leaned against him. 'No. I simply tire of my own company and thought perhaps I'd venture out to visit Mistress Marguerite.'

'Are you sure? It is cold out there.'

'If I wear my fur-lined cloak I will be warm enough.'

'I will see you to her door.'

'Richard, I am well able to make my way down the path alone. It's not as if I will get lost.'

Both men shook their heads at that statement. Her husband lowered his arm. 'No. It has nothing to do with getting lost. Go get your cloak and I will escort you.'

Conal offered, 'I am headed to her cottage in a little while, if you want to wait I would be more than happy to accompany you.'

'Oh, yes, Sir Conal, a man sitting in on women's talk, that's just what I want.' She looked from one to the other. They were both far too willing to keep her company on her short walk outside the keep. 'What are the two of you trying to hide this time?'

They met her stare, but she wasn't backing down. She narrowed her eyes and to her surprise Conal broke the contact first. He shot a rather pleading look at Richard. 'Tell her.'

'Tell me what?'

'Come.' Richard grasped her elbow and guided her towards his private chamber. He said over his shoulder, 'Since this was your idea, Conal, you are of course joining us.'

Once the chamber door closed behind the three of them, Richard retrieved a small wooden chest from beneath his pallet. After shoving aside stacks of documents and maps strewn over the table, he set the chest down to unlock it.

He handed her a rolled missive, asking, 'Can you read?'

'Yes.' She plucked the missive from his fingers. 'And I can sign my own name, too.'

Her veiled reference to the mark he'd made for her on their marriage document drew a strangled snort from Conal and a hiked brow from Richard.

She unrolled the vellum and read the poorly written contents. Her heart seemed to skip a beat. 'This is not the same missive as before?'

Richard shook his head. 'No, this is a second one.'

'The first one wasn't quite as...detailed,' Conal added.

Isabella turned her attention back to the missive. Her eyes followed each word.

Since my attempt to poison Lady Dunstan failed to bring about her death, I fear a more direct approach is in order. After I have torn her still-beating heart from her chest, fed it to the dogs and slit her throat, remember you were warned.

Her hands trembled. Struggling for breath, she dragged her focus from the note to look at Richard.

His non-committal, expressionless look never wavered as he held her stare. To her amazement, his steady emotionless response calmed her wildly drumming pulse.

She blinked, trying to digest that realisation while

at the same time letting the knowledge that someone hated her enough to want her dead sink into her mind.

Richard pulled a high-backed chair from behind the table and guided her down on to it. 'Sit.'

Grateful, Isabella offered no resistance. Had the chair not been available, her shaking legs might not have kept her upright for long.

She handed him back his missive. 'Does Marguerite know?'

Conal shook his head. 'No, I haven't told her yet.'

'She still believes her herbs were responsible for my sickness?'

'Yes,' Richard explained, 'Mistress Marguerite was not my first concern.' He rested a hand on her shoulder. 'You were.'

'Why? Because my father will soon arrive?' She truly didn't know what was wrong with her, but the need to lash out at this threat wouldn't be ignored.

At her strident tone, Conal made a hasty exit. Richard crossed the small chamber to lean against the wall, seemingly undisturbed by her outburst.

She pointed a shaking finger at the note he still held. 'That…man…that monster poisoned my wine, threatened to cut out my still-beating heart and feed it to the dogs, and to slit my throat. Yet, here we are, going on about our day as if nothing is amiss.'

Richard shrugged, but still his expression hadn't changed. Although his eyes seemed to glimmer in an oddly distracting manner. She mentally shook off the distraction.

'I could have been taken, killed at any moment and once again you didn't see it as important enough to warn me.'

Again he briefly lifted one shoulder.

She gasped. 'You truly don't care about me in the slightest.' Her stomach twisted and knowing that she was as worthless to him as a flea made her throat burn. 'What is wrong with me? How many times have you told me that I am nothing more than a means to an end, yet I keep hoping that some day there might be something more. I could be violently murdered and the only thing you would care about is that Glenforde arrived on Dunstan so you could claim vengeance for your first wife and child.'

Isabella stopped to drag in a much-needed breath of air. She wrapped one arm around her now-churning stomach.

'Are you done? Have you spilled all the accusations you can?' While she couldn't read his blank look, his deadly tone was clear. She'd gone too far.

She nodded.

'You are certain there's nothing else you wish to add?'

She shook her head.

When the missive left his fingers to fall to the floor, Isabella knew she should run. But her legs refused to listen to her head. Instead they kept her frozen in place, permitting him to grab a handful of fabric at the front of her gown and jerk her to her feet. And when the chance to struggle presented itself, still her body would not comply. She remained limp and compliant as he marched her to the back of the chamber and through the door to his inner sanctuary.

He pushed her into the room and slammed the door closed behind them. 'Now it is my turn.'

'Richard, I'm sorry.'

Ignoring her, he said, 'Let's take your complaints one by one, shall we?'

He shoved her down on the bed, then paced before her. 'It's true that it would be upsetting for your father to arrive only to find you dead. But is that my main concern? No. I don't fear your father any more than I do anyone else. He's a man, that's all. He can die just like the rest of us.'

She shivered at that thought, but kept her lips pressed tightly together.

'Yes, the man who wrote that threat is a monster. But the only person who has gone about their days as if nothing were amiss is you. You're so observant that you haven't noticed you are watched and guarded every single minute of every single day. You have not been alone for one heartbeat since the day you arrived on this island.' He stopped before her and leaned over so they were nose to nose. 'Not one heartbeat.'

He straightened and resumed pacing. 'As for me not caring about you. Since the day after Christmas, Conal or Matthew have guarded you each day and tried to catch up on their duties each evening. That's why Marguerite hasn't been told anything—Conal has not had the opportunity to see her for longer than a few stolen minutes at a time. At night you are guarded by me. I have sat on the floor outside your chamber door, my sword at hand, ensuring your safety. I have delayed repairs on my ships, rearranged shipping schedules to see to your well-being. Not my men. Me. To ensure you are not again poisoned, I personally have tasted every bit of food or drink prepared for you and then made certain that food or drink was delivered to you by Hattie or me. That's how much I do not care for you.'

She wanted the floor beneath the bed to part and just swallow her whole. Dear Lord, how could she not have known?

'I can tell you what is wrong with you.' Again he leaned close. 'You are so damned concerned about tomorrow, next week, next month, that you can't see what's right in front of you today, this moment. That's what's wrong with you.'

He walked away. 'I am gladdened to know that what I freely offer is not enough for you.'

Somehow she found a way to swallow her groan. What had she done in her haste to lash out at him from fear? Had she destroyed everything?

He glared at her. She knew he wasn't finished and that the worst was yet to come. She took a deep breath and bowed her head, knowing she deserved every bit of his anger.

'Yes, Glenforde will die. By my hand. I long for the day I shed his blood.'

She flinched when he roughly grasped her shoulders. 'Agnes did not deserve to die in such a horrific manner. Alone. With no one to protect her. Not even the husband who had promised to keep her safe.'

She ached at the anguish in his voice, knowing there was nothing she would ever be able to do to ease the pain he suffered at their deaths. And now relived because of her.

'Lisette was a six-year-old child. She had been loved and cosseted each and every day since her birth. She had no understanding of the pain and agony being inflicted on her the last moments of her short life. *I* kept her safe during the storms that frightened her so. *I* kissed the scrapes and bruises away to make them feel better. *I* protected her when she did something to anger her nursemaid or mother. *I* held her when she was sick. But when she needed me the most, *I* was not there.'

Isabella let the hot tears fall from her eyes. Sorrow and shame that she had pushed him to this state tore at her. How would she ever be able to make this right for him? How could he look at her? How could he bear to be in the same room with her?

He pushed her on to the bed, falling with her to gather her in a tight embrace. 'Isabella, do you not understand?' He shoved his fingers through her hair, forcing her head back and placing his lips near hers. 'I cannot go through that again. Not with you.' His kiss was rough, demanding and far too brief. 'Especially not with you. I would die.'

She raked her fingers through his hair, clasping his head in her hands. 'Richard, I'm sorry, I'm sorry,' she repeated over and over, choking on a sob. She asked, 'What can I do? Please tell me what to do.'

He released her to push up and rest over her on his elbows, his hands cradling her head. 'Trust me. Let me do what I must in my own way. I do not avoid you out of spite, or any lack of desire. There is nothing I want more than to taste you, kiss you, feel you beneath me and hear your cries of fulfilment.'

Her cheeks flared with heat and when he tilted his hips to give her proof of how much he wanted her, she choked back a soft, strangled gasp.

'Conal and I have narrowed the culprit threatening you down to three men. We are certain this is same man who helped Glenforde on to Dunstan. We are so close to snaring him. I am watching you, always watching, waiting for him to make a move.'

Why didn't they just toss the three men into a cell? When she opened her mouth to ask, he shook his head. 'Let me do this on my terms. Mine.'

She closed her mouth.

'I will not tell you who we think it might be, for fear you would do something reckless that would show our hand before we are ready. I promise, it won't be long. I want this taken care of before your family and Glenforde arrive. The weather is breaking early this year. They could be here any day now. Soon, this will all be over with.'

'And then?'

'And then Glenforde dies, Isabella. You need to make a choice before that day arrives. If you want any type of future on Dunstan, do not plead for him.'

'Plead for him? Oh, Richard, I have not been completely honest with you. I care not what you do to Glenforde. I never have, not really. When you kidnapped me, I'd just come from seeing him kiss and fondle his whore in my father's hall. And when he spied me, instead of stopping his betrayal, he kept his stare pinned on me while he lifted her and carted her into an alcove.'

She took a breath, then continued. 'I suffered that humiliation from him just hours after he had knocked me to the ground for disagreeing with him about my sister and what he considered her unseemly infatuation with Charles of Wardham. And this is why I don't think he will come for me, he has no reason, or desire, to do so.'

'Does your father know any of this?'

'No. I was trying to determine how to tell him when you found me.'

'Then rest assured, he will come. Your father will see to it. Glenforde is too much of a coward to admit to your father what he had done. He would not risk your father's retaliation. So as far as Lord Warehaven is concerned, you and Glenforde are nearly betrothed.'

She wasn't convinced he was right. 'I'm not so sure about that.'

'If your father doesn't convince him, then Glenforde will be led here by his greed. You are too wealthy an heiress to let slip through his grasp.'

'We shall see. Besides, my choice was made many weeks ago. Do what you must to banish your ghosts, that is all I care about. Glenforde concerns me not at all.'

'That's what you say now. But you have no way of knowing what choice you will make when that moment arrives.' He rested his forehead against hers. 'But I pray your words prove true. And if they do, when all is said and done, we'll have to get busy working on that child you want.'

She knew that no matter how many times she told him her choice was made, it would only be her actions that convinced him in the end.

'Conal waits for us.' He kissed the end of her nose before standing up and offering her his hand. 'And you wanted a visit with Marguerite.'

Richard pulled her closer to his side and tucked her hand beneath his arm. 'You are freezing.'

'No, actually, I am more than fine. The fresh air feels lovely.'

Conal, walking on the path a little ahead of them, laughed. 'Spoken like a woman who doesn't have to be out in this...*lovely*...weather every day.' He paused, turning to offer her his added assistance crossing a huge puddle. 'See, someone could drown in that.'

She laughed at him as Richard picked her up and handed her across the water to Conal. The man had been complaining since they'd left the warmth of the Great Hall. 'The trees are starting to bud. Soon the buds will swell.'

At the men's sniggers, she bumped Richard with her hip, hastily adding, 'Into leaves. I swear the two of you act like randy youths at times.'

'That's because we're constantly surrounded by beautiful women.'

Conal grunted his agreement at Richard's claim.

Isabella rolled her eyes. 'You mean like the young serving maid?'

'She's not old enough to be beautiful yet.' Richard shrugged. 'Right now, she's just young. A reminder of years long gone.'

'So only old women can be beautiful?'

Conal glanced over his shoulder at Richard. 'Talk your way out of that one.'

'Mature, I meant mature.'

'Isn't that simply another word for old?' Isabella couldn't help tease him. After what she'd put him through he needed a light-hearted moment or two.

'I—uh…I meant…'

Conal laughed. Isabella giggled, asking, 'So, am I old and beautiful, or young?'

Without missing a step Richard reached over, grabbed her and swung her up against his chest. Her breasts pressed against his hard muscles, nose to nose, her feet dangling. She wrapped her arms around his neck and hooked her feet about his thighs.

'No matter how beautiful the serving maid might become, she will never be as lovely, desirable or tempting as you.'

Conal groaned. 'God, I wish the two of you would stop.'

'He has no reason to talk.' Isabella whispered, then added, 'Please, let me.'

At Richard's nod, she said loud enough for Conal to hear, 'You're just jealous, Conal. But it is your own fault, you know.'

'Beg pardon?'

While Richard stopped, to let her slide down the length of his body until her feet hit the ground, she explained, 'There is a beautiful woman who would move the moon and the stars for you if you but asked. And yet she lives alone.'

The man waved his hand in the air as if brushing away flies. 'You, too?'

'You can't expect her to wait for ever.' She raised her voice more as he picked up his pace. 'One day while you're dawdling, someone else will sweep in and steal the prize.'

Richard sighed. 'And if that day comes the man will be miserable.'

'Then I suggest, for his own good, he be prodded a bit more.'

'Is that an order?'

Isabella wrinkled her nose, debating. 'Does his happiness affect Lord Dunstan's?'

'Yes.'

'Well, then, of course it's an order.'

'Very well, I'll take it under advisement.'

She poked him in the ribs. 'I suggest you do a little more than that.'

'Yes, my lady.'

They rounded the last curve on the path leading to the midwife's cottage. Isabella stopped, holding Richard from approaching. She nodded towards Conal and Marguerite standing in the doorway. 'Perhaps we should just let them be.'

'I have some business with Father Paul.'

'Then we'll go to the church.'

As they walked past Marguerite's cottage, Richard briefly explained where they were going to Conal.

Marguerite pulled Isabella aside, to ask, 'I know it has been many weeks, but you've had no lingering effects from the poison in the wine?'

'Ah, Conal told you.'

'That's what he was just explaining when the two of you arrived.'

'No. I seem to have survived. My dignity, on the other hand...'

Marguerite laughed at her. 'I'm sure by now everyone has forgotten, but if not, what's a little sharing of bodily functions amongst friends?'

That made Isabella laugh wryly. 'That's what you're going to call it? A little sharing?'

'Why not? Anything else sounds too vulgar and unrefined.'

'Isabella?' Richard interrupted them and she took her leave of Marguerite, promising to return soon.

He led her away from the cottage, stopping just outside the church door. 'I'll just be a minute or two. Do you want to wait in the narthex or out here?'

'I'll stay out here if you feel I'll be safe.'

He nodded. 'I'm sure of it. But if anything startles you, or gives you pause, scream. You do know how, don't you?'

She pushed him towards the door. 'Go.'

Once he disappeared inside, she pulled her mantle tighter about her, rubbing her cheek against the soft fur and strolled the muddy grounds in front of the church. Spying the small cemetery, she opened the gate and took a seat on a bench.

The headstones in front of her were those of Dunstan's wife and daughter. Isabella shivered. Of course they would be. At times their ghosts hung over Richard like a black cloud, so why wouldn't she choose a spot directly in front of them. As if she needed a reminder of the mental anguish she'd needlessly caused him a short time ago.

She leaned forward to read the carved words. The one for his wife simply said *Agnes of Dunstan* and the date of her death. But the one for his daughter read: *Lisette, Beloved daughter of R. Dunstan.*

Isabella frowned. Something was off with these inscriptions. His daughter was beloved, but his wife wasn't? And why wasn't Lisette the daughter of R. and A. Dunstan?

She reached out to touch the girl's stone, wishing it would give her an answer, but the sound of approaching footsteps made her pull her hand back.

Richard sat down beside her.

'That was quick.'

He nodded and took her hand.

When he threaded his fingers through hers and held on tightly, she silently cursed herself. Why had she come into the cemetery without thinking? He'd told her he'd only be a minute, she should have known that he'd find her here.

'We can go.'

He relaxed his hold. 'No.' He reached beneath his mantle and pulled out a leather scroll. 'Here, this is for you to keep.'

'What is it?'

'We don't know what's going to happen when your father arrives. He or your brother could run a sword through me without warning.'

'No! Richard, they wouldn't do that. I won't let them.'

'If I was your father, I would make certain you weren't anywhere near.' He leaned over and kissed her cheek. 'It's all right. Who knows, I could some day die in my sleep. But either way, you need to know what is yours.' He tapped the scroll. 'This is our marriage contract. Keep it close.'

She slid it beneath her cloak, intending to secure it behind the girdle wrapped low on her waist.

'No. Read it first.'

She opened the end and pulled out three rolled-up sheaves of parchment. The first page was just the who, what, when and where of the ceremony, which she shuffled to the back after a quick glance.

The next page was a list of what he would gain from marrying her. It was brief. And contained one line—simply her. No dowry, no exchange of gold, land or any other material wealth. Just her as his wife. She wasn't too certain this agreement would be considered binding with such an exclusion.

The last page was a list of what she gained from marrying him. It, too, was brief. And contained one line—Dunstan Isle and all of its wealth, warehouses, ships, buildings and land.

'Richard!' She pushed the pages into his hands. 'No.' Flustered, horrified by what he'd done and greatly awestruck, she said, 'Fix this. You will fix this. The minute my father arrives, you will fix this.'

'Everything here is mine. Nothing is entailed to the crown. I am free to do with it as I please.'

'No. You *will* fix this. If not for me, then for any children we might have.' She tapped the pages he still held. 'This makes me responsible for Dunstan. I cannot hold all of this safe. I cannot offer the ships protection once they set sail. If anything were to happen to you, I could lose everything you and your father and his father worked so hard to build. I could leave our children with nothing, not even a place to live.'

When he didn't say anything, she repeated, 'You will fix this. Why on earth did you do such a thing?'

'These were drawn up before I left Dunstan set on kidnapping you. At the time I thought it fair. You would give me the opportunity to avenge my wife and daughter, and in return, I would give you all.'

Isabella was dumbfounded and, for one of the few times in her life, utterly speechless.

'Even now, I still think it a fair exchange. Isabella, you have given much to Dunstan and its people.'

'I cleaned your keep. That is all. Even that act was more for selfish reasons than anything else.'

'Your selfish act made the men remember they were supposed to be civilised and not barbaric animals, made the women more willing to return to the keep.'

'I cannot speak for the men, but the women came to work and were useful.'

'Useful? Is that what you call climbing around on ladders and doing work more fit for men?'

'I had no men to use. So we managed on our own.'

'And whose fault was that?'

'Yours.' She paused, then admitted, 'And mine.'

He patted her hand. 'I willingly share the blame in that. But trust that if need be, Conal and Matthew would keep you safe. You would lose nothing. They will fight for you, Isabella, the men will follow your orders. For the most part, they are good men. A little rough around the edges, but good men.'

'No. You and my father can decide this. Even he would not be so greedy as to permit you to give it all away.'

'Again, it is mine to give.'

She wasn't going to keep arguing this with him. He could do that with her sire, because she wasn't about to step into what was rightfully her father's place in this negotiation.

'Tell me, is this the same type of agreement you signed with Agnes?'

'No.' He looked down at her. 'We are sitting here before all that remains of the woman. Is there anything you wish to know?'

She turned her face away. There were many things she wished to know, but hadn't he had enough this day?

'I would rather get all of this behind us now.'

Sometimes she wondered how he so easily read her thoughts. She leaned her head against his arm. 'These grave markers, they are odd to me.'

'How so?'

'Richard, if I ask you something about your wife, will you answer me honestly?'

'Isabella, you know that if you ask me something, I will tell you the truth. So, if you ask me something, you'd better be ready to hear the answer.'

Was she ready? Probably not, but to put it all behind them, it had to be asked. 'Did you love her?'

'Yes. With all my heart.'

She closed her eyes. He'd warned her not to ask unless she was ready to hear the answer. But she'd gone ahead and asked anyway. So she had no one to blame for this sudden pain in her stomach, or her inability to swallow past the growing lump in her throat but herself.

He draped his arm around her and pulled her closer to his side. 'Until I learned that love is just a myth, a tale devised by troubadours to lure the foolish into believing their stories.'

'What happened to make you think that?'

'She never belonged to me. She belonged to another, but I didn't know that until it was too late. Her father didn't deem the other man worthy of his daughter. His need for fast gold didn't permit him time to consider his daughter's wants or desires.'

'Most people don't get the opportunity to choose their spouses.' She laughed softly at the irony of her statement. She had been given the chance and she'd let it slip through her fingers, only to end up being forced into a marriage she hadn't wanted and now did.

'No, they don't. But unbeknownst to me, she'd already chosen her lover, months before she ended up in a marriage bed with me.' He nodded towards Lisette's stone. 'She wasn't my daughter.'

Shock froze her tongue for a minute. This was unheard of. Granted, her own father was a bastard, but his sire had been the king. For a woman to give birth to another man's child while that man still lived was more than adultery, it condemned not just the mother, but also the child to an unimaginable life. She'd heard stories of families setting the child aside—literally setting the newborn in the cold to die. 'And yet she bears your name.'

'What else should I have done? She was an innocent child. Nothing of what her mother had done could be placed at her feet. And by the time she was born, I wanted someone to love, someone to cherish.'

He looked down at her. 'Don't for one moment think I don't understand your need, Isabella. I do.'

'And Agnes?'

'Oh, she lied well at first. She was gentle, loving, kind and attentive to my face.'

'So, how did you find out it was lie?'

'Something seemed off, just a little wrong. Nothing major, an odd look, a distracted kiss, a small flinch at my touch, so I started watching and intercepted one of the monthly missives she'd supposedly written to her father.'

'It wasn't to her father, was it?'

'No. It was to her lover, telling him all about his child that she carried, how horrible it was to be in my presence, how sickened it made her whenever I so much as touched her and supplying him with enough information about Dunstan that he could have led an attack and succeeded in taking over my keep.'

How any woman could stoop so low was beyond her understanding. 'Oh, Richard, I am so sorry.'

'Yes, well, not as sorry as I.'

She was beginning to understand why he placed no faith in love. 'What happened after that?'

'Just what one would expect. She cried, swore it was over, promised to be a better wife. I was young and foolish enough to believe her.'

'And you gave her another chance?' Isabella could hardly imagine him doing so.

'Of course. Until right before Lisette was born and a missive from her lover found its way to my office at the warehouse.'

Isabella cringed.

'They had never stopped writing to each other. They made jokes about how gullible I was and how easy it was to lie to me. Worse, she had been sending him gold.'

'Your gold.'

'She had none of her own. He was saving it up to buy a ship and hire men to come kill me, so the two of them could marry and live on Dunstan as the lord and lady.'

'Oh, my.'

'That was nothing. When I confronted her, she turned into a shrew, spewing her hatred for me, my men, my keep. Everything I held dear became a target for her hate.'

'And Lisette?'

'It was worse for her, because I loved her so. Sometimes it would get so bad that I'd take the baby and we'd sleep aboard one of the ships.'

'And yet you flog yourself for not being here when Agnes was murdered. Why?'

'Because I refused to petition for a divorce based on a false claim of kinship, she remained my wife. It was my duty to keep her safe, no matter what.'

Isabella wanted to pull him into her arms and soothe the furrows from his brow. She took his hand and stood up. 'It's turning cold. Come, let's go back to the keep.'

He rose and stared at the gravestones. 'Do you know what the real horror is in all of this?'

The things that had been done to him weren't enough to be considered horrible? She leaned against his chest. 'No. Tell me.'

'The man she claimed to love and who claimed to love her, the man who was Lisette's true father, is the same man who killed them both.'

Isabella's knees buckled. From somewhere outside of her body, she watched as she slowly slipped to the ground at his feet.

Chapter Eighteen

A demon chased her. One with claws and glowing eyes. Blood dripped from his jagged teeth. He lunged at her.

'No!' Isabella awoke from the nightmare.

'Shhh. It's all right.' Gentle hands pulled her back down on to the bed.

She curled into the warmth of his chest, asking, 'How did we get here?'

Richard laughed softly. 'You do realise that you aren't that heavy, don't you?'

'You carried me?'

'Would you rather I'd left you in the mud?'

Snippets of their conversation at the cemetery flooded her mind until they filled in all the blank spaces. She rose up to stare down at him. 'Oh, Richard, I am so sorry. How can you stand the sight of me? How can you not despise me?'

'For what?' He slid his hand up her arm, across her

shoulder, to rest against her neck. 'You have done nothing. You are most assuredly not responsible for Glenforde's actions.'

When she shook her head, he eased her down on to his chest, admonishing, 'Don't be foolish, Isabella.'

'Make him die slowly. Cut him into tiny pieces, one slice at a time.'

She felt his sigh before he said, 'You have overheard far too many conversations between the men.'

'It couldn't be helped. You were the one who told me to listen to gossip and who gossips more than the men?'

'I can't argue with that.' He rolled her over on to her back and propped up on his elbow to look at her. 'How are you feeling?'

'Like a fool for swooning like a spineless maiden.'

He curled his finger around a wayward wave resting over her shoulder. 'Other than that.'

She shrugged. 'Fine. I simply fainted. Which is odd considering I never faint.'

'You are certain?'

'Yes. Why?'

'I gave Conal the night to spend with his lady. Matthew needs to be relieved so he can check things at the wharf. So I need to take his place.'

'Can you not guard me just as well from here?'

He laughed. 'No. It would be too…distracting.'

She reached up to stroke his cheek. 'Richard, please.'

He grasped her hand and kissed her palm. 'No. It is best if we wait.'

Frowning in confusion, she asked, 'Wait? For what?'

'Until all of this is over.'

'What on earth for?'

'If anything goes wrong, Isabella, I wish not to leave you with a babe in your belly.'

She tore her hand from his and grabbed the front of his shirt. 'If you have any doubts about your victory, I suggest you wipe them from your mind right now. Otherwise you are just asking for something to go wrong.' She pulled him closer. 'Do you hear me?'

He blinked. Twice. Then peeled her fingers from his shirt. 'I am fairly certain I don't need you telling me how to fight.'

'Obviously someone needs to.'

He shoved himself off the bed. 'Are you seeking to anger me for any particular reason?'

'Anger you? No. I'm angry enough right now for the both of us. I am seeking to force you into getting your mind straight.'

He swiped his sword from the floor. 'I know how to use this.'

'I would hope so.'

He headed for the door. 'Fear not, I do.'

'Good! I am glad!'

He swung the door open and shouted back at her. 'Good!'

Isabella sat up and threw a goblet hard enough to bounce it off the closed door. Only to hear a fist pound on it twice from the other side.

She threw herself back down on the bed, closed her eyes and in the quiet chamber counted out loud, 'One. Two.'

The door slammed against the wall of the chamber. 'And another thing.' He stormed across the room and fell on to the bed atop of her.

She circled her arms around him, asking, 'Which other thing?'

'How did you know I wasn't angry?'

'By the look in your eyes and your shouting. You never shout when you're enraged. But, I could ask you the same thing.'

'And I would give you the same answer.' He trailed his tongue along her lips.

Isabella sighed. 'Do you truly have to go sit in the corridor all by yourself in the cold?'

'No. I could get the serving maid to come sit with me.'

She tugged a lock of his hair. 'Go ahead and try.'

He slipped his tongue between her parted lips,

stroking and teasing until she moaned. With a lighter kiss, he said, 'Yes, I do have to go. And I fear I should do it now. Matthew is beside himself with worry over our shouting.'

'Ah, Matthew needs to stop being so serious all the time.'

'I'll be certain to tell him that.'

Isabella released him. 'Go.'

'If you need me, you know where to find me.'

'Goodnight, Richard.'

The sound of Hattie whistling as she moved about the chamber brought Isabella's eyes open. She squinted against the sunlight streaming in.

Hattie placed a gown across the foot of the bed. 'Oh, you are awake.'

Isabella didn't answer since that had been Hattie's reason for whistling in the first place.

'Lord Richard sent up a trunk from the warehouse. I had the men set it just inside the door.'

She swung her legs from beneath the covers and sat up on the edge of the bed. An odd aroma wafted across her nose, making her stomach gurgle suspiciously. 'What is that smell?'

'What smell?' Hattie came closer.

Isabella's stomach rolled and she slapped a hand over her mouth. She couldn't possibly have been poisoned again, she hadn't eaten or drunk anything. The chamber wasn't spinning like a top and her mouth didn't feel as if something furry had crawled around inside of it. She looked around the room and spied food on the small table in the alcove. 'What is that?'

It hit her a second before the woman answered. Moody as a fussy old woman, then fainting yesterday. Now sick to her stomach? No. Impossible. Well, perhaps not impossible since they did make love, but unlikely since they'd only done so a few times—three to be exact—once the night she'd been poisoned, Christmas Eve and Christmas night. Surely it took more times than that? She couldn't be pregnant.

Hattie rattled off the list of items on the table. 'It's just bread, cheese, some porridge and...' She paused to stare at Isabella and then smiled. 'Oh, goodness. Are you going to lose that wager? Will there be a babe before summer arrives?'

Keeping her hand over her mouth, Isabella shook her head, hoping to disabuse the woman of such a notion. If she was correct, the child wouldn't arrive until the end of summer, meaning she would prove those holding the wagers wrong—Richard hadn't taken any liberties before they were wed.

Hattie rushed into the alcove and came back with the crust from the bread and a cup of water. 'Eat this.

Slowly. Then lie back down for a few minutes. I'll have Mistress Marguerite get you some ginger root.'

Isabella nibbled on the bread. 'This can't be happening now.'

As Hattie went to the door, Isabella called out, 'Wait. Who is out there on guard duty?'

'Sir Conal.'

'No. No. Don't say anything to him.'

Hattie walked back towards the bed. 'My lady?'

'I want to be the one to tell Richard, later. After...' She trailed off, uncertain how many of the details Hattie knew about Richard's intentions.

'After he deals with Glenforde?'

'Yes.' She sighed with relief at not having to come up with some story that she'd not be able to remember a day from now.

Hattie frowned, making Isabella worry the woman wouldn't see her point, but then the frown disappeared. 'I won't say that I like it, but I do understand your reasoning.'

'Thank you.'

'Well, Lady Isabella, you best hope it happens soon, because you won't be able to keep this a secret very long.'

If she truly was with child, and this wasn't some sort of joke nature was playing on her, the last thing she wanted to do was keep it a secret. She wanted to shout it from the battlements.

Time would tell.

She eyed the domed trunk near the door and quickly dressed, shoving her feet into her stockings and shoes, while Hattie tried to braid her hair at the same time.

Once dressed, Isabella walked over to the trunk. She ran a hand over the travel chest, admiring the workmanship. Domed so any water would run off and wrapped in waxed leather to protect the goods inside.

Unbuckling the leather straps, she lifted the lid, letting it fall backwards as she gasped at her first glance of the contents. She dropped to her knees to slowly pull out one item at a time.

Finely woven linens and wool fabrics were folded inside. Some lengths were sun-bleached, some left natural and a few were dyed the most wonderful shades of blues and greens. There was enough fabric to make clothing for at least five people.

When she'd considered asking to borrow money for cloth, she'd never dreamed of purchasing this much. She brushed the soft linen against her cheek— nor had she dreamed of anything this fine.

Beneath the linen and wool was a separately wrapped package. Isabella laid it on her lap to unfold the soft leather—the wrapper alone was fine enough to use for clothing items. She peeled back the last fold and blinked at the brilliant green, almost emerald, cloth.

'Hattie.' She called the woman over. 'Is this what I think it is?'

Almost afraid to touch the fabric, for fear of ruining it, she wiped her hands on her gown and then ran the tip of one finger along the edge.

Hattie touched the length. Picking up a corner she inspected it, then declared, 'Silk.'

'What am I supposed to do with silk?'

'Make a gown, I'd imagine.'

'With silk?' And then for what event would she wear the gown? She'd never had a garment made of silk before, there'd never been a need. She wasn't certain her parents owned anything made of silk and they'd attended court more than once in her lifetime.

She rose to stretch the length of silk carefully across the bed. It hung over the far side and had she dropped her end, it would have fallen on to the floor. There appeared to be enough fabric for two gowns—or a gown for her and a formal tunic for Richard.

Since the fabric was unadorned, she could embellish it in any manner she desired. Isabella picked at a corner with a fingernail. She was certain the tightly woven threads would ensure whatever she decided to make would last a long time.

'Lady Isabella, look.' Hattie pulled strips of embroidery work from the chest.

Isabella ran her fingers through the embellished strips. As if the silk wasn't enough of a luxury, these pre-embroidered pieces would save immeasurable time.

She looked at the bottom of the chest to find everything she would need—from pins and needles to shears for cutting the cloth, smaller scissors for snipping threads and an array of flaxen threads dyed to match every colour of fabric she'd received.

He'd lavished far too much on her. If his warehouses were anything like those on Warehaven, they were full of costly, precious goods. Goods meant to be sold or bartered at other ports. The value of the silk alone would feed the people in the keep for over a season. She shouldn't accept this, she should make him put it back in his inventory.

Isabella lovingly ran her hand over the silk and brought the soft linen to her cheek once again. Perhaps, if she used everything carefully, making certain to put each inch to proper use, she could make both of them clothes that would last for years, ensuring his inventory hadn't been squandered.

She needed a place to sew. Looking around, she

decided that with a chamber the size of this one, it shouldn't be too hard to make space for a workroom.

'Hattie, have a couple of the men bring up a table and bench.' She walked around the chamber, until sunlight fell across her face. 'We'll set it up here, beneath the window opening.'

'That is not necessary.'

Isabella disagreed. 'There is no better place.'

Hattie walked to the door, beckoning. 'Follow me.'

Intrigued and a bit confused, Isabella trailed behind the woman. Instead of turning left outside of the chamber door, Hattie went to the right. She walked past the first door, but swung open the door to the chamber at the end of the hall.

Isabella stopped outside the chamber. 'Richard gave orders not to open these two chambers. What have you done?'

From behind her, Conal said, 'He changed his mind last night. A couple of the women and some of the men worked all night to remove the bed and clean the chamber as best they could. I am surprised their attempt didn't waken you.'

She took a few tentative steps into the room. With an additional window, even more sunlight streamed into the chamber. Between the two far windows there were two padded armchairs with matching footrests, a small round table sat between.

Curtains draped the entrance to the alcove. A long cushioned bench lined the back wall inside.

While the walls of the chamber lacked a fresh wash of paint, they were clean. The floor shined as if it were newly polished.

'Will it suffice?' Conal asked.

'Oh, yes. It is perfect.'

'Good, because that clatter coming from the stairwell is the men bringing up a table and benches.'

It didn't take long for the men to set up a trestle table and to drag the domed chest from her bedchamber into this one. To Isabella's delight, two of the kitchen maids came up to ask if she'd mind letting them help in their spare time. They loved to sew, but rarely got the chance any more.

She welcomed the offer of assistance, knowing that if she was left to do it alone she'd quickly run out of excitement for the task and would still be sewing garments come next winter.

The light had faded before she realised the morning that had given way to afternoon was now turning to night. She'd spent the entire day measuring, cutting, piecing, pinning and sewing.

Pushing away from the table and up from the chair, she stretched before leaving the sewing chamber to head to the Great Hall and help set up the evening meal.

She stopped in the corridor outside the door to speak to Conal. 'I never said thank you.'

He slowly brought his lumbering frame up from the floor and shook his head, sending the wildly curled mass of red hair flying. 'For what?'

'For helping with this.' She waved towards the door. 'And for seeing to my safety. I do appreciate it.'

'You're Richard's wife, of course I would see to your safety.'

'Even so, I still thank you. It's almost time to eat, so I'll see you below.'

She nearly skipped down the stairs. For the first time in what seemed ages, she felt…happy.

'Lady Isabella?'

Surprised to see Father Paul in the keep, she paused at the bottom of the stairs. He hadn't shown his face here since the Christmas feast, so she found it odd. 'Father Paul, can I help you with something? Would you care to join us for the meal?'

'No, no. I just wanted to ask you if you had a chance to look over your marriage contract?'

'Oh, yes I have.' He'd probably been as shocked by it as she had. 'And I assure you, it will be changing soon.'

'I assumed that would be the case. But there were

a few things I wanted to go over with you, it won't take but a minute.'

She waved towards the high table where the chairs were already in place. 'Certainly, why don't we have a seat?'

He looked around and then wrinkled his brow. 'I would prefer somewhere more private. It is a lovely night. Can we not just step outside away from this throng of curious ears?'

Isabella glanced over her shoulder and didn't see Conal behind her. Richard had told her to trust no one other than Conal and Matthew. He hadn't mentioned Father Paul in that short list, so she wasn't certain leaving the keep with him was a wise idea.

'I'm not sure.' She motioned behind her. 'I'm not supposed to leave without Sir Conal and I don't know how Richard would feel about this.'

'I completely understand. But I am certain your guard only stopped to use the privy. Fear not, Lady Isabella. I can put you at ease.' Father Paul called over one of Dunstan's men. 'My good sir. When he comes down, could you tell Sir Conal that I have taken Lady Dunstan just outside into the bailey for a word. We'll be right outside the doors.' He turned back to her. 'Will that ease your worries?'

Something prompted her to say no. But he looked so sincere and with one of Dunstan's men standing by to let Conal know where she was, what would be the harm? Isabella motioned towards the double doors. 'Lead the way.'

She followed him outside, glad that he'd been correct about the mildness of the weather. While there was a slight nip in the air, it wasn't frigid. And while the breeze in the bailey might make it feel colder, here in one of Dunstan's countless small courtyards, they were protected from the ocean wind.

Father Paul didn't slow his stride. Instead of stopping just outside the door as he'd suggested, he kept walking.

'Father Paul, isn't this private enough?'

He stopped and came back to her side. With a pointed nod, he tipped his head towards a small gathering of women. 'I wish them not to overhear business meant for the Lady of Dunstan.'

She rolled her eyes. Now he was worried about how things looked or sounded? 'Fine, let us go.'

She glanced back at the women to see if they'd taken offence at the priest's words and spotted Matthew standing off to the side. He held a finger to his lips, silently telling her not to alert anyone to his presence.

Isabella stumbled, but quickly regained her footing. Dear Lord, not the priest. Father Paul was the man seeking to kill her? A man of God? No. It couldn't be.

'Are you coming?' He'd paused in front of the postern gate. The portcullis was raised.

'Yes. Yes. I stumbled over my feet, a clumsy habit I have.'

'That is understandable as the ground is uneven in these godforsaken courtyards.'

Isabella raised a brow at his insult. She liked these courtyards and had every intention of planting roses along the wall come spring. Some of those trailing ones like Marguerite had along the one wall of her cottage garden.

They would smell wonderful and look beautiful as they climbed up the wall here. Isabella's gaze followed her thoughts and met the frigid sapphire glare of one guard peering over the wall at her.

Even if he was dressed as a guard, she recognised that glare well. And from the complete lack of visible emotion, he was livid and very dangerous.

She quickly lowered her gaze. Someone would die this night at Dunstan. From the resolve etched on her husband's face, she was certain it wouldn't be her.

'Come, my lady. We can talk right out here.' Father Paul took her elbow to lead her under the gate and out into the bailey.

Now her legs trembled. But she wasn't certain if it was from fear of Father Paul, or Richard's anger.

She moved her arm, to free herself from the priest's hold, but he tightened his grasp and whistled.

Instantly a man led two horses to them. Father Paul shoved her towards the now-mounted rider, who easily grabbed hold of her wrist. She recognised him as Father Paul's deacon at the church. Both men of God were involved in this?

'No!' Isabella struggled. 'Release me!' She dragged her feet and hung from his hold, making herself as heavy as possible, so he couldn't pull her up on to the horse.

At her first scream the heavy portcullis to the main gates started to groan as they were lowered to close off the only escape from the inner yard.

The bailey, which a heartbeat ago had seemed empty, now appeared to fill with men. Armed men.

A strangled gasp from the man holding her wrist drew her attention back to him. His hold instantly fell away as he frantically waved his hands at the arrow sticking through his shoulder. She hit the ground, quickly scrambling away from the horse's shod hooves.

Father Paul's shoulders slumped. He dropped the reins to his horse and stood there.

A hard hand grasped her upper arm, dragged her

to her feet and shoved her against Conal's chest. 'To your chamber.'

'Richard, I—'

He didn't spare her a glance, instead he turned away to deal with Father Paul.

Conal put his hands on her shoulders to spin her around and pushed her towards the keep. When she dug in her heels, he paused long enough to ask, 'Are you going to walk like a woman, or am I going to toss you over my shoulder like a sack of grain?'

'You would shame me in such a manner before all of Dunstan?'

'In a heartbeat.'

She stormed towards the keep, shouting, 'You're as bad as he is.'

'No. I'm worse.' He caught up to her, to add, 'Because, at the moment, I don't care about your tender heart.'

When they entered the Great Hall, he placed one large hand on the centre of her back and pushed her directly to the stairs. She felt every pair of eyes glued to her. She swore she could hear their curious thoughts wondering what she'd done.

Isabella kept her chin high, refusing to bow beneath the stares and marched up the steps to her chamber.

Conal opened the door and pushed her inside. Before closing the door he suggested, 'Don't grovel, that will only set him off more.'

She stared at the closed door. Grovel? What made him think she'd ever grovelled before anyone?

No, there were no worries on that. She'd not grovel. She would simply explain why she'd left the keep with Father Paul and he would understand the dilemma she had faced.

Doubtful.

To keep her hands and mind busy, she went to the chest of linens in the corner and pulled a bedcover out. She spread the cover on the bed and then re-folded it. She repeated her actions until she heard the distinct sound of heavy boots heading up the stairs.

Her pulse quickened, certain from the determined stride it was Richard. She looked down at her hands to reassure herself that she was in complete control of her emotions.

The chamber door banged against the wall, making her jump. Isabella turned around and gasped at the stranger barging into her bedchamber.

His frown was so fierce that it seemed to form a single line above his eyes.

She knew instantly that the crazed berserker stalking her was her husband, but she backed away from the fiery blaze of his steady stare until her retreat was stopped by a solid wall. All of her calmness fled. 'I had no choice.'

Still intent on explaining, she continued, 'He made everything seem so normal. What else was I going to do?'

He didn't appear to be listening to her. She pointed a wavering finger at him. 'You never told me he was one of the men you were watching, so how was I to know?'

He didn't answer. Instead, he flung his cloak on to the bed, tore the sleeveless tunic bearing Dunstan's colours over his head and dropped it to the floor.

She held her hands up, as if they'd offer any protection and tried once more to reason with him. 'He said we were only going right outside the doors.'

He lunged at her, shoving her arms aside and pinned her against the wall.

Before she could say anything else, before she could even so much as catch her breath, he claimed her mouth in a kiss that curled her toes and set her mind spinning.

His face was cold. His fingers, tearing at the laces of her gown, shoving the fabric off her shoulders, were nearly freezing. But his kiss...his kiss was, oh, so hot.

She shivered when the cool air of the chamber rushed across her naked shoulders. Their tongues tangled and she moaned softly, forgetting her intention to calmly explain herself to him.

He answered her with a throaty growl, roughly pulling her gown and shift down her arms until they slid to pool at her feet. He then picked her up and deposited her naked on the bed.

Before she could complain of the cold, he was on the bed, pushing her legs apart to shatter her thoughts with his mouth.

Isabella tugged at his hair. When he grasped both of her wrists with one hand she had no choice but to let the out-of-control spiralling quickly take her over the edge.

'Richard!' she cried out. 'Please.' Wanting more than just the wickedly wonderful feel of his mouth, she wanted him to fill her.

He released her wrists and loomed over her. Grasping her chin firmly, he glared down at her.

Startled by the fierce glimmer in his eyes and the hard line of his mouth, she touched his cheek, whispering, 'What?'

'You were perfect.'

She frowned, uncertain what she'd done to be described as perfect.

He released her chin, wrapped his arms tightly about her as he entered her, claiming harshly, 'I have been worried sick that when the moment came, you would give all away.'

She returned his desperate embrace and managed to choke out a strangled, 'Thank you,' before her tears mixed with her laughter.

Laughter of relief at his declaration when she'd been so certain he was angry, and tears because the heart others had declared too tender was shattering from the pain of unreturned love. It was lost. Well and truly lost without any chance of ever saving it from hurt now or in the future.

From the way he made love to her, she wondered if perhaps his heart wasn't as unaffected as he claimed.

Even if that were true, she knew that she would never hear the words from his lips. But perhaps, if she listened closely, she could some day hear the whisperings of his heart.

Richard grumbled something she couldn't quite make out, but she completely understood his growl against her lips. He'd sensed her wandering mind and wanted her full attention.

She curled her legs around his waist, more than willing to give him all the attention he desired.

Through a clouded haze of pure lust, Richard couldn't remember a time when he'd ever wanted a woman as much as he did his wife right now. He knew there was nothing tender, nothing gentle in his touch, or his kiss.

He'd watched the priest closely this day and knew by the man's odd comings and goings that he was planning something. Hours of worry had chased away his ability to be easy. He knew she was safe, and well, but he needed to hear her cry out with abandonment.

From the tightness of her legs wrapped about his waist and the way her body met his, he doubted if his wife was feeling ill used. Still, he forced himself to rein in the unbridled lust, to regain some measure of control.

Chilled to the bone, he shivered. Gathering her closer, he let the heat of her body seep into him, warming him and chasing away his inexplicable concern for her well-being.

Richard groaned in frustration. It wasn't enough to just be skin to skin, he needed to be closer. But the way to accomplish that oneness he craved glimmered just beyond his reach.

Troubled by his inability to fulfil this unnatural need, he focused on the spiralling physical need driving him on.

Isabella curled her fingers into his back and arched her hips, seeking release from her own needs. He let his wavering control slip, quickly bringing them both to completion.

Unable to breathe past the hard pounding of his heart, he rolled off of her, kicking the cloak off the end of the bed.

Isabella placed a hand on his chest and laughed weakly. 'This can't be good for our hearts.'

He lifted her hand to his lips, kissed her palm and then lowered their locked hands back on to his chest. 'If this is the way I must die, at least I will meet my maker with a smile on my face.'

Once he regained his breath, he asked, 'Did you receive the chest of fabric?'

'Yes, I did.' She slipped her hand from beneath his and sat up to look at him. 'Thank you, but you needn't have taken so much from your inventory.'

He guessed from her cocked eyebrow that she was about to berate him. Seeking to stave off an argument, he said, 'I wasn't aware that I suddenly needed someone to manage my inventory.'

'I—'

He grabbed her shoulders to pull her back down against him. 'Not tonight, Isabella. This may well be our last night together.'

She drew lazy circles on his chest with her fingertips. 'And why is that?'

'Your father's ship is anchored off the coast.'

'Ship? As in one?'

'Yes.'

'No.' She sat back up. 'That is not right.'

'I thought the same thing. It made no sense that FitzHenry would come to rescue the granddaughter of a king without an army at his back.'

'Have you checked the cove?'

He stared at her, wondering what had made her decide he was suddenly too dense to protect his own island and people. 'No. I never would have thought to check the one place Dunstan had proven vulnerable in the past.'

'Truce.' She held up a hand. 'I am sorry. Of course the cove is guarded. What will you do now?'

Richard groaned. 'There isn't much I can do until they disembark from the ship.'

Isabella ran a hand down his arm. 'You need not fear my father.' When he stared at her, she at least had the decency to wince at the foolishness of her claim before adding, 'True, the two of you will most likely exchange blows along with a great many angry words, but once he knows I am safe and well, he will listen to reason. He may not like it, but he'll listen to it.'

'So while he and I argue, his force will seek to lay waste to my ships, warehouses and village. Little comfort there, Isabella.'

'No. His men will not raise a sword until they are ordered to do so. And they will not be given that order until my father knows of my well-being first. I guarantee you that he will not recklessly risk my life in such a manner. My mother would not stand for it.'

Before he could respond, the sounds of battle floated up from outside. Richard rushed to the window to tear back the covering.

He watched as flaming arrows flew across the battlements, setting one of the outbuildings on fire.

A heavy pounding beat on the chamber door. Richard waved at Isabella to cover herself, and called out, 'Enter.'

Conal burst into the room. 'We are under attack.'

'Don't let them burn the place down. Open the damn gates and meet them head on.'

Conal headed back downstairs, shouting orders before he'd hit the stairs.

Richard picked up the clothing he'd tossed on the floor, pulling each piece on as he retrieved it.

'You aren't going to give them entrance?' Isabella held the covers to her neck.

'Yes. Do you think it could be your brother?'

She shook her head. 'No. My father would not risk the sole heir to his shipping empire so foolishly.' She frowned, then said, 'I don't know how it would be possible, my father never would have given him command of a ship willingly, but I suppose it could be Glenforde.'

'We'll know soon enough.' Richard tugged on his boots. At her quickly indrawn breath, he explained, 'There is one ship. It can only hold thirty to maybe forty men.'

'If that many.'

'Most of Dunstan's men are inside the walls. They can easily dispatch them to their maker.'

'They disembarked ready to fight.' She pointedly ran her stare down his body. 'And they are protected by armour.'

'Then I guess I need be more alert. Stay here.' He strapped on his sword as he headed for the door. 'Bolt the door behind me.'

Chapter Nineteen

Isabella scrambled from the bed and hastily dressed. Laces to her gown half-undone, her hair in disarray, she opened the chamber door and slowly stuck her head out to listen.

The sound of clashing swords lessened, as if fewer and fewer men were engaged in combat. She leaned back inside the chamber, turning her attention towards the open window. Gone were the earlier shouts of men.

Unable to bear not knowing the outcome of this brief battle, she stepped into the corridor and paused to listen to the sound of two men arguing—rather, one arguing, the other seemingly goading the first one on.

While she didn't need to see the men to know that the second one, with the deeper and decidedly steadier voice, was her husband, she did want to discover the identity of the other man. With her back against the wall, she side-stepped to the stairs.

'Give me my woman, Dunstan.'

Isabella bit hard on her lower lip to keep from screaming.

Glenforde had arrived, ahead of her father. Something was mostly definitely wrong. As she'd told Richard, her father never would have given an unseasoned sailor command of any of his ships—not even one of the small river barges. Nor did she believe for one heartbeat that her father would not have come to Dunstan in person. It wasn't in his nature to permit someone else to stand in his place.

She needed to go down there. Isabella stepped away from the wall and looked down at her gown. But not like this. Glenforde would think she'd been made a prisoner, or worse, if she appeared at Richard's side looking like a well-used whore.

'Pssst.' From the shadows on the other side of the stairs, Hattie tried to get her attention.

Isabella pointed at the door of her chamber and the maid nodded. They both hurried as quickly and quietly as possible into the bedchamber. Hattie dropped the bar across the door, while Isabella tossed back the lid of her clothes chest.

There wasn't much to choose from: the gown she'd worn when taken from Warehaven had been patched, even the patches had been patched, the one she wore now was torn and filthy from tussling in the bailey, or there was a deep forest-green one that she'd worn at Christmas.

'Too bad you have no court clothes.'

She shook her head at Hattie's lament. 'No. The last thing I want to do is have Glenforde think I dressed for him.'

The tunic Richard had dropped on the floor caught her eyes. She pulled the green gown from the chest and retrieved the tunic. 'These will do nicely.'

'What do you want with a guard's tunic?'

She held it up against the green gown. 'The colours, Hattie. Dunstan's colours.'

'Oh, that'll be sure to get him riled.'

'That is the plan.' Isabella tugged at her gown. 'Help me.'

With Hattie's help she was dressed in short order and sat on a bench, scrubbing a wet rag across the dirt on her face, while the older woman combed and captured her wild hair into a matronly plait down her back, complete with blue-and-green ribbons giving her hair a splash of Dunstan to help get the point across—she was Dunstan's.

Rising, she pulled the tunic over her head, laughing at the length. The man's short tunic fell to her knees. Hattie draped a girdle made of golden links low around her waist, then reached into the pouch hanging from her side. 'You might want this.' She handed Isabella the wedding band she had thrown at Richard on the night of their marriage.

'Where did you find it?'

'Lord Richard pressed it into my hand on his way down the steps a few moments ago. He said the choice was yours.'

He still thought there was a choice in this? Isabella slid it on to the ring finger of her left hand, then asked, 'Ready?'

'No. But there'll be no putting it off.'

Hattie fell into step behind her, wringing her hands and muttering under her breath.

Isabella did her best to ignore the woman, pausing at the top of the stairs to place a hand over her grumbling belly and take a deep breath before heading down the stairs with as much dignity befitting the Lady of Dunstan and a daughter of Warehaven.

'I'll not tell you again, Warehaven's bitch is mine.'

She arrived at the bottom step in time to say, 'I am sure Cecilia would disagree.'

As calmly as possible, she'd made a reference to her father's breeding bitch. The hunting hound had bit Glenforde twice, drawing blood both times. Obviously, everyone should have taken heed of the dog's warning.

Both men turned to stare at her. Richard's eyelids

lowered slightly, his mouth lifted into that come-hither smile that made her want to act a fool.

Glenforde's eyes narrowed in what appeared to Isabella as outrage. He took a step towards her. 'Thank God, we have been so worried about you.'

'We?' She made a show of looking around the Great Hall. 'I don't see anyone here but you. However did you manage to arrive ahead of my father?'

He shrugged. 'The rudder on his ship broke and I wasn't willing to wait while he made repairs, so I came ahead. Oh, Isabella, I was so anxious to get to you.'

The sound of her name coming out of his mouth made her want to gag and she doubted his tale of a broken rudder. Her father's ships were always inspected. A broken rudder didn't just happen unexpectedly. At her prolonged silence, Glenforde took another step closer. She fisted her hands at her side.

Thankfully, Conal got to her first and offered his arm. 'My lady.'

She tried not to roll her eyes at his overly formal manner and asked softly, 'How fare the village and the men?'

'The village is intact. One man lost, one injured. Marguerite is seeing to his wounds.' He handed her off to Richard and took up a position behind them.

Richard squeezed her fingers lightly before placing them on his forearm. 'I told you to stay upstairs,' he said, in a whisper meant only for her.

She placed her left hand atop of his, making certain to thumb the ring so it spun on her finger, drawing his attention. 'My place is here.'

Isabella glanced around at the upturned tables and benches, then asked, 'What have you done to my hall?'

When he didn't answer, Conal replied over her shoulder, 'Bit of a disagreement.'

Glenforde raked her from head to toe with his stare. 'You seem whole.'

'Why would I be otherwise?'

'You were taken captive, kidnapped—how were we to know what treatment you'd endure?'

She saw no point in dancing around the truth. 'Please, spare us your lies. Everyone in this chamber knows full well I was taken as bait to lure you back to Dunstan. And now, here you are.'

'Yes, here I am.' Glenforde eyed her carefully. 'And there you are, dressed in his colours, toying with his ring upon your finger. Tell me, whore, did he make as good a lover as I did?'

She felt Richard's arm tense beneath her touch and wanted to scream at him not to listen to the lies. Instead, she confronted Glenforde directly. 'Since I have never shared your bed, it is impossible to make a comparison.'

'You can do so after we wed.'

'I am already wed.'

Surrounded by men who would gladly see him dead, Glenforde drew his sword, announcing, 'Then it seems I must make you a widow first.'

Richard wanted to laugh in his face, but first he needed to make sure Isabella was under control. When she opened her mouth to respond to Glenforde's threat, Richard said, 'Enough,' and pushed her against Conal's chest, ordering, 'hold her.'

He ignored what sounded like her hiss of displeasure. But he didn't care, this was not her fight. Her part in this was over.

Richard tapped the blade of his sword against his leg. 'Since we have witnesses, yours and mine, gathered, why don't you explain to everyone exactly what this is about?'

He wanted to hear Glenforde's confession, wanted all to know how vile this man truly was and what harm he had brought to Dunstan, before he ran his sword through Glenforde's black heart.

'You wronged me first, Dunstan.'

'Did I now? Let's bring your brother into this conversation, he had a different story that I'm sure he'd like to share.'

Matthew dragged Father Paul into the Great Hall. Isabella and Hattie gasped in surprise. Richard had been shocked at first, too. But it explained much. He'd been betrayed by the man who had helped him devise this plan to get Glenforde back here, the same man that everyone on the island had trusted since his arrival just under seven years ago—after Agnes had requested a full-time priest take up residence on Dunstan. When she'd offered up the name of a priest she knew and trusted well, Richard had had no reason to think otherwise.

He pointed his weapon at Father Paul. 'Go on, tell everyone how I wronged Glenforde first.'

'You didn't, my lord.' The man had the decency to hang his head. 'You didn't know she was in love with another until it was too late.'

'And who helped Agnes remain in touch with her lover?'

'I did.'

'Who saw to it that they were able to share personal, intimate moments alone while I was at sea?'

'I did.'

'Now, tell us why you would do such a traitorous thing.'

'Because he is my brother.'

'Enough of this.' Glenforde shoved Father Paul aside. 'I can speak for myself.'

Richard smiled. 'And I would welcome your explanation.'

'How many men have you killed, Dunstan?' Glenforde jabbed his weapon towards Richard.

Unwilling to die, or be seriously injured so soon in this fight, Richard stepped back from Glenforde's reach. 'Outside of battle, none have died by my hand.'

'You are a ship owner. I doubt if you have been in so many battles that you cannot remember them.'

Richard shrugged as he and Glenforde circled each other in the centre of the hall. 'I try not to take the memories of battles off the field.'

'There is one I am sure you didn't forget. Northallerton.'

Richard's stomach churned. Yes, he remembered that battle. It had been his first experience at taking another man's life. For nearly two hours they'd fought King David's men hand to hand. Many had fallen that day. 'That was years ago. Why speak of it now?'

Glenforde swung his sword and Richard stepped into the blow, blocking the other man's blade with his own. Their blades slid along the other until the guards met, bringing them nearly nose to nose. 'Do you remember puking after you severed a man's head from his body?'

Richard shoved free. Unfortunately, yes, he did remember that, too. He'd taken his share of lives that day, but that one had been the first.

'No!' Father Paul's shout rang in the Great Hall. 'He killed Alan?'

'Yes.' Glenforde's lip curled in a snarl. 'Our brother died because of this man's lust for blood.'

'Lust for blood? It was a battle. All there followed their commander's orders.'

Glenforde lunged towards him again. 'Alan was but twenty.'

'And I was sixteen.'

'His wife had just had a baby and no returning husband.' Raising his sword over his head, Glenforde brought it down, missing Richard as he spun away. 'While you came home to marry my betrothed, I was tasked with taking my brother, my dead brother who I watched you kill, home to his wife and child.'

While that explained Glenforde's anger, it didn't justify what he'd done to Agnes and Lisette. 'So, instead of coming after me, you took your rage out on an innocent woman and child?'

'Innocent?' Glenforde's high-pitched shout grated against Richard's ears.

The man came at him again, swinging his sword wildly. Thankfully, Richard was quick enough on his feet to keep out of the blade's way. At the rate Glenforde fought, he would wear himself out quickly. 'Did you know she was again with child?'

Surprised by that piece of information, Richard said, 'It wasn't mine.'

'Nor was it mine. She took great delight in telling me so, over and over, even after I had taste of what she thought to keep from me.'

'You were surprised that the whore slept with another man? You found that reason enough to rape her and then take a knife to her?' Richard ducked away from another swing of his opponent's weapon.

'No. She was already dead by the time I carved her up.'

No sane man would have reacted so violently. Respond in anger at that sort of news? Yes. Leave her? Yes. Rape and kill her? Never.

'And had that little brat done as I said and shut her mouth she might still be alive. But, no, she kept screaming for you. Had I not stopped her, the entire island would have heard her.' Glenforde rushed him, aiming the point of his sword at Richard's neck.

Richard sidestepped and swung his fist, making contact with Glenforde's mouth as he came close. 'She was just a baby.'

'What do you care? She wasn't even yours.'

As he expected, Glenforde was now trying to make him angry enough to lose focus. It wouldn't work.

'Just like that one over there isn't yours. At least she won't be once you're dead.' Glenforde laughed. 'I can't wait to teach her how to be a proper, obedient wife.'

Richard narrowed his eyes. He'd see Glenforde in hell before he'd allow the man to touch one hair on Isabella's head. 'Bold talk for a coward.'

'Coward?' Glenforde grasped his sword with both hands. 'I'll show you a coward.'

The man came at him, swinging his weapon in a chopping motion like it was a battleaxe. Richard backed away, leading them in an ever-narrowing circle, making sure the sharp swords were nowhere near the onlookers gathered along the walls.

Glenforde's blade came close enough that Richard felt the whoosh of air as the weapon barely missed the side of his head. He heard Isabella's gasp and the distinct sound of flesh meeting flesh. He could only assume Conal had quickly slapped his hand over her mouth.

When Glenforde screamed in rage at yet again missing his intended target, Richard knew it was time to end this before the man directed his anger towards an innocent bystander. And before he, too, became tired enough to make what could be a fatal mistake.

He planted his feet and beckoned Glenforde to charge him. 'Come, it is time to join your beloved Agnes.'

'Wade, no!' Father Paul rushed forward, trying to stop his brother from walking into what would be his death by putting himself between the two men.

But Glenforde was moving too fast and was unable to stop his momentum in time. His sword sliced through his brother's unprotected chest. Father Paul fell to the floor, dead before his fall was completed.

Without sparing a moment for the brother he'd just killed, Glenforde jerked his weapon free and slashed at Richard.

He held his ground, deflecting the blows until the muscles of his arms and shoulders burned with the effort.

Then Glenforde made a mistake. He turned his gaze from Richard, towards Isabella. The moment he took a step in her direction, Richard rammed his blade home.

Glenforde's weapon fell from his hand. He stared at Richard and whispered, 'She was mine.'

He hung on to the weapon as Glenforde crumpled to the floor, a look of surprise frozen on his face for all eternity.

With a foot on Glenforde's chest, Richard pulled his blade free and tossed it across the room. He stood over the dead man. Why did he feel no satisfaction in Glenforde's death? Why wasn't he consumed by relief now that he'd doled out his revenge?

No, it wasn't relief or satisfaction flooding him. It was guilt.

Guilt for everything he'd done of late. Glenforde's last words echoed in his mind. *'She was mine.'*

Yes, he'd been right. Agnes was his and Richard had no right marrying her. No right keeping her confined to this island once he'd discovered she belonged to another.

'She was mine.'

Yes, she had been his. And so had Isabella.

It didn't matter if in the end Isabella would have wed Glenforde or not, she deserved the choice.

She been forced into a situation not of her making and he'd been the one who had done the forcing.

No, it wasn't relief or satisfaction he felt. It was guilt and shame.

He had to make this right. The only thing left of this thirst for vengeance was Isabella, an innocent in this entire plot. He had to make things right for her. Otherwise, he'd not be able to live himself.

'Richard.' A gentle touch, a soft voice floated through the fog swirling about him. Yet he had no wish to deal with Isabella until he could decide how to do right by her. He shrugged off her touch and searched the hall. Finding Conal, he gritted his teeth a moment and then said, 'Get her out of here.'

'Richard!'

He heard her scream as Conal took her to the stairs.

'Richard, please, I love you.'

He heard her declaration as he slammed his chamber door behind him.

Love. What did she know of love? Nothing. He'd done well in teaching her lust, and desire, but nothing of love.

How could he when he didn't believe in love?

But Isabella did. He knew that and suddenly that fact made all the difference in the world to him. She deserved the chance to find this love she so craved.

Her connections were mighty. She was the granddaughter of a king. Surely Rome would grant her a divorce and permit her to marry someone else.

Richard's chest tightened at that thought. He shook off the regret teasing him. This was the right thing to do. The only fair thing he could do. Some day, Isabella would see that.

Isabella sat on the edge of her bed and waited, just as she had for nearly the entire night. And still he didn't come.

What had she done to anger him so?

She knew that at first he'd most likely been busy clearing the bodies from the hall, and rounding up Glenforde's remaining men, but surely that wouldn't have taken all night?

A knock on the door made her jump. 'Enter.'

Conal and Matthew entered the chamber. Neither looked as if they'd found any rest during the night. But they were more than simply tired, they looked... sad...distraught.

'Lady Isabella.' Conal stepped forward. 'Your father's ships will dock within the hour. You need to meet him at the quay.'

She rose. She'd looked forward to this for so long, yet now that the moment had arrived, she longed for more time. 'Richard will meet me there?'

'No. I will escort you.' Matthew twisted his hat in his hands. 'You need pack what things you want to take with you back to Warehaven. Two of the chamber maids will be along to help.'

Her heart seemed to freeze in her chest. 'The only thing I wish to take is Richard.'

'Isabella, that isn't going to happen.' Conal sighed. 'He wants you gone.'

'And he couldn't be bothered to tell me that himself?' She tried to fight through the pain lashing her. 'Where is he?'

The two men looked at each other. Finally, Conal stepped aside. 'His chamber.'

As she marched by them, Matthew touched her shoulder. 'He will not change his mind.'

She stared up at the man, noticing that her vision was clouded. She hoped it was from rage and not tears. 'I deserve an explanation.'

The two maids met her halfway down the stairs. Isabella paused long enough to say, 'Use the smaller chest to store my clothes and the fabric. That is all.'

She wanted nothing else. Just the things she'd worn here and the fabric he'd taken from his warehouse inventory specifically for her. She would use it for the baby.

Everyone in the Great Hall paused to look at her as she came off the last step. She turned to them to ask, 'You have nothing else to do?'

Thankfully, they all hung their heads and went about their tasks.

Isabella didn't pause to knock on his chamber door, she shoved the door open and crossed the room to the rear door, shoving through that one, too.

He rose from the bed as she entered. Only to be knocked back down on to the mattress when she shoved against his chest, shouting, 'What is wrong with you?'

'I didn't think you would take leaving here this

hard. You are going home, isn't that what you've always wanted?'

His sarcastic tone did not fit the anger shimmering from his eyes. She couldn't quite put her finger on it, but the two emotions did not fit. Not with Richard. He could be sarcastic and teasing, or angry. He was never both. 'No. And you know better. We were supposed to start working on a child when all of this was over.'

'I changed my mind.'

'You what?'

He shrugged. 'I changed my mind.'

She put her fisted hands on her hips. 'Richard, what is going on here?'

'Nothing more than what I'd planned all along. You did your part. You lured Glenforde here. He is now dead. So you are free to leave.'

'And if I wish not to leave?'

'I will have Matthew place you aboard your father's ship. You are not staying here.'

She fell to her knees before him. 'What did I do?'

He reached towards her cheek, then drew his hand back. 'You did nothing, Isabella.'

Her name didn't roll off his tongue, he didn't drag it out, as if cherishing each letter. 'Richard, I love you.'

'You don't know what love is.' He rose, pulling her up with him. 'But you will some day.'

She threw herself against his chest. 'Don't make me go.'

He encircled her in his arms and for a moment held her close. Then, holding her at arm's length, he asked, 'Don't you see? This is the only thing I can give to you. The chance to find this love you so desire. Isabella, you will never find it here, you know that.'

'We are married.'

He brushed wayward strands of hair from her face. 'And you know as well as I that your family can see that corrected.' He cupped her cheek. 'One day, this will all be nothing more than a dream, a nightmare better left forgotten.'

'But—'

'No. I'll hear no more.' He released her and walked away, to pause at the door. 'Go. Your father will dock soon.'

She reached a hand towards him. 'Richard, wait, I—'

He had to stay to hear what she had to say. Instead, he walked through the door, out of the chamber and out of her life.

Chapter Twenty

'Lady Isabella, your parents wish a word.'

Isabella turned away from the servant sent to summon her to yet another discussion with her parents. That's all they'd done of late—discuss her future.

She had no future, why couldn't they understand that? She was married to a man who no longer wanted her. She was pregnant with no possibility of being granted a divorce. So, without Richard, there was simply no future.

'Are you coming, my lady?'

Isabella sighed. 'Tell them I'll be down in a few moments.'

None of these discussions did anything to lift the pall that had surrounded her from the moment she'd left Dunstan just over a month ago.

'Isabella!'

She groaned as her mother's shout sped up the stairwell. She took a deep breath and headed for the Great Hall. There was no choice—if she didn't go down there right now, her parents would only come up here.

One of the lookout-tower guards nodded as he walked past her on his way to the doors. Normally the lookout guards only came to the keep when something dangerous, like being under the threat of attack, was about to happen. Otherwise any needed information was shared via riders whose only task was to deliver any messages from, or to, the lookouts. She frowned and joined her parents at the table. 'What was he doing here? Is something wrong?'

'No.' Her father waved off her questions. 'Everything is fine. He was anxious because one of the riders became a little sidetracked this morning and didn't show up at his post on time.'

'Oh.' She took a seat. 'You wanted to see me?'

'Yes.' Her mother tapped a missive that was on the table before her. 'We have heard from Matilda.'

'And what does she say this time, Mother?'

'It seems no divorce or annulment is required. That Father Paul was not a priest. He'd not yet been ordained and had no right to marry you in the first place.'

Isabella wanted to laugh, but knew if she did that she'd only start crying—again. There was no humour in this situation, but it seemed to her that everything had fallen Richard's way, even down to having a false priest marry them. She was certain he didn't know that was the case, she didn't believe him that devious.

She looked at her father. 'Then I suppose you can stop going over that marriage contract.'

'You need to think of the child.' He leaned his forearms on the table. 'I agree with your aunt in this. We feel that your marriage was valid and she intends on taking possession of Dunstan for the child, of course.'

'No.' Isabella jumped up from her chair. 'She can't do that.'

'She can do just about anything she wants. But why would you care?'

'He would have nothing.'

'Who would have nothing?' her father asked.

Her mother explained, 'The child will be set for life, Isabella.'

'Richard. Richard would have nothing.'

'After what he did to you, taking you from your home, getting you with child and then sending you back to us a disgraced woman? Nothing is exactly what he deserves. He should be grateful if he escapes with his life.' Her father's voice deepened to a menacing tone.

She defended Richard. 'He most certainly did not

get me with child alone and we thought we were married, so how am I disgraced?'

Her father slapped his palm on the table. 'You defend that pig to me?'

'That pig, as you call him, is the father of my child.'

'Yes, well, thankfully Matilda and your father are seeing that situation is changed as quickly as possible.' Her mother sought to calm the tempers flaring at the table.

Isabella gasped. No, they couldn't be thinking to wed her to someone else. 'I am not going to marry someone else.'

'You are carrying a child, you need to think of his or her future. You most certainly will marry and the quicker the better.'

'Father!'

'Don't you use that tone with me. No, you will listen, Isabella. I know what it is to be a bastard, but at least I was the king's bastard. The child you carry doesn't even have that benefit. How do you think it will be treated if there isn't a strong man around to claim responsibility for it?'

'And who do you think is going to believe I got married and delivered a legitimate child a few months later?'

'It won't matter. As long as the man is powerful

and rich enough to stare down the naysayers, all will be fine, you know this.' Her mother reached out and clasped her hand. 'Isabella, what does this man hold over you? Why can you not get him out of your mind? He was evil, a thief who stole my daughter away in the night and nothing more.'

'Mother...' Isabella paused, trying desperately to not sob as she'd done so many endless nights since returning home. She swallowed. 'Mother, he... I...'

Knowing she was losing this battle with her emotions, she slid to the hard floor on her knees before her mother and buried her face in her mother's lap. 'Mama, I love him.'

Her mother combed her fingers through her hair and gently eased her up from her lap. 'Child, why did you say nothing before now?'

'Because it wouldn't have mattered. Nothing would change. You could marry me to a dozen different men and my heart would still belong to the knave who stole me away.'

She heard her father's chair scrape across the floor and his approaching footsteps as he came over and placed a hand on her head. 'Is this man your choice?'

'Yes. Yes, he is. But I'm not his choice.'

Her father and mother exchanged a look she couldn't decipher before he said, 'I need to think about this a little while.'

She bowed her head. 'Father, there's nothing you can do.'

'That might very well be true. Time will tell.'

One of her father's men entered the hall and requested a moment with the Lord of Warehaven.

She couldn't hear their whispered conversation, but knew by the brief exchange that it couldn't have been too important. Her father returned and once again shared an odd look with her mother before whispering something in her ear.

Isabella narrowed her eyes. They were up to something. It was useless to ask, because she knew from experience they would only deny her charge.

Her mother patted her shoulder. 'Come, give your father some time to think about this and we will talk again later. Right now, you can join me in the kitchen. You've sat in your chamber sulking far too long. It is time you show me what you've learned about running a keep.'

She rose and followed her mother while her father disappeared into his private chamber.

Once they reached the kitchen, her mother studied the herbs hanging over the work table. 'Isabella, run out to the herb shed and bring back some rosemary and perhaps another bunch of lavender.'

Reaching up to touch the rosemary already present, Isabella asked, 'What are you making that will require so much?'

The cook leaned in to say, 'I've a couple of new recipes I wish to try.'

She shook her head and headed for the rear door, only to be stopped by her mother. 'Change your shoes. It is still damp out there and you will only ruin those slippers.'

Isabella spun around to go back up to her chamber to exchange her soft slippers for a pair of sturdier boots.

Isabella tromped through the bailey. It felt good to get out of the keep even if it was just for a few minutes. The air, while still just a little chilly, was fresh and felt good against her cheeks.

She nodded at one of her father's guards, and continued to the small shed alongside the stables.

She wished her sister was here. But Beatrice had been sent north to stay with Jared and Lea right after the kidnapping. Her parents had had no way of knowing if their younger daughter was also in danger, so she'd been banished to safety.

If Beatrice were here, she'd have someone to talk to, someone who would understand how lonely and confused she felt.

Isabella reached to open the door to the shed, only

to have a large work-worn hand slapped firmly over her mouth.

She opened her eyes wide in shock as she swallowed the scream she'd been so eager to let fly.

'My, my, what have we here?' the man standing behind her asked softly over her shoulder.

He ignored her struggles to free herself, to ask, 'Why, I wonder, would Warehaven's whelp travel this far from the safety of the keep?'

He leaned closer, his chest hard against her back, his breath hot across her ear. 'Unescorted and unprotected.'

The deepening timbre of his voice acted like a drug-laced wine, soothing her brittle nerves and setting her blood afire.

She went lax in his hold and, as soon as his vice-like grip loosened, she turned around to rest her cheek against his chest, savouring the feel of his arms around her, the familiar scent of his body and the steady drum of his heartbeat.

Then she shoved against his chest, freeing herself from him and from all the things she'd never thought to feel again, demanding to know, 'What are you doing here?'

'There were some things left unsaid.'

'No. I think you made yourself perfectly clear. I'd served my purpose and you had no use for me.'

She turned to leave, before she humiliated herself by bursting into tears. She didn't want him to know how badly he'd hurt her.

He grasped her wrist to prevent her escape and tugged her back around. 'We are going to talk, Isabella.'

'Are you kidnapping me again?'

'I can't very well kidnap my own wife.'

'We aren't married, Dunstan. Your priest wasn't ordained.' She leaned closer to peer into his eyes. Even though she knew better, she couldn't resist vexing him. 'But you probably knew that didn't you?'

'What are you accusing me of now?'

'Wouldn't that have been the perfect ploy? Make me think we were wed so I'd come to your bed easier and then, when all was said and done, cast me aside because after all we never were truly married.'

'You have a mighty high opinion of us both, don't you?'

'What do you mean?'

'For one thing, Isabella—' his warm breath against her ear as he rolled her name off his tongue made her shiver '—I doubt I would have had to wed you to coax you to my bed. And if coaxing had failed, you would have been powerless to stop me from taking you any time I so desired.'

Horrified by the truth behind that statement, she stomped her foot. 'Why you...you...low-life scum.'

'And in the second place, I may be low-life scum and a black-hearted knave, but I'm not devious enough to have planned everything quite that thoroughly.'

She curled her upper lip. 'That much is true. You probably don't possess the—'

He placed a finger over her lips. 'Careful. You don't want to say something you'll regret now, do you?'

Isabella shook her head.

He extended his arm and, to her surprise, Matthew handed him a cloak.

She nodded. 'Sir Matthew, 'tis good to see you.'

'You, too, Lady Isabella. How are you?'

'I was fine until a few moments ago.'

Richard cleared his throat. 'If the two of you are done?'

After Matthew stepped back into the shadows, Richard slung the cloak about her shoulders, pinned a brooch in place, then pulled up the hood and tucked her hair inside.

'So, once again you think to disguise me enough to walk through the gates?'

'No. You will walk through the gates, disguised

or not. The cloak is to ensure you and the baby stay warm.'

She grabbed his arm. 'You know.'

'Of course I know.'

'Who told you?'

'Conal.'

Ah, Conal had most likely received the news from Marguerite, who'd received it from Hattie, proving the grapevine on Dunstan was alive and well.

'It is yours.'

He jerked back as if her words had threatened to bodily attack him. 'Why would you say such a thing?'

'I didn't want you to think I'd slept with another man.'

'Don't be foolish, Isabella, it doesn't suit you.'

She hadn't been trying to be foolish. She'd been thinking about Agnes and Lisette. It was important to her that he know this child was his. Did that not matter to him?

Richard placed his palm against her cheek and it was all she could do not to lean into his touch. She'd missed him—she'd missed the warmth of his caress so very much.

'Isabella, if I know nothing else about you, I know without a doubt that you are honourable and faithful. I've no fears that you would have taken another to your bed.'

When he dropped his touch, she nearly cried at the loss tightening in her throat. He took her hand. 'Come, we have a great many things to discuss.'

He headed towards the gates, Matthew leading the way. Isabella noticed the decided lack of guards in the gate tower. 'Does my father know you are here?'

'Let's see, this is an island. I sailed around the south-west corner yesterday. Depending on the speed and diligence of his outlooks, I'm fairly certain he knew within hours I had arrived. Obviously, he gave safe passage, because I docked at his wharf unimpeded. So, yes, Isabella, I imagine he does.'

'So this was planned?'

'No. I've not spoken to him yet.'

A terrible thought tripped across her mind. 'He did not send for you, did he?'

Richard's bark of laughter drew the attention of people passing by. 'Send for me? Like one of his paid men? Not hardly, Isabella.'

'Oh.'

'What were you thinking? That your parents sent me a missive telling me what to do? You know better than that. I'm here of my own accord, have no fears on that score.'

Actually, even though she'd never admit it to her

parents, just knowing he came here on his own did make her feel better. Although, with the guard from the outlook tower visiting the keep personally, and the obvious lack of gate guards, added to the guard who'd spoken to her father and the looks her parents had exchanged, she wondered if they'd sent her out here on purpose. She wouldn't put it past them. Especially not after she'd so openly declared her love for her husband.

'They have been planning my future.'

'Good for them. I hope you and your new husband will be very happy together.'

Her feet dragged of their own accord. She stared at him. If he wasn't here to apologise and take her home, why was he here?

Her stomach churned until she had to ask, 'Why are you here?'

'To talk, Isabella. Did I not already say that?'

'You sent me away, there is nothing left to discuss.' To her horror she burst into tears. God's teeth, she was tired of these tears, these sudden bouts of sadness so overwhelming that she wanted nothing more than to fall to her knees and sob.

He swung her up into his arms and lowered his lips to her ear. 'There is much to discuss. Now, hush.'

She fell silent and rested her cheek against his shoulder, for now content to do nothing more.

Once they reached the wharf, Richard boarded his ship, docked at the furthest end and carried her to the privacy and protection beneath the covered aft castle. He lowered his arm to permit her feet to land on the deck. 'Stay here.'

She heard him order the men to disembark and telling Matthew to stand guard on the quay, then he returned.

A sudden bout of shyness swept over her. She didn't know what to say, had no clue what to expect. She studied the cabin. Tableware and food were set out on a linen-covered table near the bed. Two high-backed armchairs flanked the table, near dwarfing it in size. Light from the many-armed candle stand in the corner flickered across the table and bed.

Richard pulled a pillow from the bed, placed it on the back of one of the chairs and held out his hand. 'Come. Sit.'

'I'm not hungry.'

He didn't argue. Instead he stepped closer to pick her up and deposit her in the chair before taking the seat across from her. 'I am.'

Calmly, as if he hadn't a care in the world, he snagged an apple from the plate of fruit and idly began to slice it with his small eating knife. He then did the same with a pear, slicing, placing a piece on his plate, slicing again to place a piece on hers. All the while watching her, his expression placid, giving nothing of his thoughts away.

But she knew by his smooth, unlined, unsmiling face that he was angry.

Unable to bear the uncomfortable silence, Isabella asked, 'Are you ever going to tell me exactly what you are angry about now?' Not that he had any reason to be outraged about anything.

He paused to angle the tip of the knife towards her stomach. 'Why wasn't I told you carried my child?'

That's what had him in this mood? 'I tried.'

'When?'

'The day you threw me off Dunstan.'

'I didn't throw you off Dunstan, I sent you home to your parents. And, no, you didn't try to tell me then.'

'Yes, I did. You cut me off.'

'Ah, when you said "but" before I walked out of the bedchamber?'

'Yes.'

'And we both know you are so meek and mild that you never would have thought to scream at me through the door, or follow after me or tried a little harder to tell me.'

She'd give him that much. Perhaps she could have tried harder. 'Would it have made a difference?'

'To your staying on Dunstan? No.'

'Then what difference does it make?'

'I deserved to know.'

Isabella closed her eyes and took a deep breath. She opened them and leaned forward, her elbows resting on the table. 'Richard, what is this about?'

'I need to decide what to do about my child.'

'Your child?' Shocked and dismayed, she leaned back in the chair. 'Your child?'

'Yes, my child. The heir to Dunstan.'

'This is our child, not yours.'

'You are the granddaughter of a king. Your future is secure. The child's future is Dunstan and it needs to be raised knowing what his or her place is in this world.'

'I am the child's mother.' She leaned forward again. 'And your wife.'

'Isabella, you deserve more than I could ever give you.'

So that's what this was about? He thought her above him? This needed to be put to rest now.

'Don't you see? Your father can secure you a husband who will be able to provide you with everything I can't. But I will not permit my child to be a part of that agreement.'

She watched him closely and asked, 'So it bothers you not if I wed another as long as you possess the baby?'

He hesitated slightly before saying, 'You need do what you must for your future.'

Isabella's heart leapt. There, there it was, she nearly swooned with relief. She easily ignored his words, they were meaningless. His hesitation and that brief shimmer deep behind his sapphire gaze told her everything she needed to know.

The question now was if he would ever permit himself a long enough moment of weakness to realise it. She had to take the risk no matter how much pain it might cause to him, or her.

Isabella rose. 'Perhaps you are right. I do need to see to my future, since it is plain you care not.'

She clasped her hands before her so she would do nothing foolish like reach out to him and walked purposely towards the doorway.

Something behind her fell heavily to the floor. 'Isabella, please understand.'

Without turning around, she said, 'Oh, I fully understand, Richard, once you sated your thirst for revenge you had no room left in your heart for me. You made that clear.'

'No. You are wrong.' The heavy sadness in his tone nearly caused her to turn around, but she stayed in place, waiting for him to say what they both needed to hear.

'When I stared down at Glenforde's dead body I

felt no satisfaction. None of the relief I'd expected came from his death. I realised in that moment that revenge no longer filled my heart, it was too full of you to permit something as vile as vengeance any room.'

She gripped the beam of the doorway, to keep from turning around and throwing herself in his arms too soon. 'Yet you sent me away.'

'I ruin everyone I touch. I couldn't let that befall you, too. Not at my hands.'

'Self-pity does not suit you.' She needed more than his explanations and self-accusations, they would not suffice. She wanted his apology for the hell he'd put her through. She turned around to continue her confrontation, only to gasp at the sight before her.

'Richard?'

The sound of something heavy hitting the floor a few moments ago had been him. He was on his knees, on the cold hard deck, staring at her. His eyes glimmered, creases cut across his forehead and the tick in his cheek beat rapidly. 'Isabella, I am sorry. So sorry for all I have done to you. I never should have used you in such a manner. Please, tell me you understand that I need to make up for the wrongs I have committed against you. I only care about what is best for you.'

He hadn't said 'I love you,' but he had apologised

and she was certain that one day his heart would prod him to say the words she'd waited a lifetime to hear. For now, it was enough that her heart melted at the honesty of his reply.

But she groaned at his misplaced reasoning and walked back to him. 'Richard, the only thing that is best for me is you. That is all I need, all I'll ever want. Do my needs not matter to you? Do you think another husband will make me not long for the lust I feel at your touch? Do you think he will appreciate me desiring another in our marriage bed? Do you truly believe that a huge keep, filled with servants, men and gold will begin to make up for the love I hold for those at Dunstan?'

He wrapped his arms around her. Resting his head against her belly, he whispered, 'I may never be able to give you all your parents can.'

'Oh, you mean like their lectures on how I should comport myself, what I should or shouldn't do? Trust me, my love, you excel at that. Or did you mean the keep? Warehaven is under my mother's command, not mine. Now that I've had a taste of it, I would rather have command of my own abode, thank you very much. Or were you referring to my father's temper tantrums?' She threaded her hands through his hair and held him tightly to her. 'Yours are so much more enjoyable.'

'Does this mean you will forgive me? Will you come home?'

'Richard, I would like to see anyone stop me.'

The sound of boots hitting the deck outside the cabin and the jingle of amour prompted her to add, 'I believe we have company.'

Richard rose and gathered her into his arms. 'I care not.'

'You had better care, young man.'

Isabella laughed at her father's growl. 'Father, I'd like you to meet my husband, Richard of Dunstan.' She turned to Richard. 'This grousing warrior is my father, Randall FitzHenry of Warehaven.'

Her father glared from one of them to the other. Finally, he asked, 'Ah, so this is the knave who despoiled my daughter and left her dishonoured?'

Richard bowed his head. 'Yes, sir.'

'What have you to say for yourself?'

Richard squeezed her fingers, and raised his head. 'I would do it all over again, sir, without a second thought.'

Her father tried his best to look angry. When that didn't work, he tried to look shocked, which only made Isabella lean her head against Richard's arm.

'Give him but a moment, he'll settle on one or the other.'

Finally her father motioned Richard to join him. 'Come along, it seems we need to revise that farce of a marriage contract you drew up and find a real priest.'

Chapter Twenty-One

Isabella stared out of the window of her chamber at the rising sun. Richard had spent the last two days ensconced with her father, working out the details of their marriage contract. They'd start early in the morning and end late in the evening.

Her parents had assigned him to a chamber at the other side of the keep with orders not to even consider visiting this one.

She had barely got the chance to see him, let alone talk to him.

The ceremony was slated for today. Since there were so many here from Dunstan to attend the wedding, her mother had decided to use the church in the village instead of the family's private chapel in the keep. Richard, Conal and the others would gather outside the church soon, if they weren't already there.

She'd been thrilled to discover that Marguerite,

Hattie, some of the maids and others from Dunstan had made the journey to Warehaven. It pleased her to know Richard had been confident enough of her love for him that he'd come prepared for another wedding.

And she'd been delighted to learn that once they returned to Dunstan another marriage would take place. Marguerite was finally going to make an honest man out of Conal—at least that had been his explanation. Isabella was happy that they'd decided to wait until her return before exchanging their vows.

'Looking for someone?' her mother asked from the doorway.

'Is Father Bartholomew ready?'

'I'm sure he is.' She draped her cloak over a bench. 'Come, let's get you dressed.'

Her mother helped her into her gown, then drew her into an embrace. 'I will miss you so.'

'Mother, I will be closer at Dunstan than Jared is at Montreau.'

'It is different with you. You are my daughter, Isabella.'

'You are planning to come to me at the end of summer, aren't you?'

'Child, I wouldn't miss this birthing for anything in the world.'

Whether it was having Richard so close and not

being able to talk to him these last couple of days, or carrying a child, or once again leaving Warehaven, or just the simple fact it was again her wedding day, Isabella burst into tears. 'Mama, I am so scared.'

Her mother laughed softly. 'I would be concerned if you weren't.' She stood back and smoothed one of Isabella's braids. 'You are strong and healthy. Richard will be there. Your father and I will be there. All will be well, Isabella, I promise you.'

She sniffed and wiped at her eyes. 'I'm sorry. I just… I don't know. I just feel so…weepy.'

'I hadn't noticed.' Her mother chucked her under the chin. 'Dry your eyes. Don't let your father, or husband, think I've been tormenting you.'

Isabella laughed. 'I'm fine.'

'Good. I need to make sure your father is ready before I leave for the church. He will meet you below.'

Isabella smoothed the skirt of her green-silk gown. She, Marguerite, Hattie and her mother had worked tirelessly to turn the length of silk into a gown for her and a tunic for Richard. They'd trimmed both garments with slivers of blue ribbon.

Slipping on her grandmother's torque, the best piece of jewellery she owned, she took one last look around her chamber and smiled. It would be the last time she'd have to sleep alone.

Isabella met her father at the foot of the steps. He took her hand. 'Are you ready?'

'Yes.' She was more than ready.

'Your mother has already left for the church.'

'Then we should join her.'

He led her out to the courtyard and a waiting horse. 'Do we really have to do this?' she asked.

'Your mother and I were wed in rush with very little ceremony. We weren't present when your brother wed Lea. So, yes, Isabella, we are doing this as properly as we can in the time allowed.'

With the assistance of her father and a guard, she mounted the ribbon-bedecked horse without further argument.

On foot, her father took the reins and led the way to the village church. There, he helped her down, led her to the door of the church, placing her at Richard's left side and stood between them, stepping back only after assuring Father Bartholomew that there was no reason they should not be wed and that he was freely giving her to Richard.

This time, when she said her vows, nobody had to force her hand, or say the words for her.

Richard handed the priest their two gold bands, which Father Bartholomew blessed and handed back.

He slipped the ring on to her finger, saying, 'With this ring, I thee wed.'

His hands were steady, his voice strong, while her hands shook visibly as she slid the band on to his finger and her voice was little more than a hushed whisper, when she repeated, 'With this ring, I thee wed.'

And when they knelt inside at the altar for the priest's blessing it was all she could do not to cry. She wondered if she would always be this weepy. Or if, eventually, she would regain control of her emotions.

A nudge from Richard drew her out of her musings, reminding her where they were.

When the ceremony ended, and they left the church, she noticed that all of Richard's men had green-and-blue silk ribbons tied around their arm.

She glanced at him, realising that she hadn't seen his ribbon because it was made of the same fabric as his tunic.

She reached over and touched the ragged scraps of fabric. 'And where did you find the scraps?'

'I have my ways.' He shrugged. 'I can't tell you all of my secrets, Wife.'

She rolled her eyes. 'Fine. Keep your secrets, then.'

Later, after the meal, Isabella slowly walked around the perimeter of the Great Hall. Between those from Warehaven and Dunstan, the hall was crowded. Much to her mother's delight—and her dismay as the walls seemed to close around her.

'Come.' Richard hooked his arm through hers. 'We're going upstairs.'

She slipped her arm free. 'No. Our friends and people are here from Dunstan. We'll stay.'

'Isabella, I can see that you're ill. Besides, your mother just ordered me to take you from the hall. Who am I to disobey a direct order?'

'I can manage on my own.'

'I never said you couldn't. But I've no wish to let you sneak off without me.'

'I wasn't going to sneak off.'

He leaned close and whispered against her ear, 'Ah, but I was. See, perhaps you weren't aware, but this is my wedding night and I've every intention of wickedly seducing my bride if she'll let me.'

She laughed softly at his teasing. 'Oh? And what exactly did you plan to do?'

'Well, first I thought I'd kiss her senseless until her toes curled and she needed to hold on tightly to keep from falling.'

Isabella shivered. 'And then?'

He put his arms around her, pulling her into his embrace and started backing her slowly towards the stairs. 'Then I planned to remove her stockings. One at a time so I could slowly trail my hands over her shapely legs. Stopping only to kiss her ankles, then her knees and her luscious thighs.'

'Mmm, that sounds wickedly lovely—and then?'

'I'd loosen the ties of her gown and slide my hands ever so slowly up her body, feeling the warmth of her flesh all the while pushing her clothing up until I could pull it over her head.'

'Oh, my. Then she'd be naked.' Isabella's heart raced at the images his words created in her mind.

'Yes, she would. She'd be naked, hot and needy. Better still, she'd be completely and totally at my mercy.'

Breathless, she asked, 'And then what would you do with her?'

'I would stroke and taste her most intimate flesh until she repeatedly cried out my name in wild abandonment. I would make certain she begged until she could withstand no more.'

Isabella thought she'd faint with need right then and there. But she wasn't yet willing to cry surrender. 'And then?'

In a deep, husky whisper he answered, 'And then, that very moment before I claimed her as my own, I would tell her that I have finally found the one thing that I thought would for ever elude me, the one thing that makes me complete.'

'And what might that be?'

'Love, Isabella. I would tell her how very much I loved her and how I couldn't imagine ever living without her at my side.'

Knowing that everything she'd ever wanted, ever desired, ever dreamed of, was now within her reach, Isabella looked up at him.

His shimmering brilliant blue eyes met hers without wavering.

She placed a hand against his cheek and whispered back, 'And she would vow to hold your heart gently and for ever close.'

* * * * *